VIOLENCE OF ACTION

A Mercenary Tale

Phillip D. Holt

TEAMRAZOR

A **Team Razor** Book

Second Edition for North America published in 2025 by TM RZR LLC.

All inquiries should be emailed to info@tmrzr.com

Author: Phillip D. Holt, Captain, USA (Retired)
Copy Editor: Savannah Lani Murray
Formatting & Editing: Markus Taylor
Cover Design: Beth Lehman
Focal Liaison: Jessica L. Kunze

ISBN: 979-8-218-58813-7

For Michael "Big Mike" Duskin
Chief Warrant Officer 2
KIA October 2012
Afghanistan

This tale's beginning can be traced back
to a botched response to the Big Guy's question.

TM RZR directly supports the
Three Rangers Foundation's
mission of empowering past and present
Comrades from My Ranger Regiment,
our Veterans Gold Star Families,
and Veterans of affiliated Support Units.

www.ThreeRangersFoundation.org

PREFACE

After the Battle of Mogadishu in October 1993, Special Operations Command (SOCOM) realized that an urban environment would be the terrain where a potential enemy might next choose to fight. *Desert Storm* had demonstrated how easily the U.S. military could win a traditional set piece battle. Open terrain, it seems, is no place to challenge American military might. But Operation *Gothic Serpent* in Mogadishu, although an operational success, illustrated a weakness in the vaunted US doctrine of air supremacy. Urban environs also complicated the credo "never leave a fallen comrade to fall into the hands of the enemy." Those two weaknesses, coupled with the subsequent withdrawal of the US military from the Horn of Africa, smelled like failure to our future adversaries. SOCOM knew this and took measures to prevent further exploitation of its doctrine.

Urban Warfare became *the* contingency for which SOCOM began to prepare, and none too soon. In the period between Somalia and the opening salvos of the War on Terror, one additional chapter was added to the Army's premiere leadership manual: an addendum concerning the terrain of the coming battle. The relatively low casualty figures in Iraq and Afghanistan are partly due to this proactive addition. This new chapter in the US Army Ranger Handbook is a compilation of lessons learned from Operations *Gothic Serpent*, *Just Cause*, *Urgent Fury*, and individual campaigns in Vietnam and Korea. This did not have to be.

Great War I & Great War II provided many a lesson in urban combat. Employing tactics that worked in the last conflict is an American military tradition. Sadly, the United States pays for this custom by the body bag.

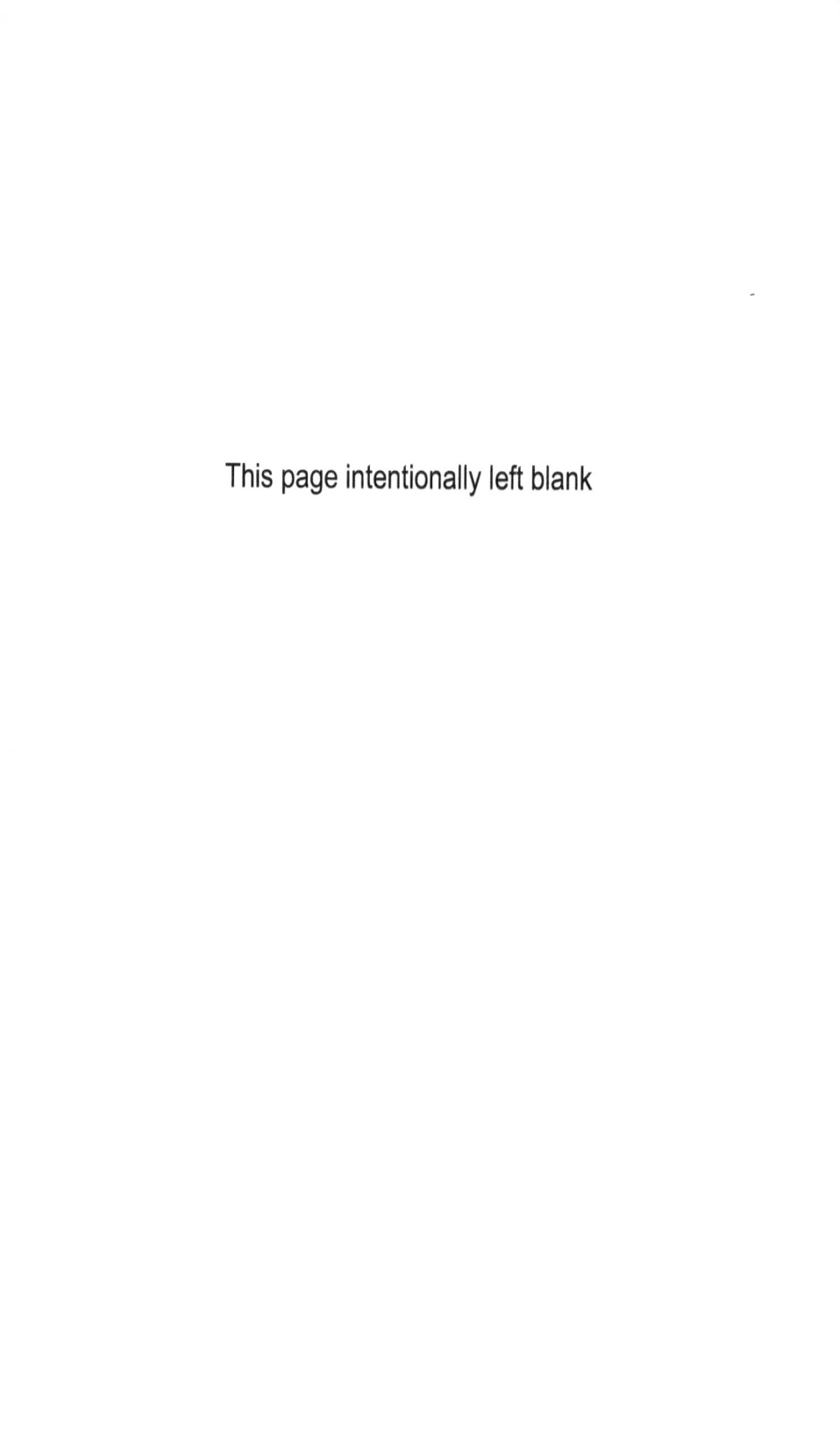
This page intentionally left blank

HANDBOOK

Chapter 14
Urban Operations

14-2. Principles of **MOUT** (Military Operations in Urban Terrain)

a.   Surprise. Strike the Enemy at a time or place or in a manner for which he is unprepared.

b.   Security. Never permit the Enemy to acquire unexpected advantage.

c.   Simplicity. Prepare clear, uncomplicated plans, and provide subordinates with concise orders to ensure thorough understanding.

d.   Speed. Allow rapid Action to serve as Security.

e.   **Violence of Action.** Eliminate the Enemy with sudden, explosive force.

MUZZLE AWARENESS

A la guerre comme àla guerre.
"When at war, act like it."

The double-barreled shotgun recoiled in Sal's hands as he attempted to bust the door down. However, the dual impact of 12 gauge slugs had done nothing to jar the door from its frame. The ballistic breach had failed, and this was unexpected.

"Metal door here!" Sal yelled back to the team leader.

"Shit!" was the sharp response. Sepp briefly wondered why the primary method of entry had stalled out. His mind then raced to solve the problem. He carried a backup doorknob charge, but that was useless on metal. Sepp decided to kick the door in with high explosives.

"Joe, water charge." Sepp used his command voice to convey the order over the headset. "Sal, back away!" he relayed with hand signals. His eyes were always forward, focused on the breach point. The door was coming down. That wasn't the problem. Precious time had been wasted due to poor intelligence. As always, time was the driving factor.

Without a word or a wasted moment, Sal retreated down the coarse brick stairs, holstering his sawed-off shotgun as he moved toward Sepp. Bounding past him on the way up the stairs was Joe. He was carrying a bag of water and an O-ring initiator.

Joe worked quickly, making up for lost time. He let his M4 rifle dangle from its figure-8 bungee cord sling and magnetically connected the IV bag to the metal door. IV bags are meant to deliver fluids to the wounded, but when a detonation cord is properly wrapped around one, an IV bag becomes something else entirely. Joe activated the ignition element and relayed "Fire in the Hole" three times over into his microphone as he made way for the impending blast. Sepp crouched to make room for the retreating breach man. They huddled tight to the retaining wall, one man on each side of the stepway. Both were covering their night vision goggles, waiting for the detonation. As they took cover, Sal re-took his place as the #1 man, moving toward the breach mere seconds before it existed.

Krummph! The light came first, closely followed by the sonic wave. The det cord exploded, but the IV bag reduced and redistributed the force. A quart of saltwater knocked on the metal door at just above the speed of sound. Instead of concentrating kinetic energy at a focused point, the liquid force spread out to form a footprint-sized area. Amid the acrid smoke of the explosive and the buffer's saline mist, the strike effectively kicked in the door.

The sound of the explosion was stark but somehow distant to the ears of the team. Over time their hearing had been dulled by acoustic trauma. Still, it was a familiar break from the silence. Displays of firepower comforted these men; such was their habituation with violence.

Looking up, Sepp could see that the water impulse charge had functioned according to plan. The shadow of a silhouette faded into the darkened breachway. Sepp gave the signal to enter the home, knowing full well that the team was moving of its own accord. He used his left hand for the command gesture. His rifle was always pointed to the twelve o'clock.

Perched in his sniper hide, Chuck had witnessed the effects of the water impulse charge. Through the scope mounted atop his big-bore rifle, it looked as though someone had popped the flash on a camera from behind the house. The light was stark to him, as any bright light is when viewed through night vision goggles, but contrary to movie fiction, the light was in no way painful. Rather, the brief illumination left a bothersome photoburn on his vision. Chuck blinked rapidly to remove the after-effect and then reacquired his target, a transformer atop a utility pole.

A shower of sparks fell, accentuated by the absence of light that the round had created. Chuck moved the massive rifle away from the transformer and trained it back upon the objective. It was in time to see US MARSHAL on the tag of Joe's jacket briefly illuminated by the cascade of sparks. He made a mental note to bring up at the post-mission review and returned to his job as the over-watch for the team.

The scope that Chuck peered down was mounted atop a Barrett .50 caliber rifle. A monstrosity of a weapon, the fifty cal is capable of splitting an engine block in half, to say nothing of its effect on a soft, fleshy, human target. It was Chuck's job to incapacitate external threats to this operation. He saw nothing of concern but continued to scan the streets with a diligent paranoia.

Sepp had a glimpse of the #1 man moving into the objective (the OBJ). Shrouded in his all black uniform, Sal was an anonymous specter to most, but Sepp recognized the familiar gait. Sal was the most attuned to the boiled down essence of rapid violence, and so Sepp had chosen him to lead the team into the house. It was Sal's job to determine the *path of least resistance* into the OBJ and then to move along that path. Sal was free to decide the best avenue toward this purpose.

Sal knew that the team had to get *into* the house; they could not stall in the doorway on the attempt. Doorways, in this line of work, are known as fatal funnels because in passing through them, groups of men can have their movements bottlenecked and thus be killed in mass.

3

Knowing this, he barreled into the house with a reckless disregard for his personal safety. He knew it was the only way to get the job done.

Sal disappeared into the darkness of the OBJ, relying on his night vision goggles to enhance his sight. He followed the wall to his left, knowing that Joe, the second man in, would follow closely behind. If the first man has the left side, and the second has the right. Up and down are likewise assigned sectors. In this manner, rooms, corridors, and staircases can be effectively sectioned into areas of responsibility. In the lexicon of soldiers and cops, this technique is known as "slicing the pie." When divided into smaller sections, an objective, like a pie, can be more easily devoured. Each man on the team knew and had trained on which section was theirs and how to react if the man ahead was killed or incapacitated.

After Joe entered, Dognut followed close behind. James Smith had grown to like this cruel nickname. He lagged outside for a brief moment in case the room was too small to accommodate three men. "Dognut," he said into the headset, "going in."

Sepp was mission leader and so entered behind the shock troops. As he bound over the concave remnant of the door, Sepp noted the effect the explosive had made. Beautifully bent, and somewhat polished by the blast of salt water, the door was now a Salvador Dali masterpiece.

Killingsworth and Matt followed closely behind Doc, the team's tall and almost too thin excuse for a medic. Matt and Killer were heaving the belt-fed guns. These two men each carried the stumpy M249 SAW. They would only get to play if serious firepower was required. Matt and Killer, with their Squad Automatic Weapons, entered effortlessly as the tail of a snake creeping down a rat hole. Matt quickly fish-hooked and took up station at the doorway. His SAW was trained back outside the breached door. It was his job to provide rear security. Killer hurried forward, bypassing Matt, for it was his job to watch the team leader's back. He

4

was on standby to hose down any spark of resistance that the lead element could not decisively overcome.

Deep within the house, Joe reached his limit of advance. He positioned himself as close as possible to a doorjamb. It was scant protection but Joe was willing to take whatever he could get. He popped the safety off the Flash Bang with his teeth, pulled the grenade-style pin out of it, and tossed the pyrotechnic into the room. The Flash Bang is, in actuality, just a large firecracker. The Flash-Bang is aptly named because *flash*ing an intense white light and exploding with a *bang* is precisely what it did.

Joe waited just long enough for the dust to begin to settle and pivoted into the room. He let loose a controlled three-round burst from his rifle as he did so. In the green/black of his night vision goggles, the man dropped like a sack of potatoes into the smoky, swirling aftermath of the Flash Bang. Turning right, Joe was about to fire when the infrared tactical light on Sal's weapon illuminated a second silhouette. It was not his sector of fire, but that was a mere technicality.

Sal was as quick to kill as Joe, and as swiftly as the target had presented itself, Sal had taken the man/silhouette down with a three-round burst. *Just like over there,* he thought for the umpteenth time. The triple impact of 5.56mm bullets hit the man's chest at close to 2,500 feet per second; the bullets tore through his internal organs and impacted the bone mass of the spinal column.

What followed demonstrates precisely why the US military adopted 5.56mm bullets during the early 1960s. After shattering the third thoracic vertebrae and disfiguring itself in the process, the 5.56 round then ricocheted downward, ripping its now jagged form through the lungs, liver, and stomach until it met with the pelvic bone. From there, it bounced again, lacerating the femoral artery leading to the man's left leg. After all the damage the tiny bullet had caused, it slowed to a halt within the tough muscle mass of the man's thigh.

Had this mess been made within the sterile confines of a hospital's surgery ward, there still would have been little to do beyond rifling through the dead man's pockets for loose change. This was a planned consequence of government research and funding.

Three rooms deep into the house, a burp of light twinkled in a smoke obscured corner, and three or four rounds just missed Sal and Joe. Crouched in response to the incoming fire, Joe had chunks of plaster fall over the extended barrel of his weapon. Some obscenely outdated wallpaper held together the irregular shapes of drywall. The shots were haphazardly discharged from behind the couch.

Murphy's Third Law of Combat: *Nothing draws fire, like fire.*

Dognut took his time to aim and then chimed in with a controlled burst of his own. From fifteen feet, the couch looked no worse for wear, but a reflective pool of blood began to ooze from beneath. Still, the danger was not yet neutralized. Intelligence reports were specific about four men being inside the objective, and the team's reconnaissance had verified this; Sepp could only think *three corpses ain't four corpses.* There was one more man unaccounted for. *Perhaps he will just give up*, Sepp thought wishfully. *Not likely,* but possible.

His greatest concern was that the last man was a resident of the house. He could have knowledge not gleaned from schematics. Floorboards that creaked, and reinforced hiding spots. Men like that would have too many advantages to be defeated easily. Restricting the target's ability to defend or retreat was the paramount goal of the team during this phase of the operation. *Never permit the enemy to acquire an unexpected advantage.*

Sepp's concerns were for naught. The one survivor was an amateur who believed a few un-aimed shots could ward off a team of professionals. That man was wrong about many things that day, and this just happened to be one of them. Sepp pointed toward Killer, and then toward the wall the man was using as cover. The belch of 5.56mm rounds tore through the sheetrock as easily as they had ripped through the man's shirt. A deep, thick, gurgling noise emanated from around the corner. It was hard to listen to.

As the liquid death rattle faded, the team members each switched the dial on the flashlights affixed to their weapons from infrared to non-tactical white light. As always, it was an unpleasant scene. The bodies of men are no match for the violence within their minds. The number and lethality of weapons toted into the objective might have seemed inordinate to the untrained eye, but that is the way of all police and military agencies. Governments operate this way because the method is so successful. Military mistakes cost lives and lives are assets. Sepp's team was no different here for their tactics than any other paramilitary organization in the world. They were different for other reasons.

Surveying the detritus of battle, Sepp mused that Von Clausewitz had it wrong. *Politics is an extension of war by lesser means*, not the other way around. War must be the primary purpose, for it gets all the funding. *Whose budget is larger*, he asked himself, *an ambassador's, or a field general's*?

Sal announced the mission success call word, "Joy" three times for the sake of absolute clarity. Just as 'Fire in the Hole' is announced three times to communicate danger. He made his way past Matt and out toward the team van that Sepp had moments before beckoned onto the scene. By locating the drug money, the team's primary objective was achieved.

Beyond their physical security, all things were secondary to that end. Sepp thrice repeated the call word over the radio, and then returned his attention to physical security.

Dognut soon followed with a report of his own, "Bossman, Dognut got the dope!" He never was one for protocol, but it made no difference. Locating the cocaine was important, too; the stuff had to be taken off the streets. As

7

planned, they had hit the objective right in the middle of a drugs for money exchange.

Sepp paused and surveyed the wreckage. Four men in various states of disrepair were strewn about the floor plan. Blood was pooling and congealing on the hardwood floor. The smell of copper, gunpowder, and lacerated bowels hung heavy in the room. It always does when a plan comes together. Sepp and Doc began to search each of the deceased. It was a gruesome task, but a critical one. Agents of the local, state, or federal governments were not, and could not be, targeted by the team. Undercover cops are sometimes wired for sound. That could lead to all manner of unpleasantries for the team's collective good.

Sepp's technique for ensuring that no one was playing possum was to give each corpse a hard jab to the eyeball with the business end of his rifle. He learned in Iraq that this was a great way to reveal a faker. Having been in Afghanistan, Doc preferred to give each body a hard kick to the crotch. Both techniques confirmed expectations. *These four were toast.*

The body searches revealed that these men were nothing but typical gangbangers. None of them carried military grade handguns or were wired for sound. Sepp left the crime scene with a vague sense of security and two blood-wet latex gloves.

Outside the objective's house, Chuck watched as Matt retrieved Claymore anti-personnel mine from a small tree along the driveway. In extremis, that man-killer would send steel ball bearings into any law enforcement agency that attempted to encircle the OBJ. Chuck smiled at the thought of Matt's lethal instincts, knowing that a team comprised of such men was unstoppable.

As Doc entered the van, their driver, Chicken, quelled the police lights and the van moved toward Sepp's position. Sepp quickly mounted up and gave the nod to move to Chuck's pickup point. The team was quiet within the confines of the vehicle as they helped Chuck hoist his rifle into the back. Sepp removed the magnetic SWAT emblem as Matt and Doc unfastened the emergency lights from atop the van. With the façade removed, the team began the egress phase of the operation.

Chicken pulled onto a side street surrounding the OBJ, vanishing behind the curtain of night. As he did so, Sepp pulled the plug on the van's radio and cellphone jamming device and turned on the police scanner. He listened intently to the voice traffic. The fire at the warehouse was now under control, but the majority of the local precinct's manpower was still involved with the regulation of traffic into and out of the area. Sepp smiled. Arson had been their first criminal act of his day.

Sepp knew that the fire's diversions wouldn't last. As soon as they quit jamming the phones, calls would filter into the police dispatch. It was only a matter of time before the police figured out that they had no one in the area and that something very bad had gone down. But by that time, the team would be long gone. They were not simple highwaymen; they were highly organized, highly motivated criminals. And as with all past operations, they were not going to be caught this time either. This team had many advantages that would play in its favor; high on that list was that they had all been trained by the same sort of men who would be sent to capture or kill them.

In the outskirts of town, Sepp ejected the unspent round out of his M4 and tossed it out the window. Chicken seemed confused by this action, but Sepp paid him no mind. Sepp had learned the hard way in Iraq that the M4 is designed to chamber a round and then to fire it. The firing pin inside the weapon can actually touch the small mercury primer at the base of the round. Over time this causes a dent to form. This small depression in the primer potentially makes the bullet a dud round. It was such a dud round that had almost cost Sepp his life over in the Land of Allah. Sepp consequently never re-chambered a round; *bullets are meant to be shot. It is what they do.*

9

Rolling past the city limit sign, the van suddenly swerved over three lanes of empty road before it regained its trajectory.

"What the fuck, Chicken?" Sepp said none too politely. Getting pulled over by the cops is the last thing they needed.

"You see that fuck'n car, man?" he asked of Sepp. Sepp had seen the abandoned vehicle but didn't think anything of it.

"Man, that fucking shit fired up my PTSD, dude. Thought I was back in Haji-Stan." Chicken had driven his entire combat tour and was a little sensitive to roadside threats. He wiped the sweat from his brow and shook his head in embarrassment. The team's collective Post Traumatic Stress Disorder was yet another failing that Sepp had to account for when preparing for missions.

"I feel you, brother, I feel you," Sepp said as he lit a menthol cigarette for his buddy. He squeezed Chicken's shoulder after dampening the Zippo. It was a genuine show of empathy. *We all have our demons.*

Their safe house was a rental garage an hour away. It provided the team with a place to count, sort, and divide the loot, as well as to have one of their infamously long After Action Reviews. During this briefing, the team would go over every phase of the operation detail-by-detail, critiquing their performance. But before any of that could occur, each man took off his cumbersome body armor and changed into their street clothes. Large amounts of bottled water were also consumed, for violence is thirsty work indeed.

"...and that was when I noticed the US MARSHAL tag on Joe's jacket," Chuck explained during the last phase of the AAR.

"OK, people...lesson learned," Sepp interceded on Joe's behalf. And that was that. The only thing that did not go according to plan was inconsequential in the team leader's eyes. It was time for everyone to go their separate ways.

The loot had totaled twenty-five thousand each. It had already been divided and then greedily placed within each man's personal bag. Sepp had asked that a small portion be allotted for a former teammate, and all had agreed to a slight pay cut. Their total take was not enough money to risk one's life for, but it had only taken two weeks to earn. Sal and Dognut were tasked with disposing of the drugs. They put the large bags of white powder into a duffle before they left together. Sepp watched them depart before returning to his job of packing up the donation money. The other team members left at odd intervals after the money was divvied out. Chuck waited around to have a private word with Sepp.

Chuck led off with a softball, "You know, man, there's talk in the team about the dope,"

"I know," Sepp replied, waiting for the changeup that he knew would surely follow.

"They think that this is a fucking waste. They think we should be selling it and tripling the cash that we're making. And they got a good point. I think that the Twins," as Sal and Dognut were known, "are gonna sell that dope instead of burn it."

"They might at that," was Sepp's only response as he stacked his portion of the money into a rifle case.

Chuck could tell that the problem was not new to Sepp, and that it had already been thought out to what Sepp would term *its logical conclusion*. Chuck was frustrated, but left it at that.

After securing the clasp of his Pelican brand gun case, Sepp felt compelled to speak, "You wanna know why we do it this way?" it was a rhetorical question. "Why we nickel and dime this shit instead of just knocking off some fucking Al Pacino in his goddamn palace? Because my way we don't get killed, and we don't get caught either. That is why we do it my way, because my way is safe and smart. You guys know how to pull triggers, but there's more to it than that. A lot more."

Sepp was obviously angered by the challenge to his infallibility, so Chuck decided to change the subject. No reason to raise the man's ire.

"So, where you off to this time?" he asked.

"Way down south, man, way down south...gotta get out of this country, it's full of fucking thieves," Sepp jested.

It made no difference telling Chuck, but Sepp would never let on to his real destination. He had always been secretive that way.

"See you in a month, brother," Sepp said, turning his back to Chuck, "I'll find something real good for the boys, something that'll give us some time off."

Chuck smiled goodbye, for he knew that when he said something, Sepp meant it. And that in turn meant *real* money was on the horizon. Chuck's financial goals weren't lofty. He was growing close to his. And that was the kicker. Each man had sworn to play out this little game until his written goal was met. Failure to do so in the absence of death or debilitating wound would mean the "100 Dollar Bill Plan" would go into effect.

"Don't spend it all in one place, man," Chuck said to the closing door.

The $100 Bill Plan

In the event that any one of us decides to place his own priorities before that of the team, here in shall lay a damn good reason not to. If any member of the afore said team shall deviate from their written and stated financial goals, then that man shall bear this burden of punishment from all the living members of the team:

You might elude us for a while, perhaps years. But in the end, you will be held accountable for your transgressions. One day, when you're safe in your new life, you will come across a $100 Bill. You will take note of it. You will reach down to pick it up and place it into your pocket, happy in your good fortune. That moment shall be your last. The trigger shall then be pulled, and your death shall then fulfill thy obligation to said team.

The Undersigned Agree With this Very Real and Legally Binding Document:

Doc
Sepp Lokken
Chuck Wilson Jr.
Salvador "Sal" Calipari
Clarence "Chicken" Pandy
Tomas "Killer" Killingsworth
James "Dognut" Smith
Matt McCall
Joe D. Shifflett

This was in no way, of course, a legal document. It was but a simple pact accepted and signed by simple men. Legality notwithstanding, it was not less, but a greater pact for the men that chose to sign it. These men knew little of the law and cared even less for the conventions of the civilized. All they knew of law was concealed within the magazines of their weapons. In there was the only maxim that truly mattered: The Law of Retaliation.

ILLUMINATION ROUNDS

*"A Prince should therefore have no other
aim or thought, nor take up any other thing
for his study, but war."*
-Niccolo Machiavelli

Detective Jenna Penning was not the first to the crime scene, far from it. As the head of the Major Crime Unit, it was not *her* job to be the first there; it was her job to be the Lead Investigator. She quickly asserted authority by placing her people into key positions. Forensics, lab, and coroner's findings would all flow through her before official reports were made. The local sheriff was none too happy to take orders from a woman, but he possessed a clear enough sense of professionalism to toe the line and to make sure that his men did likewise.

After the obligatory briefing, Jenna's first few minutes were spent wondering about the crime scene, observing and listening to the uniformed officers discuss what they were experiencing. Jenna saw herself as an artist in this regard. She had once read that Michelangelo only freed his great statues from their stone, that *David* was already there, trapped in the marble. Major cases were like this for Jenna, where the bad guys always lurked within the stone-like lack of evidence. She was, as one of her colleagues had put it, a "tough bitch." A subordinate member of her Major Drug Interdiction Team had once drunkenly stated, "She might not wear the pants in this family, but she wears the strap-on."

An attractive thirty-three-year-old native of Miami, Jenna was tanned, fit, and married to the job. She typically wore her blonde hair in a ponytail that stuck out the back of one of her ball caps. None of her clothing ever covered her well-formed posterior. *Vanity, thy name is woman.*

She was indeed a beauty, and that was but one of her assets. Jenna also happened to be an encyclopedia when it came to the law. She had been under fire on multiple occasions and had acquitted herself as well as her male counterparts. When relocated to the Major Case Squad, Jenna quickly moved up the chain of command until she was running her own special branch. It wasn't Robbery Homicide but the hardcore Gangland Interdiction. She had worked tough cases and simple cases and thought that she had *been there, done that, got the T-shirt, and already lost it.*

This case would be different from all that she had previously experienced; that much was painfully obvious to her. The dead men had each been hit at least twice, with no missed shots. Professionals did this. The dead had not made an effective defense of their lives. All *their* rounds had already been accounted for in the plaster walls, the pockmarks identified on the old wallpaper with a black "X" marked with a Sharpie. None of their defensive shots had found their mark. The number of spent casings matched the slugs in the walls. What stood out the most was the back door of the residence had been breached with a clever explosive technique. One of the uniformed officers had to explain it to her, and he had clearly been impressed with the ingenuity.

"I've only seen this shit in training. It's really tight work, ma'am." The officer was a former Marine, and a veteran of Fallujah. His respect for the water impulse charge had, in turn, impressed Jenna. She did not understand how to blow a door down with water, but the Marine had said that the use of a water impulse charge showed a high level of expertise with demolitions.

The blown transformer had been punctured by an, as yet to be identified but no doubt, large caliber bullet. Forensics was working to determine the exact type of round used. The shot was fired from the rooftop of an abandoned house across the street. The rifleman left *Royale* brand cigarette butts around the chimney, but no spent shell casings were recovered. The butts were on route to the lab in hopes that some dried saliva on them would provide a biological fingerpost. Detective Penning was already wrestling with doubts about that. *The sniper had collected his brass but not his own biologicals?* The fissures cracking her preconceived notions of the crime scene began to appear as crow's feet around her pale blue eyes.

Amid the controlled chaos within the police line, Jenna ran scenarios to herself... *Perhaps a team of Colombians had been hired to kill one of the parties, and stole the drugs and the money on top of the fee for the hit. It was a possibility. Maybe there was another explanation.* One of the victims was one Carlo Vandingo (aka) "Dirty" Sanchez. He was not currently under surveillance, but one of his lieutenants happened to be. That same lieutenant had lost his police tail three days prior to the crime. *Perhaps the man had orchestrated a coup attempt within the Mexican Cartel.* Jenna wasn't sure about anything, really; all that she knew was that a drug war loomed on the horizon. *Shit like this does not stop without more bloodshed in its wake.*

Jenna was at the rear of the house, strangely fascinated by the mangled door when she overheard two uniformed cops, "To hell with 'em, goddamn druggies got what they deserved one way or another. Who really gives a fuck who did it?"

A far more frightening thought entered Detective Penning's consciousness. It rekindled her inquisitive mindset. The absence of shell casings could mean several things. First, it could mean that the perpetrators of this crime were using revolvers. Those weapons don't eject their spent shell casings but rather hold them within their cylinders.

17

Secondly, it could mean that the perpetrators collected their brass after the fact. The logistics alone for such a task was implausible, and therefore not likely. The third possibility was that these men (*females did not do this*) were using some device to collect the expelled brass on the fly. This possibility solidified a single thought in Jenna's mind. *These guys are cops, or military, maybe even a rogue police squad. No shell casings but cigarette butts? The cigarette butts are a red herring. Someone wanted the dope and the money, and had ruthlessly killed everyone in the house to get it.* These were now made into facts in her mind. Their self-evident nature excluded all other possibilities.

The neighbors on the block maintained that they had not called 911 because there was already a police van on scene. However, one man's statement claimed that his cell phone was interrupted around the time of the crime, and was restored only after the shooting stopped. Detective Penning had a feeling that when she checked the calls placed to the power company, she would find that they all went through after the crime was committed. *So, they are killing the power, jamming the airwaves, putting on a front that they are the police, and then taking the drugs and money and disappearing.*

The thought idled in her mind, stirring further questions. After a moment of lateral drift, she wondered how many cops had seen through this and let it slide. The hairs on her neck raised when Jenna realized the same type of crime had probably happened before.

She had a contact in the D.C. office of the F.B.I. and decided to run her theory past him before filing the official report to her captain. But first, she needed to contact the Fire Marshal about the warehouse fire that had consumed most of her precinct's manpower. She already suspected what she would find there. Jenna was a stranger to words like *chance* and *coincidence*.

18

"I hate hippies. I really fucking hate 'em," Missouri State Trooper Ross declared to his partner as traffic rolled by their Patrol cruiser.

"Yep," was the reply given by Sergeant Colt. Busting dopers was the single purpose of the day's patrol. Speeding tickets were an unsaid sidebar for these two. Their patrol captain had his agenda, and they had theirs. The silence lingering between them was in no way uncomfortable. They had known each other long enough not to feel the need to fill the void.

Colt's instincts were almost supernatural when it came to sniffing out drug runners. Ross knew it had more to do with Colt's personal history with dope than from any paranormal source, but what Colt said or did not say on his application was his own business. The two men had come a long way together through mutual trust. There was little second-guessing between them. Each man was focused on oncoming traffic, scanning for the telltale signs of drug runners trying to get their wares to the market cities of the Midwest. Interstate 44 is the front line in the war on drugs, and Trooper's Colt and Ross counted among its most decorated soldiers.

The two met at the United States Army's School of Infantry in Fort Benning, Georgia, some eight years ago. From there, they attended the Army's airborne school, again at Benning. They took another chance together and signed up for the Ranger Indoctrination Program, better known as RIP. The acronym is never lost on the candidates, who refer to the course as Rangers In Pain because there is no Resting In Peace to be had there.

Having never served in any regular Army units, they knew no other military than the Ranger Battalions and were thus known as "Batt Boys." Just getting into the Ranger Battalions is an insanely rigorous task, so their bond had been strengthened further. They had then both been assigned to Bravo Company and so had endured even more shared trauma. Their bosses had mostly been in Mogadishu on that hellish day back in '93, so they had received a rough initiation. Their training was incredibly harsh; this was rightly so, and they knew it. While enduring the rigors of a peacetime army they had in turn prayed to have their own battle, to prove their own mettle.

The War God answered when those motherless bastards attacked the Eastern seaboard. No thinking soldier was pissed about the wreck of United Flight 93, for that was America's first strike back at the terror. It was a successful operation carried out by civilians with absolutely no training. *God Bless 'em.*

However, two combat tours are more than one can rightly expect from a man when war has not officially been declared.

US Declarations of War by Acts of Congress:
1. United Kingdom – 1812
2. Mexico – 1846
3. Spain – 1898
4. The Great War – 1917, Twice.
5. World War II – 1941 & 42, Six Times.

The US has never declared War on the nations of Korea or Vietnam. The US never declared War with Terror, Drugs, or Poverty.

So, after serving out their enlistments with SOCOM, the two men decided to get out while they still had their limbs and lives. Like many soldiers, the two aspired to become police officers. They decided to go home and try out for the State Police. That was three years gone now, so the Batt Boys fought in the other unending, undeclared war: The War on Drugs.

The high pitch of their radar gun went off as a three-year-old white Bavarian Motor Works 315i cruised past their concealed position. The two men paid no heed to the machine's chirp or the red display that clocked the vehicle's speed at 76 mph.

"Hippies, you said."

As the good Dr. Thompson once wrote, *"The long hair arouses contempt in the cop heart."* You know, they don't bathe properly."

"And you know we're not in the 60s anymore?"

"Just because they no longer call themselves that doesn't mean they're not. They still cover up with that nasty patchouli."

Colt laughed. He'd only smelled it once when Phish was in town. The only people wearing it seemed to be spoiled rich kids pretending to be hippies. It was the marijuana that he smelled. He was good at sniffing out potheads because he used to be one of them. Ross didn't seem to mind because Colt could score a bust, and with a bust came accolades. Accolades meant promotions, and so it was decided.

A late model VW van is suspicious, but not really an excuse to pull someone over. However, as it lumbered by at a smooth 59 mph, Colt noticed a Grateful Dead sticker on the shiny rear bumper, and in the great state of Missourah, that is probable cause.

"Oh Shit, Bob," was all that Slim Truex could muster under the circumstances. He had a freshly rolled joint in one hand and a bag of weed between his legs. The rolling papers were lost in his nervous fright. *The papers always get lost.*

"Don't turn your head, man, be cool," Bob chided. They were busted and knew it. No sense getting upset about it. There was only a small amount of grass on them. They only smoked joints, so there wasn't even any paraphernalia. Still, the flashing lights and the blaring siren sent his blood pressure racing.

Ross was pleased to see them decelerating and crossing lanes to pull onto the right-hand shoulder. *Damn the fools who pull off to the left just because they're scared or trying to show their obedience. Those idiots don't seem to realize that both they and the patrolmen will have to pull back into speeding traffic.*

As always, Ross and Colt let the offenders stew in their vehicle for a while. This served the dual purpose of allowing for a thorough plate check and increasing the stress on the occupants. The plates had come back clean, but it was during the wait that Sergeant Colt noticed that the van was in immaculate condition; that is if you could look past the Deadhead 'Steal Your Face' logo. Or is that painted on? *Damn, it is. It was a perfect rendition.*

Slim and Bob lived a good life. On the road, they're what Deadheads called Trustafarians. A play on "trust fund" and "Rastafarian," they are usually spoiled kids spending their family's hard-earned cash on dope and "finding themselves." The term matched them to a T. They lived off a huge trust fund set up by Bob's late father, a big-time televangelist out of Dallas. Never the religious type, Bob decided to hit the road with his buddy Slim and do what they loved to do. Both men had worked hard to become ASE certified mechanics and liked to tour the nation following various bands. Once Jerry Garcia died, they kept on trucking with the band of the day. *Phish, Widespread Panic, whomever.*

The mission never changed; Bob and Slim stayed in various parking lots, fixing the inevitable breakdowns. Stoners aren't the greatest caretakers of their rigs. It was a point of pride that they never passed by a stranded vehicle without an offer to help. They never accepted a monetary payment, well maybe the occasional joint or an offered sexual favor from the pretty ladies, but that doesn't really count. The only things the guys ever took away were a Polaroid of the people they had helped and the feeling of a job well done. The photo album on the van's console bore

22

testament to this life choice. It was one that the two men were justifiably proud of.

Trooper Ross approached the van, noticing the pungent smell of marijuana emanating from it. He held up his clipboard between himself and the driver's side window. Most people don't know that these clipboards are wrapped in bulletproof Kevlar, but they are. Cops take all the advantages they can get because they take more risk than most people.

"License and registration," he quickly demanded. Ross hated it when people asked him what the problem was. He always got to that part in accordance with his own schedule.

"Ok, Ok, Man." Bob immediately regretted his choice of words, but they had already flown from his mouth. Ross's response to this familiar address was predictable.

"Are we fishing buddies?" Ross said with a tone of agitation. Bob knew what was coming.

"Boy, don't you ever address law enforcement with that damn word. You see this rank on my sleeve? It means Corporal. You can call me that. You can call me 'officer,' 'sir,' hell, even 'trooper' will do, but don't you ever call me 'man' you got that, hippie?" Ross jabbed the clipboard at the driver.

Bob did, and nodded with a very polite "Yes sir."

"What the shit we got here?" Colt had snuck up on the passenger's side of the van, scaring the bejesus out of Slim. He and Bob instinctively looked over at the other Patrolman, giving Colt his chance.

"I 'm talking to you, boy." Their heads whipped back to the driver's side. Colt and Ross did this on purpose, of course. They called their little game the Tennis Match because they could keep those heads going back and forth like spectators at Wimbledon. The cops continued their spiel until the obligatory vehicle search took place. Slim tried to assert his constitutional rights, protecting him from unreasonable searches and seizures, until Trooper Colt

23

informed him that the alternative was to wait right here until a warrant was cleared. That bullshit cleared up in a hurry. The van was duly searched.

"Well, well, well, what have we here?" Colt stepped out of the passenger's side door of the van and confronted the two hippies, who were now leaning against the van's hood under the watchful eye of Trooper Ross. In Colt's hand was a small black cylinder with a grey cap.

"A thirty-five-millimeter film canister, lookie here. Damn, you hippies are stupid, musta thought that this here is our first day on the job," his voice dripped with sarcasm as he shook his head, dumbfounded. He handed the 'evidence bomb' to Ross and went back to his search.

These might have been hippies, but they sure took good care of that vehicle. The only thing that cluttered the front of the rig was a photo album. Colt sat in the passenger seat and thumbed through it. He had a new appreciation for these two young men. Maybe he could work a deal.

Trooper Colt stepped out of the van, to confer with his colleague.

After doing so, he shot a look at the hippies. "We're taking you downtown, punks. You're looking at five years for this. With that pretty, long hair, you'll be the belle of the ball."

What happened next was a first for both officers. Bob fainted. Just flat out collapsed. It was the funniest thing they had seen on the job.

They helped him up. "I was just fucking with you," Ross said. "Seems you two boys are decent folk when yer not gettin' stoned as you drive down our nation's highways. We're gonna let you go. But you don't get to keep this." They watched sadly, but still relieved as their buds were poured on the ground and swept away by the wind.

"Before you go, we have a mechanical job for you."

Slim perked up. "Sure, anything."

Three hours later, Bob and Slim were finishing a complete tune-up and lube job on the First Baptist Church's

'Meals on Wheels' van. Reverend Dobbs brought everyone a glass of homemade lemonade and informed the two civilians that break time had arrived. Colt and Ross grumbled, but Reverend Dobbs quietly insisted.

"Those boys are *his* people too," the Reverend said. "Especially when they're doing *His* work."

Colt raised his glass in a toast with Ross. Bob and Slim smiled at each other as they downed the thirst-quenching treat. They had just done what they both loved to do, fix good people's cars. What made them smile most was the kind bud they knew was in Slim's underwear.

Belize is a stable nation within a historically unstable region. The former British Honduras is now a Mecca in the sport diving community, and a hotspot for international tourists. Sepp's plane landed at the Belize City airfield. As he stepped from the aircraft, he was consumed by the warm tropical humidity. That was going to take some getting used to. He was familiar with the dry, desert air. At least here Sepp wouldn't be in full tactical gear.

The airport in Belize is one of those places where only a ceiling is required. There are no walls to hold in air conditioning even if there was any. Sepp was well rested. There's no jetlag when you stay in the same time zone. He retrieved his scuba gear from his checked baggage, examining it to make sure it had not been damaged in transit. Experience had taught him that this was the only place where blame could be placed on the airline. His Dräger rebreather had cost him upwards of five thousand dollars and he was damned if it was gonna get jacked up by TACA airlines without due compensation. Upon inspection, all his gear was in order, the rebreather as well as the extras.

The customs office comprised of a small tollbooth looking structure within the airport proper. There was no activity within it. A fat guard and a skinny dog were deep in siesta as Sepp passed through Belizean customs.

A ten-minute ride later, Sepp was heading down an aluminum dock leading to his water taxi. A boat with four 150cc outboard motors was waiting. To the unsuspecting tourist, the ride was a total nightmare. Buffeting atop small waves that lead out to barrier reef islands, the small boat seemed to be heading straight toward a mangrove isle. But just as the entirety of the passengers was sure that an unseemly death was about to be had, the pilot made a hard cut to port. The new vantage afforded by the turn allowed for a view of the small gap between what had previously appeared to be a single land mass. The rest of the passengers let out a whoop that lingered between the trees. Sepp gave a savage howl, for to him, life was a danger area, and the best way to move through one of those is with great rapidity. It was the way Sepp lived his entire life. He departed the vessel feeling alive. The driver received a large tip for his theatrics.

Caye Caulker, as it is written, is pronounced Key Caulker by the natives. Really just a small strip of deforested mangrove and coral, Caye Caulker is paradise. Simple, quiet, and sunny. The island lies about a mile from the Barrier Reef. It is not the Great Barrier Reef, but it is the second largest reef in the world. Sepp had come for the diving, the sun, and the snorkeling. Well, the booze and the women, too. Where the liquor flowed loosely, so did the ladies. Before vacation could begin, there were ventures that needed attending. Those tasks he reluctantly deemed work.

Sepp first took the money he had concealed in his dive gear and visited the local bank. He opened a savings account with a generous sum deposited and prepaid for a safety deposit box. Sepp was well aware that the mangrove islands had been ravaged by a hurricane; there was money but no real wealth being stored at the bank itself. Instead, he was safeguarding some modest cash and a few key documents. This was not unlike the other banks that he had visited throughout his journeys. The Caribbean was his

26

favorite haunt, but there were European and South American banks as well. If he found himself in Asia, a wire transfer or a quick trip on a false passport to the South Island of New Zealand would have to be made.

After his business at the bank was completed, Sepp visited one of the many dive shops that lined the waters of Caye Caulker. The name "Bob's Dive Emporium" tickled his fancy, so he booked tomorrow's trip to the Reef with Bob himself as the guide. A few years ago, his PADI credentials as a certified Dive Master would have been more than adequate for the trip. But in this day and age, Bob wanted to see his dive log. *It's an insurance thing, you see?* The log was proffered, and after conducting some business, Bob recommended a bar at the northern end of the island.

With his work complete, Sepp ambled down the sand-covered thoroughfare that comprised Caye Caulker's main street, the only sounds being the wind through the trees and the occasional hum of a golf cart passing by. No gas powered vehicles are allowed for normal use on the island, though there are a few golf carts allowed for the convenience of wealthy residents. At the far northern extremity of Caye Caulker lies the bar called "Patty's at the Split." It is a typical beach bar but without the beach. Partly because the juvenile island was of mangrove origins, there were no sandy strands of beach. Patty's husband had fixed all that by constructing a pier that served instead of a beach. The actual *Split* was the result of a hurricane slicing a channel through the northern end of Caye Caulker Island. But that was long ago, now the channel provides a good snorkeling experience for the beginner. Sepp noticed a few of the women in the loungers were topless. *There's nothing like a woman's bare breasts to put a man in a good mood.* Drinks were in order.

"Barkeep, I think that this situation demands some heavy drinking," Sepp said in his most convincing southern accent.

"What'cha haven, Sailor?" the actual Patty of "Patty's at the Split" asked.

"That obvious?" Sepp played into her incorrect assumption. "Can you make me something with tea?"

"Ice Pick is yer best bet there. Tall glass of sweet tea with a shot or two of Stoli vodka, topped with a wedge of lemon."

"That'll do just fine, ma'am. Make it two and make them doubles." Sepp was ready to get his swerve on right then and there. He pounded the first drink and before he could ask, a second one replaced the empty glass.

A topless beauty selected the lounger facing him. That couldn't have been a coincidence. Her body was tight tanned and fit. It was clear that she had spent much of her time in the Caribbean nude sunbathing. Her golden hair was almost dreadlocked by sea salt and a shoestring budget. Elke was her name. She was a Dutch beauty from some small town outside of Amsterdam that she assured him was close enough to be Amsterdam itself.

Elke was in that particular stage of womanhood that men find irresistible. Playful in mind, and a woman in body; her innocence had been surrendered, but her essence was still fresh. Sepp was relatively young at twenty-nine, but this nineteen-year-old had all the men in the world wrapped around her finger.

Two bottles of Belikin beer shook on the rickety excuse for a nightstand before it fell beneath the weight of clothing flung off in a frenzy of sexual appetites at their zenith. Sepp's physical condition was the product of years of self-discipline. He was in fantastic shape; his body was peppered with battle scars enhancing his masculinity in her blue eyes.

In contrast, Elke was flawless. Every curve on her sunkissed body was stunning. What pleased him most was how she surrendered herself to his command. She liked it rough which was fortunate because Sepp knew of no other way.

Taking her from behind, Sepp was watching Elk as she watched herself in the mirror. Really all he wanted was to see her beautiful face. But she didn't need to know that. Elke loved the dominance. She saw him lower himself out of view, feeling the kisses down her curves. He paused and she quivered. Elke grabbed the bedpost with both hands. She felt him lick as her knees began to shake. Elke regained her strength as she watched Sepp bind her wrist to the bedpost. Ja Meester, Jaa!

He was back to fucking aggressively. Sepp had already taken her to the very top twice with his mouth and fingers. But no man had ever given her an orgasm from penetration alone. Elke could feel the tightening in her stomach as another was building. She looked back at Sepp, shocked. Sweat streamed down his face. A bead fell from the upturned lip of his satisfied smirk. His eyes were closed, letting his energy slap into her own.

Elke's core shook as the orgasm took control of her body. The bedpost Sepp had bound her hands to broke off as she let the island know that she had just had the fucking of her life. The scream of delight was a Dutch phrase that Sepp took to mean 'Yes, God!'

She collapsed on the bed as if her bones were made of Jello. Her hands curled up, shaking uncontrollably.

Elke's dripping wetness and obvious satisfaction meant it was his turn. She rolled onto her side, presenting herself. He eased inside her gently and fucked with raw abandon.

Sepp was getting close. She could tell from his breathing rhythm and increased force.

She slid off of him and went to her knees. Sepp wanted to finish his way, but she had other plans.

"In my mouth," she begged.

"Holy fuck!"

29

Afterward, she fell onto her back, exhausted but thoroughly satisfied. He offered her a sip of beer. She drank a mouthful and shut her eyes. Sepp took her into his arms and set her comfortably on the bed. A cute whisper of a snore soon emerged from her beautiful mouth.

Sepp stole a cigarette from her purse and made his way to the balcony. Looking back at her on the bed, he noticed that her legs were twitching. He smiled another smile, for pleasing her had pleased him greatly. Sepp took a second drag off the cigarette, exhaled, and flicked the ember into the sand below.

The next day, Sepp passed Elke on his way to the dock. She did not accost him with any warm affection, but rather offered a demure smile. Elke's body language told him although he had left in the early morning hours, Sepp was welcome to call on her and her favors at his leisure. Sepp shot back a sated grin at her and then shook hands with Dive Master Bob.

The trip to the reef only took thirty minutes, during which Sepp prepared for the coming dive. His request was odd but Bob accommodated him without question. Sepp wanted to dive at a fairly consistent depth and to be resupplied with air tanks below the water. It was a circuitous route; the total dive time would be roughly six hours. There was some danger here, which Bob was delicate in noting. A few hundred-dollar bills assuaged the Dive Master's trepidation, and that was that. Cash paying customers are a thing unto themselves and although Bob had his theories, he kept them to himself.

Sepp drifted the entire time he was submerged, never going further down than thirty-five feet. He followed a simple route. His mind focused on a solitary aim. After five and a half hours beneath the waves, it was time to put his theory to the test. He began to ascend to the surface. And that is when the most terrible pain in his life began. His very lungs felt as though they were exploding. He thought it was the bends. Air had passed into the soft tissue of his chest, and that air was trying to vacate the body via his flesh. Hands balled up as though suffering from palsy, Sepp found that he was unable to perform even the simplest of motor functions. The pain was intense to the point of paralysis. Only the timely intervention of Dive Master Bob, who slowed his ascent, saved him from the insane level of agony that he was enduring.

The following day Sepp understood the error of his ways. Thoroughly embarrassed, he made several inquiries as to a more appropriate rate of ascent and decided not to dive again on this trip. He wore a T-shirt to the bar because his chest was peppered with what looked like a nasty rash.

His plan was to drink until the pain and embarrassment were gone. After fortifying himself with yet another cocktail at the bar, Sepp found himself in a conversation with Patty's husband, Stephen. He was a portly fella with a swagger of wealth about him. It didn't take long for him to start bragging about all the properties he owned on the island. Patty's Bar was a gift for their ten-year anniversary. Eventually, Patty eased across the bar to serve the men drinks, but mostly to join in on the conversation. Stephen took the margarita, no salt, and then admonished her for a recent weight gain.

"What did I tell you about that shit woman?" he grabbed over the bar to squeeze at her ample forty-year-old frame.

"You told me that you would still love me if I got fat, Steve," she replied.

"And," he smiled.

She finished his stock phrase. "You told me that you would still love me but that you would miss me too."

Sepp laughed heartily until it became clear that it was no joke, just the straight hard truth. The conversation grew quiet and awkward, and so Sepp decided to change the topic.

"So, Steve, are there any good properties for sale? You piqued my interest."

Stephen could tell by the manner in which Sepp carried himself that the money was there. He answered in a way that just might benefit himself financially. There was a business lot he owned with an apartment above. He told Sepp he'd let it go for only 425K. Sepp had reservations. Anything approaching a solid footing put Sepp off balance. The whole thought was like a dream, but if Elke would stay.

Chuck drove up the long driveway that led to his parent's house in Kansas. He felt shame when he saw the single star in the front window. It meant that the home had one son, or these days a daughter, fighting overseas. It was just like the home in Saving Private Ryan, only they had four stars. He held his head low as he approached the house. A profound sense of shame overwhelmed him. He felt bad that they still flew that banner and that he had betrayed that oath. He was a mercenary now, and felt no pride of it. Only the smell of his mother's baking knocked his mind back into the here and now. The aroma of homemade pies hit his nostrils as he followed the brick walkway leading him around the house and to the rear kitchen door. There, placed on the windowsill next to the wooden door lay a couple of his mother's blackberry pies cooling as in some 1950s television show. The intoxicating smell enticed him to steal a bit of the golden brown outer crust, but he dared not.

The backyard was a maze of gardens and clotheslines. The green field beyond was lush with the simplicity of the farm. Why he had ever left this place was a mystery to him. Chuck saw his mother hanging laundry on the far line and moved toward her. His approach was stealthy even with his six-foot-four frame.

"Hello, Charles," she said when he was about ten feet from her. A professionally trained sniper and he could still not get past his mother's intuition.

She moved to him and they embraced. "My boy, you are looking thin as a rail. Let's get some food in you."

And so they ate, and they talked. It was decided that Charles would spend the rest of his "leave" at the farm, helping the family tend to the soil. Chuck Sr. was skeptical of all the random time that his son had off these days. It was unlike the Army in which he served. Chuck Sr. had been in a peacetime Army and had still been gone for years at a stretch. But times had changed and he was simply happy to have his son back for a while.

Clarence "Chicken" Pandy had a very different upbringing from the rest of the team. He was born dirt poor and jet-black in South Philly. Chicken was the sort of man who had tasted acrid gunpowder as long as he could remember. He had, therefore, joined the Army via a different recruitment agency than the rest of the team. The head of a local chapter of the Bloods had given Chicken a directive. *Join the Army, go to the Rangers, and return to teach us how to kill better.* Under the threat of death to his family and himself, Chicken made it through all those long runs, road marches and night patrols. He never thought about failing. He couldn't think about that. Most of his instructors liked the way he operated. Secretly, they were happy to have a disciplined ex-gangbanger in their Army. He was not like the other recruits. He had already been under fire. He had fought in gun battles. A combat veteran for the price of a raw recruit is a good deal.

The sergeants and officers of the Regiment saw a dedicated young man, but it took the fatherly concern of a

First Sergeant (1SG) to see deeper into the man. When doing the required Preventative Maintenance on SPC Clarence Pandy's personally owned vehicle in advance of going on leave, the Company First Sergeant Travis Sage noted that the military vehicle identification sticker on Chicken's car was velcroed onto the windshield instead of properly affixed. When the 1SG inquired as to why this was the case, *a clear violation of the Uniform Code of Military Justice and a security threat*, Chicken had told him a partial truth.

"First Sarn't, all due respect, but if I leave my car in my naberhood, with that there sticker, it will be trashed and quick."

The 1SG had not totally bought that response, but it took the entire two-week leave to consider his young Ranger's situation.

Ranger tabbed and combat scrolled SPC Pandy was summoned to the 1SG's office right after the company 5-mile run that followed every block leave. Standing at a rigid *Parade Rest*, Chicken was put *at ease* and asked point blank if he was a gangster. Now, any soldier knows that admitting to something illegal to a senior non-Com is in itself a UCMJ violation. Still, something about the First Sergeant's demeanor told Chicken that it was now or never. Chicken came clean with the 1SG. The truth is painful, but it carries its own weight.

Chicken was given a promise of transfer, an immediate week of emergency leave to get his kinfolk out of Dodge, and was to be paid for the enterprise. Sadly though, Chicken had prematurely called his brother and told him of the eminent break with the gang and of the upcoming visit home to make the necessary arrangements. That was when things got jacked up. Some jackass officer, not even in his direct chain of command, had called "Bullshit" and screwed things up just long enough for Chicken's brother to accidentally sell him out. His brother was killed in a drive-by, and his mother murdered in her own home. His girlfriend made it out of the City of Brotherly Love just in time to hear that Chicken was being discharged from the Army for striking the officer who had so desperately messed things up for him. The discharge was all that the 1SG could do for the boy that he had so utterly failed. It was the only regret 1SG Sagee had about his time in service when he applied for an early retirement the following spring.

During the toil of actually leaving the Army, SPC Pandy found himself waiting in a long line doing out-processing paperwork. In that line, Chicken found himself sitting next to another soldier who offered him a way to lash out at both the Bloods, and, in a roundabout way, the Army itself.

And so, it came to pass that Sepp had entered into Chicken's life. And he was a better man for it. Sepp had never deviated from the path that he had set forth. Sepp was a white boy who had proved his worth over and over. Chicken had money in the bank and more coming every few months. The money was good and the danger always minimized. Sepp never killed when it was unnecessary. He never took the drugs to sell. The dope was always destroyed or used to gain the trust and confidence of the next victim. This he could respect about Sepp. The other white hoodlums were a different matter altogether, but Sepp was the master of them. Chicken took comfort in that.

"Hey Baby, what you got cook'n?" he asked his beautiful woman as he let his hands run over the roundness of her backside. He already knew the answer, but loved to hear her say it.

"Baby, can't you smell it." She laughed at his foolishness. He knew. Black-eyed peas over rice and hot water cornbread, *don't nothin smell like it*. He returned to the TV to catch up on all the scores he had missed due to the Operation. Betty busied herself with the plates, knives, and forks. Taking care of her man was her business. Making money was his. She knew what he did for a living, but loved him anyway. He loved her too, but the details of that weren't nobody's business but their own.

35

Sal and Dognut were tasked with the job of getting rid of the cocaine. A portion was kept as bait for the next hit, but the bulk of it was to be destroyed. The team had been built around the central theme that dopers are bad people and that killing them was a community service. It was a code that ran contrary to most people's ethics, but it had served them well enough. Sepp had sold the idea to the men on the team with the pretext that they would be helping the country by taking drugs off the streets. A certain moral high ground was the backbone of the team. Hell, Sepp even wanted to leave the stuff in the beginning. Sal had dissuaded him from such foolishness straight away. To do so would generate little respect from the police, but it would also narrow any potential investigations into the real motive behind the hits.

Sal had dumped some of the stuff into a river initially. He now laughed at his naïveté. There was so much money to be made in the dope trade that it proved too much for him and his partner in crime to give up on. Soon, the Kentucky Twins were making more money than they were on the Hits. No one on the team seemed to want to be caught with the stuff, so the two men became the default disposal unit for what was in reality, a goldmine. This suited the two quite well, but as the man says, *"When life looks like easy street, there is danger at your door."*

Their steady buyer rubbed furiously at his nose. "Goddamn, man, that is some straight up, grade-A coke. I'm gonna cut the fuck out of this shit." He rapidly expanded on his thoughts. "Where the fuck do you guys get this? No, no, I don't want to know, but goddamn it's good."

Just buck up with the fucking cash, and we'll see you next time." Sal was in a hurry to secure some female companionship for the weekend. If he waited too long, the good ones would be taken.

"You guys just don't know what you're missing. This shit will have hot ass nuggets on their knees just to taste this shit, bro." It was this declaration that stuck with the two men as they drove home to Kentucky.

Once back at the hotel, Dognut decided to come out and ask his buddy a question that had been on his mind, "Say, how much of that shit did we keep for the next score?" Dognut asked Sal. It was standard practice for the team to keep some of the stuff to help make inroads into the next drug community that they would ultimately eliminate from the face of the Earth.

"About one and a half kilos, man," Sal responded.

"Man, speak plainly, like a white American, and leave that metric shit to niggers, fags, and Europeans. I deal in pounds, so how many pounds is that?"

"That would be about three and a half pounds, *Herr Hitler.* Wanna try some?" Sal knew where this was going.

There was a Motel 76 advertisement in the distance and the trip was a long one. The idea was to stop by the motel, get a room, and try the stuff out. A few days later, they left town with a thriving addiction to cocaine.

Killer was working late in the back of his gun shop, which gave him the privacy required to destroy the team's used rifle barrels. He carefully checked the chamber of each weapon before igniting his cutting torch. He had failed to inspect them once, and the oversight had consequences, unpleasant consequences. That small explosion was how his little brother had become wise to his mercenary work. He desperately wanted on the team, but Killer would not have it. He cursed his stupidity as well as his brother's insane desire to follow in his footsteps.

The cutting was soon done. The next task was an especially soothing one for Killer to toil through. He was replacing the entire upper receiver of his backup M4 with a newer and slightly different one. The CMMG Corporation, out of Fayette had just placed its 7 1/2 inch M4 barrel on the market. Killer used a back-channel connection to acquire an unused prototype. The snub-nosed barrel was already affixed to an upper receiver, so the process was quite simple. Remove both retaining pins and switch out the entirety of the upper with the new version. This meant that he now had a ballistically untraceable barrel and an all-new sighting system to be tweaked into combat readiness.

That was the rub, Killer knew that he had to re-zero the weapon and its attached optical package to compensate for the shorter barrel. His weapon would not be as accurate as the longer barreled version, but it was lighter, more compact, and thus precisely what Killer was looking for in a close quarters battle scenario.

Doc was frightened by the sudden realization that he was driving when he awoke. The day was bright and he had plenty of rest the night before, but this had happened before, just not while driving. He slapped himself to regain his senses and as a form of self-abuse for his error. Thankfully, the road was empty. His fear was becoming a reality. He finally admitted to himself that these were narcoleptic episodes, and they were getting worse. Still, Doc was reluctant to confide his weakness to anyone. He had ably hidden it while on active duty and figured that he could continue to do so. *No use in getting anyone else involved, especially Sepp.*

"High Side! High Side!" Matt screamed at his charges. The white-water raft he was guiding just north of Dahlonega, Georgia. had just struck a rock and was in serious danger of flipping. One of the men in his rafting group was drunk and had failed to heed commands. Matt cursed the man and then used his strength to shove away from the rock. The raft low sided and eased back into the current away from the massive stone.

"You need to listen and respond accordingly, you half-wit!" he roared. The rest of the crew let out a collective gasp. Matt saw the hurt his message conveyed but still commanded the drunk to keep his oar dry for the rest of the trip. It was not the drunk's fault; it was Matt's and he knew it. No one else was driving the boat, just him. He had seen the drinking and had not said anything about it. Matt also knew he would lose this job at the pullout point, but he didn't care.

Fucking idiot, he chastised himself but looked straight at the now shamed and wet drunkard.

DANGER AREA

*"Make a fortune honestly if you can; if not,
make it by any means necessary."*
                                        -Horace, circa 21 B.C.

In late January, the team was to reconvene just outside the small Pacific Northwest town of Yelm, Washington. It was close enough to the target area of Seattle, and yet far enough south from the city to provide a safe distance for the train-up. Chuck rented a moss-strewn hunting lodge under the pretense of a frat boy reunion. There would be men, guns, booze, and of course odd hours. Late night gunfire was a given. The team would appear as a bunch of college-educated idiots reuniting to relive the debauchery of days gone by. *A good lie always has an element of truth in it.*

Chuck had set the place up right, and knew that Sepp would be pleased with it. He closed the rain slick padlock to the easement and headed for the Port of Olympia. The drive was short but it gave his windshield wipers a workout. A constant drizzle was not rain, *per se*, but a dense fog with droplets of moisture that seemed to hang suspended in the air. The winter rain in western Washington did not come and go; it just was.

After climbing down the gangway, Sepp was actually smiling as he donned a raincoat. Chuck knew his friend was a true to life ruthless killer, but he was also aware that Sepp could turn this part of himself 'on or off' at will. Chuck watched Sepp sign for his car keys, wondering when his Boss was going to turn that part of himself back on. Sepp was too friendly, *like he must have been before he had seen combat*, Chuck guessed quite correctly. The truck had a Panamanian registration. Chuck wanted to ask if he had driven it from Panama, but he did not. Sepp did not like questions of that sort.

People always told Sepp that he should buy an American made truck, and he always replied that he was a combat vet of the United States Army and there was a rebuilt Chevrolet 350 under the hood of his '72 Land Cruiser. He figured that the truth of the matter should suffice. He was fascinated by the truck and began to pamper it as such. As Chuck watched Sepp evaluate the entirety of the rig, the change in his boss was slow but sure. Sepp went from his beer and pizza routine to his deadly serious mode. All the particulars were checked and then rechecked. It wasn't that Sepp babied the rig; it was more like when a soldier cleans his rifle before a mission. There was love and devotion in what Sepp did, but it wasn't out of affection either, more out of *need*. Chuck realized that Sepp did everything out of a certain need. He required the truck to function perfectly, or to at least be intimate with all its failings. That way, he could anticipate its failures. Sepp did this with all his tools, and with the team. While watching Sepp check the oil's texture, Chuck knew that he and the rest of the team were simply parts to be cleaned and checked by the Boss. There was sadness in this, but also a shaded beauty. Chuck knew that this was as close to love as Sepp would ever get. Even after all the missions that they had worked together, Chuck surmised there was an immeasurable distance between him and Sepp. What Chuck didn't know was that Sepp held him in a genuine regard. He actually liked Chuck, and that was a rare emotion for him.

After dropping off Chuck's rental car in Olympia, the two began combing through the details of the impending mission.

"How we lookin' on possibles for the medical staff?" Sepp asked Chuck as he settled into the cabin, picking the least choice spot for himself and his gear. Sepp was never one to abuse his brevet rank.

"We got some definite possibles," Chuck replied. He truly relished this part.

Mike O'Brien was lingering in his cramped office, drinking whiskey from a Styrofoam cup. He had nowhere else to go that evening. His wife left him several months ago, and he had been 86'd from the local tavern. O'Brien became a private investigator because of the TV show Magnum PI, but had to admit that he had fallen well short of the mark. It didn't help that the functioning side of his alcoholism was fading. He watched as a taxi pulled into the parking lot and around the corner. Anonymity is something that most of his clients wish to preserve. This guy took it to the next level with his ridiculous bucket hat and dark glasses. The disguise stood out on his tall, lanky frame. Mike had a feeling that this was not going to be a usual client. His instincts would prove to be correct in this matter.

Chuck saw that the private dick put away a stack of contracts and a Styrofoam cup as he approached the desk. The distinct aroma of whisky hung in the air. *It was not this man's first rodeo either.* Chuck withdrew his hand from his coat pocket and dropped its contents onto the desk. Five hundred in twenty-dollar denominations has an undeniable ability to catch the attention of your typical PI, and O'Brien proved himself to be quite average in that regard.

The job was relatively simple. Young interns at the local trauma centers were to be scoped out. He would then compile data on each prospective candidate. And that was all that the private Dick would be privy to. What O'Brien, P.I. did not need to know was that these young professionals were being stalked, so it would be easy to snatch one of them up to work on any team members who suffered worse wounds than Doc could treat. Chuck most decidedly didn't like this grizzly part of the business, but it was a necessary facet of the team's operations.

When Nick Valdosta had been hit in the Atlanta Operation, a second-year med student had saved his life but not his leg. The team may have had reservations about Sepp's leadership before then, but it had been a backup plan that they didn't even know about that had saved their teammate. They never forgot Sepp's ruthless foresight, for if he did it for Nick, he would do it for them. It was also Sepp that had set up a stipend for Nick. He didn't receive a cut per se, but there was always money sent to the Valdosta family after a score. Sometimes it was only a couple thousand dollars, but more than a few times it was considerably more. This all added up to a serious boost to unit morale. And that, too, was a planned consequence of events.

Chuck had done an admirable job, Sepp surmised as he read through the dossiers of the medical staff. Had he known that an outside agent was used, he would have been more than a little disturbed, but Sepp was unaware of his cohort's shortcut. All the prospective doctors were single, all lived in areas easy to ingress and egress, and all had surgical aspirations and/or experience. They would not be harmed, even in extreme circumstances. There was no need for that. All that had to be done was to show the candidate a simple file that listed each of their next of kin, maybe some other information that the gumshoe had gathered. All the intelligence was quite genuine, to be sure, but a straw-man in reality.

While Sepp and his team had spent their late teens and early twenties learning the trade of war, these people were in college learning more pastoral arts. Scaring them was no great achievement. It was simply business. Once they saw a photo of their mothers, or aunties and uncles, they would only do what they were trained to do. After that, a knock on the head or a chloroform soaked rag would give the team the time needed to part ways with the medical resource. Regardless, Chuck took an unnatural pleasure in making the dossiers look as CIA as possible. He even used the plastic cover sheets that he picked up at the local copy shop to augment the private dick's handy work. Sepp laughed as he tossed the folder back atop the pile.

"There is something seriously wrong with you."

"I know," Chuck deadpanned right back at him, a devilish grin forming as he contemplated his perverse satisfaction.

In the next few days, the team slowly assembled in that misty, sleeper of a town. Killer flew into SeaTac, his modest gun store in Missouri was being run by his suspecting little brother. Killer greedily opened the package that he had sent ahead. New $7^{1/2}$ inch and $11^{1/2}$ inch barrels for all of the M4's were laid out. Much shorter than their military issue cousin, the shortened barrel gave up some accuracy at three hundred meters, but their compact size compensated nicely in close quarters. Ultimately, it was an individual decision, maneuverability versus long-range accuracy. When the team arrived, some of them would prefer the 11's and fewer still the 7's. But take they would, for men are naught but boys grown large.

Chicken showed up next, with the communications equipment in tow. He had a great deal of panache for all things involving his van. The cellular jamming devices were crafted by his hands, and incorporated into his 1983 GMC *A-Team* style cargo-van. All the devices meshed into the interior and exterior so flush that only a trained observer could spot them. The spoiler on top was, in reality, a cellular jammer. The radar jammer was concealed within the grill. There was even a space in the chassis for a spare .50 caliber

45

barrel. Chicken was like Killer in that his hobby was also his trade. Few men live such a life, and they are all truly blessed.

Chicken owned a small shop along Interstate 95 near Richmond, Virginia, that sold legal radar detectors and CB radios. He made his real bread and butter in the illegal support of outlaw truckers and speed demons. Chicken was a happy man who did what he wanted to do with all parts of his life. He had already driven about 500 miles into and around the objective area, in a rental car, of course. He never advertised this to the team; it was just that wherever they went Chicken always knew the most obscure routes. Although the advent of the Global Positioning device had impacted his line of work, Chicken took the whole thing much further than that. He possessed a GPS array that would make the government nervous if they knew he had it. In fact, the taxpaying public had funded a great deal of it. Chicken was adamant that he had reallocated the GPS, not stolen it. This was an important distinction to Chicken.

Matt McCall had arrived with his usual flourish. He brought the beer and fodder for the barbeque. Always filled with good cheer, and a real zest for life, Sepp called him Falstaff. That Shakespearian moniker was lost to the rest of the team. The former Marine was a good ole boy addicted to the easy money and a rush of adrenaline. He was also a monster of a man. At 6'4" and 250 pounds, Matt was the most physically imposing of the team.

He had entered Western Washington via the rural Chinook Pass to avoid Fort Lewis but also because he loved the view it afforded of Mount Rainier. Matt had old friends at the base and made no secret that he planned to hunt and fish. Someone had to take the game in for butchering so their cover story would stand up to any scrutiny. Matt was all too happy to be the one who got to clean the game and guzzle beers. Sepp had agreed to this because it was a vital component of the team's success. The rest of his men would conduct the operations that set up the hit.

Joe arrived in his Jimmy about the time that Sepp had pulled the first steaks off the grill. Joe, a loner even within the team, was well thought of, nonetheless. He was a man of few words who only spoke when he thought it necessary. Everyone respected him for that, so when he did speak, his words had real weight with the team.

"Evening, All," Joe said slowly as he carried his gear inside. No one made an attempt to help, and no help was expected. You never knew when to talk to him. With Joe, it was best to let that sleeping dog lie. Partly because of his silent loner reputation, everyone assumed that Joe was a solid backer of Sepp, but that was an incorrect assumption on their part. Joe approved of Sepp in the past, and at the moment, he was constantly judging, weighing. His support was reliant on Sepp's ability to effectively guide the team, and so far, he had. But even Joe's icy nature was not immune to a reunion of this sort. He made his way to the table and picked out a nice T-bone steak. Eating now was important. Everyone knew that some serious drinking was about to take place.

After the keg was tapped and most of the team had arrived, Killer let it be known that he brought more than just replacement barrels. Some other surprises rattled around his big red sack of toys. He laid those out on the table for his comrades to admire. Killer was best at fabricating new weapon add-ons' and walked and talked like he knew it; pride is no sin amongst these men. The team had been using various methods for collecting all their spent shell casings, or brass, as it is more commonly referred to. Killer felt he had solved that particular problem with a fine metallic mesh bag that snapped onto the universal accessory rail atop the carbine. There would never be a missing shell case that could link the team to what they very reluctantly and seldom called a crime scene. The SAW's and the .50 cal had their own ingenious designs, also crafted by Killer. None were totally silent and all had capacity limitations before they had to be emptied, but these were merely parameters that the team had

47

to work with. *Imperfections that could be planned for*, as Sepp has so aptly put it.

Killer's next toy to show off was for himself. The ultimate weapon for close quarters battle is the 9mm Heckler and Koch MP5. The relatively high rate of fire and minimal recoil of the 9mm is due to the short case length, allowing for a reduced distance for the bolt. A smaller distance of bolt travel allows for an increased cyclic rate when fired on automatic. The 9mm round travels at about 1,200 feet per second, and the jacketed hollow point configuration is a purebred man killer. If the round makes its way through the flesh, a 27mm exit wound is the general result. The Germans learned this with their meticulous field-testing in the early 1940's. For this reason and a few personal ones, Killer was the only man on the team to carry the MP5 chambered in .45 ACP, or as it is more commonly known, the UMP. As with all the team's advances, this one needed explaining, and because this particular advance was Killer's, it was he who took the professorial podium at the onset of the beer drinking.

"After the Second World War, the .45's popularity within the ordinance community was eclipsed by the .30 carbine." Some heads turned toward other members of the team as if to say, *I have no idea what he's talking about.* Professionals are like that; they admit when they're unclear about anything. Pride is worthless if knowledge, and therefore lives, are lost because of it.

Killer continued, "The grease gun of World War II was, and still is, an effective close quarters battle weapon. The people that mass-produce these things for the various militaries of the world went 30 cal. But with the advent of Special Forces in the mid-Cold War years, the Operators demanded what worked. And what worked at the time was the 9mm Uzi. But Americans are Americans, and we tend to want to use and rely on our own American made shit. And so the Mac 9 and Mac 10 entered into our world. 9mm and .45 calibers, respectively, these two weapons represented our nation's movement toward the clandestine. Now I love the MP5. This you guys know, but this baby," he paused and took up arms, "this mutha fucker, is the shit. It spits a 230-grain hollow point, with a hollow big enough to mix a drink in, traveling at roughly 875 feet per second, which will give you one of three outcomes; first, these bullets here will rape the fucking life out of you. Secondly, an appendage hit will tear the whole limb off, and thirdly, a near miss will give a man a heartfelt brush with Jesus Christ, my personal Lord and Savior."

"OK, tough guy," Matt interjected, "so what the hell does the 'twelve' in a 12 gauge mean?"

Joe chuckled from the rear of the room, as he knew that this part of the lecture could last for hours and require a slide rule of some sort.

There are some aspects of the manly world of guns that remain esoteric. The various manuals and periodicals collected by the learned are there for a reason. The history of firearms is the history of man. It encompasses many a nation and many a yardstick with which to measure. With his vast knowledge of the art, even Killer had to check his facts twice before daring to explain just how one pound of lead, when smelted into spheres equates into an armorer's simplified expression of a twelve gauge barrel.

At once utterly confused and impressed by Killer's dissertation, the team took turns with the new toy. Matt grabbed it out of Killer's arms and then wrenched the loaded magazine out of Joe's hands. All knew what was next. Using his bulk and his natural aggressiveness, Matt sauntered to the cabin's back door. Inserting the mag into the proper port, and then chambering a round, Matt yelled, "Pull!" Nothing happened, so he turned and motioned for Doc to throw a beer into the night sky. The can fell to the ground undamaged, but the silence outside the cabin had been breached by the muffled eruption of .45 caliber automatic gunfire.

"I like it," Matt said drunkenly. And in turn, they all did. The Army calls it familiarization or *fam-firing*, and so did they, albeit with a slur. Joe was the only one to ever hit a can on the fly.

About midnight, when most of the team was good and drunk, the Kentucky Twins showed up. They had a few beers on the way but weren't too drunk to be chastised by the rest of the team, far from it. Sal had acquired a new toy of his own, and after firing the UMP, he pulled it out. The Ballester-Molina, a .45 caliber automatic pistol is in no way different from any other model 1911 chassis, but it does have a certain mystique about it, especially after hearing Sal tell the tale. According to him, the *Admiral Graf Spee*, one of Nazi Germany's more famous naval vessels, had been scuttled off the Argentine coast by its captain at the outset of World War II. The steel used to make the legendary firearm was salvaged from that very wreckage.

"Bullshit!" Killer yelled after the story was told. But it was one hell of a great tale if you're trying to sell that particular pistol. Although Killingsworth was suspicious of the story, almost everyone was glad to hear it told. Most of the men didn't care one way or the other; They were simply pleased to be in each other's company again. The men had their differences at times, but all in all, they were a close-knit group of ruffians. Throughout the lives of men, there are always bonds to be shared. In high school, you have sports teams and clubs; in early adulthood, there are fraternities and the military. Prison, in its own way, is also a fraternal organization. These men had all been in one, or all of these groups, and now the team was their new brotherhood.

As Dognut returned from the shitter, Sal stood and raised his bottle. "To the bond that ties us!"

"To the 100 Dollar Bill in each man's pocket!" Dognut smiled as he spoke. Steve Earle's *Copperhead Road* blared from within the cabin.

"I'll fucking drink to that fucking shit!" Joe spewed forth profanity in a way that infantrymen are prone to. The expostulation was the longest stream of words he had spoken in three days. They all shared a sly smile. Nothing was said,

50

but volumes were present. They would travel once more into that place and snatch from fate what they could. It was always dangerous; some might not make it back, but they would all go in.

"Speed *is* security," Chicken uttered as the men locked in a huddle-like embrace. It was a phrase particular to his role in the mission.

"Slow is smooth, and *smooth* is fast," Doc added. All eyes moved to Killer, who was the next to speak within the huddle.

"Don't forget nothing," Killer quoted *Roger's Rules for Rangers*. It was the first of nineteen rules set down by the Major in the year of our Lord, 1759.

"One shot, one kill," Chuck chimed in with the sniper's catchphrase. Everyone knew that the rule applied to them all, but to he who is in overwatch, it applies to a much greater degree.

Sal and Dognut spoke together for their mantra, "Fuck the police."

Sal added, "If you can't outthink the cops, you ain't no good to us here."

In a somber tone, Dognut raised his whiskey bottle high. "To the Airborne Ranger in the Sky." Everyone in the room had lost a buddy in the war; they all toasted with the appropriate solemnity.

Matt was next. Because of his size and southern drawl, the big guy was always assumed to be a touch slow, but he surprised them with a Hemingway quote. "There is no hunting like the hunting of man, and those who have hunted armed men long enough and liked it, never care for anything else thereafter." Although he was no soldier, Hemmingway had it right. All other occupations pale in comparison for those who have drank deeply from the Cup of Wrath and asked for more.

Joe let the gravitas of his large friend's words take hold, but as their weight faded, he added his own two cents' worth. "Trust me with your life, but not your money or your wife." It was an age-old truism amongst soldiers.

Then the team turned to its leader. Bolstered by the words and demeanor of his men, Sepp took center stage. His team was ready; all he needed to do was lead them to water and they would do the rest. He quoted an old 1st Sergeant from his days with the best that he had ever served with.

"It is all about *Violence of Action.*" And with that, they all knew what was meant. Sepp was intimating to the men that if, in all their actions from here on out, they adhered to the principle of domination, then they would succeed. General Patton had laid out that principle in more words than were needed there in the cabin when he said, "*There is only one tactical principle which is not subject to change. It is to use the means at hand to inflict the maximum amount of wounds, death, and destruction on the enemy in the minimum amount of time.*"

A rain-shrouded dawn broke late on the tiny cabin. Sepp stirred through a haze of the aftereffects of a night of hard boozing. Matt was already gone, his rifle and rig missing along with him. It was his style; booze had no lasting effect on his plans for the day. The Kentucky twins had obviously stayed up later and drank a lot more beer. They were still passed out in their soaked tents, but they somehow had the presence of mind to place them on top of a few dry pallets. *Well, at least we don't need to make it look more like a party than a tightly ran Op.* Chuck and Chicken were up, and that was enough of a quorum to get the ball rolling.

"Chuck, you and me gonna go buy some dope from yer friend's little contact. Chicken, you and Doc go recon some routes. Chuck will let you in on the Medical Staff intel later, Doc." Sepp issued his orders in a friendly manner, but they were still orders.

Later that afternoon, Sepp and Chuck were stuck in the traffic where the Tacoma Dome and the Narrows Bridge converge.

Chuck turned to his leader. "You think the Kentucky twins are using?"

"I don't know. They drink like fish and never get too messed up. I fucking pray it ain't true. Better not be. It'll fuck a lot of shit up, and that's a fact."

Chuck turned up the volume on David Allen Coe's *The Ride* playing on the radio and let the unpleasant topic drop. A few miles further, they pulled off Nugget Road and into the gravel parking lot of the "*Booby Trap Tavern.*" Sepp and Chuck shared a smile at the duality of the name. This nefarious shithole was where they were going to begin their infiltration of the Pacific Northwest's drug trade. Sepp and Chuck paused to read the sign that warned loggers to take off their boot spikes and then sauntered into the dimly lit dive bar. They made their way to the barkeep and ordered a pitcher of *Olympia*. It was good that beer was what they wanted, for Sepp learned that day that the State of Washington has two kinds of watering holes. The first is a regular bar where ardent spirits are offered alongside food. The second, known as a tavern, is strictly a beer and peanut fare. The latter is what they were in. They paid $4.50 for the undersized and overly foamy pitcher and headed to the rear of the bar near the pool tables. The place serviced the night shift from the surrounding airport and manufacturing sites. The hookers were old but still in demand.

About three games of billiards and two pitchers of something other than *Oly* later, a small Hindu looking fellow approached and asked if they were friends of Juan. They said that they were precisely those men, and asked the Hindu to take a seat with them and talk some business. Sepp would have fetched an empty mug for him but didn't want to appear overly friendly. The man returned with a schooner and joined them at their booth. After a few beers, he was ready to talk business.

53

Dopers are addicted to dope and dope dealers are strangely addicted to dopers. They hate 'em, and at the same time love 'em. The doper will wake his dealer up in the middle of the night to ask for some fronted dope. *Fronted! They don't want to pay you for it just yet. They just want it.* This is not the ideal customer. What Sepp was setting out to do was to make himself the ideal customer. The kind who doesn't complain about quality and only occasionally about quantity. One who always pays up front and in cash. No DVD players or old TV sets in trade. Sure, he would wake you up in the middle of the night, but it was to make you a thousand dollars.

And this is just what Sepp became, the perfect customer. He used a fake ID card to cut out a line right there on the table. Doing the coke in front of the Hindu showed the law meant little to him. A drunk tried to score a free hit. Sepp pushed him roughly to the ground and then tossed the douche out the back door, bloodying the man in the process. The altercation was duly noted, but no one called the cops from the *Booby Trap* that afternoon. Sepp and Chuck earned what the tough guys call "street cred." Two loggers at a Golden Tee arcade game took note of the ass whipping, made sure that it did not go too far, and then returned to the sixth hole, which presented a bitch of a water hazard and a nasty crosswind.

Sepp soon placed an order for 30 grams of the good stuff. There are approximately 3.5 grams in an 8-Ball, the bulkiest amount that street people buy in. Kilos are for the big fish, so 30 grams was a large purchase by street standards. Sepp knew that the little fish would have to go to his supplier, and that Chicken was trailing the guy. The big fish would never deal with Sepp, but Sepp didn't need to meet the big fish. Chicken was on it. Chuck already knew where the Hindu lived. By following him, it was only a matter of time before the men with the kilos could be targeted.

To best fit in with the surroundings, Matt purchased himself a "Washington is Bigfoot Country" T-shirt. He thought the garment was just too rich to pass up, but he never thought it would lead too much beyond a few stares from the locals. But on his way to purchase some beer and ammo, a funny thing happened because of that T-shirt. The man ahead of him in the checkout line took note of his shirt and said, quite matter of fact, that he had a genuine Bigfoot story, although he used the term "Sasquatch" rather than Bigfoot.

"Yeti is also an acceptable term for them," the man said, "no reason to be insulting to the big fellas," he said. This comment got Matt's attention as well as the female clerk's.

"All right, I'll bite," Matt opened the door, knowing full and well that he could not let this opportunity pass him by.

The man was well versed in the art of storytelling and began by casting a serious eye on Matt and the clerk. "Well, a few years back, a buddy and I made our living stealing cars and selling them for scrap down by Lake Tapps." A good story is always self-deprecating. *No one wants to hear about all the men that you've beat up. They want to hear the story about how you got yer ass kicked.*

"Anyway, we're down there and all a sudden all the hairs on our necks rise. Felt like we was being watched, ya see."

Matt knew this feeling. During the USMC Scout Sniper course at Quantico, he was taught not to look at the eyes of a potential target. Even from a thousand meters, people can sense these things. Neither the Marine Corps nor the Army NCO Corps can prove this to be true, but they teach that it is. *Better safe than sorry.*

"Well, we all start running, all directions but the way we felt was wrong. And just as we get out of eyeshot of the cars, a mighty banging begins. Had to have been the Yeti protecting his territory. We never did see it, but them things are out there, I tell ya," He ended his tale with an extension of his hand to the clerk. She gave him a quizzical look before handing him an assortment of nickels, dimes, and pennies. The man wasted no time waiting for any validation or rebuttal; he simply walked out the door, vanishing behind the curtain of rain.

"I... well, I'm just not sure of what to make of that," Matt flatly addressed the bemused clerk.

"The rain," she said. "It does that to some people."

Back on mission, the team followed every contact that the Hindu made. It would only be a matter of time before a target presented itself. Just as they divided rooms, the team would break down a complicated task until one member found the source of the dope. The plan was standard by now. They would snatch an inside man, extract the needed information from him, and then make the sudden, lethal strike.

Dognut and Sal had separated in Seattle to check on some leads. Gas Works Park was their rally point. A promontory thrust from the chilly confines of Lake Union, the park's kite hill provides a stunning view of the Space Needle and of the grayish cityscape. It was near to raining, as usual. Downtown was beginning to glow with an urban hue. A stiff wind created a rough turbulence that prevented their conversation from being easily overheard.

"Jesus, man, have you ever seen so many fleece-wearing, biodiesel driving, hybrid folks in yer life?" Dognut's lazy southern accent bit into the wind as the two mercenaries approached each other on the concrete platform atop the grassy knoll.

"Dude, I heard on the radio that this was the seventeenth straight day of rain, fucking seventeen." Sal shook his head in amazement. A seaplane climbed through the heavy air, ascending over the rusted petroleum tanks that give the park its name. Its engine's blast temporarily canceled out any attempt to communicate verbally.

After the plane passed by, Sal spoke, "Man you think this city is bad. You ought to check out Olympia. Can't throw a rock down there without hitting one of them granola eating mother fuckers."

"My guy is an Oriental fellow." Sal was referring to his assigned man to follow. "No shortage of those round here neither. Hell, the state of Washington could export Rice Eaters if they wanted."

"When is one of these guys going to pan out?" Dognut asked. "We need to get more Go-Caine." He was fiending and didn't care that he advertised this to a fellow junkie. The urgency in his voice was followed with a clenched jaw. Sal knew that his buddy was jonesing and that his own addiction needed to be served.

Dognut spoke before thinking about the consequences of doing so. "Let's just kill a crackhead and smoke his shit," It was surprising that the logic flowed so easily to that conclusion. Both men realized that this is what they now did for a living. To kill a single doper or ten was no different to them any longer.

Sal sighed as the two men exchanged a look of understanding. They walked down the windswept slope and headed to the University District.

Everything was occurring within the parameters of the team's normal template, when something unexpected took place. Normal men would call this luck. But not Sepp. No, he did not know anything about luck. Sepp deemed these eventualities as inevitable.

Sal had decided to follow his assigned target aboard the *Victoria Clipper* hydrofoil to British Columbia. It proved to be a serendipitous event. While looking for a little cocaine, Sal found the mother lode of heroin.

Chang Yau adopted his American name, Eric, mostly because Americans couldn't pronounce his Chinese name easily. He also found his workmates were incapable of learning it. Regardless, Eric was the alias that he used when he was dealing cocaine for the Anglos, and Yau was what he used when he was dealing heroin for the Chinese syndicate. He had been making money on the side with cocaine when Sal tracked him to the home of his true masters.

After he returned from British Columbia, Sal and Dognut stun-gunned Eric outside of an all-night eatery in Seattle's Chinatown. Sepp nurtured this level of independent thinking and action in the team, which proved to be effective on this day. But the team could not know about what he had planned. Only Sal and Dognut had both the moral ambiguity and the clarity of vision for this particular task.

"Look at this little Chinaman that Dognut got us. This and about two keys of China White Horse says Dognut done good!" Dognut was an arrogant sort even when he had little to be prideful of. And with the abduction of Eric proving so clever, his third person was even more full of itself.

Sepp looked down at the fierce Asian man. He had been stun-gunned, hoodwinked, flex-tied, and then stuffed into a rental car's trunk. He was not a happy man. Chang "Eric" Yau wore a mask of rage, and as soon as the duct tape came off his mouth, he became a vocal man. The stream of obscenities rolling out of his mouth did little to anger the men. Just the opposite, they started to laugh. That Chinese fella cursed their families, their friends, their genitals, and their mothers in particular. Sepp laughed out loud and then spoke to Sal in a whisper. Just because the Chinaman was speaking Cantonese did not mean that he could not understand English.

Sal nodded, then applied a liberal amount of ether to a rag and covered the Chinaman's face with it. Sal never did care much for blathering. While their captive slept, Sepp and Sal did a little arithmetic concerning heroin and US dollars. There was a great potentiality presenting itself. *A gift from God, one not to be shunned.*

Eric awoke from his haze a much more subdued man than he had gone in. He was naked and bound now but no longer had the pillowcase over his head. The place he was in was creepy as hell. It looked more like a serial killer's home than the abandoned hunting shack that it was. He could see his captor's faces, and knew he would not survive this encounter. It made his mind sharp and focused. Sepp was in the rear of the room, watching from afar. It was Sal's collar and Sepp was going to let him run this show. Sal walked up to the bound man and asked him quite politely if he spoke English. Eric was born and raised in Hong Kong and let Sal know this.

"OK, Chinaman," Sal began with no real malice, no racial hatred. He had simply been raised to refer to all Asians as Chinamen. It just so happened that Eric was of Chinese descent. "What the hell you all got going on in Victoria? I know where, but I need to know how many men are there, how much dope is there, and when there is gonna be more." Sal was good at this part. He knew how long to let his words sink in before continuing.

"You, my new Chink friend, are gonna tell me what it is that I have just asked you about. I'm not gonna threaten you. I am not gonna beat you. I got no time for that. Tell me, and do so now." Sal kept his calm composure even when Eric spat at him in response. Wiping the blood off his face, Sal smiled wickedly, and motioned to Dognut.

"Why don't you go into the kitchen and fetch me that blender?" His voice was soft and his face pure menace. Dognut reappeared with an old secondhand store-bought blender in his hands, its stubby little electrical cord augmented by a thick, orange industrial-sized extension. Sal pulled off the glass pitcher, revealing the sharp tines still affixed to the electric motor. Horror gripped Eric as he heard Sepp point to the blades and say, "Hey man, that will splatter something fierce. I got a better idea. Just bear with me."

Sepp took out a tube of Superglue and firmly sealed the pitcher over the blades.

"That ain't gonna do shit," Sal complained. He continued venting his frustrations until Sepp cracked the glass against the side of the cast iron fireplace. He handed the blender back to Sal. The bottom of the glass pitcher had stayed put in testament to the strength of the glue, but the jagged remnants of thick glass now poked up around the metal blades, presenting a gruesome contrast. Looking more like a cruel flower concocted in the mind of a mental patient than a broken appliance. The instrument was now ready for duty. Sal hit the "puree" button and the resulting torque caused the blender to jump to life in his hands. Despite Eric's protestations, Sal eased the jagged glass and rotating blades against his delicate flesh. The first use of the modified blender was somewhat mild and mainly to prove to Eric that they weren't fucking around, but it didn't produce the amount of information or details they desired. The next two applications were more forceful and longer in duration.

Eric told them everything that they wanted to know. When they were satisfied with the intel, Sal took him to the wood line and put a bullet through the back of his head. Eric preferred that to living even another second. His thin eyes thanked Sal in the end. Sal, in response, felt that he had done his good deed for the year.

Sal and Dognut went back to join the team in Yelm, leaving Sepp to take care of the body. He insisted on being

60

the one to take care of the mess. *If you want a job done right, do it yourself, especially when cokeheads are involved.*

When Sepp returned to Yelm, he laid out the new plan for the team. "Ok guys, here is the real meal deal. We need to shift fires. There's new intel that a major dope deal is going down in four days, twice the cash but twice the danger." He could tell that they were all interested, so he continued. "We can either nickel and dime this shit in Seattle, or head north for some real money."

"How good is this intel?" Matt had to ask.

"It's solid," was all that Sepp revealed.

"Where the fuck did it come from? And why are you the only one that knows?" Matt shifted his stare to Dognut, who shifted uncomfortably under the big man's gaze.

"I got the intel. It's good," Sepp ceded some ground, but not enough for Matt's liking.

"Look, I know these fuckers we hunt are grade 'A' assholes, child poisoners and such, but isn't there some line out there that we ain't supposed to cross?" Matt said, getting a touch hostile.

"Look, Matt," Sepp said as he scanned every man's face. "I just buried a Chinaman up in the Olympics with my bare freaking hands. If you ain't comfortable with this, perhaps you signed up with the wrong gang."

"Sometimes we gotta kill some folks, just to get to kill some other folks and get the score we need. Any man here got a problem with that? I'm sure there's a $100-dollar bill out there just waiting to be found." Sepp let the threat hang in the air as he took the time to look each man in the eye. It took a good thirty seconds to do so. Sepp never once blinked.

"Are we clear?" he finally asked. The silence in the hunting lodge became a collective consent to proceed.

It had to be a waterborne Op. There was no other way to get to Victoria with all the gear by land or air. 9-11 had seen to that. And with only four days to plan, this had to be run smoothly yet with a rush. Chicken and Chuck headed to British Columbia to do the onsite recon. It was only logical that the driver and the sniper would do this. Although the infiltration and exfiltration of the team would be waterborne, they had to have ground transport once on Canadian soil. Chicken would do a familiarization run into and out of Canada, and Chuck and his rifle would be left on site to radio back data to the team as well as to cover the ingress to the target house.

Doc was trying to make sense out of the mess that his medical support plan had been thrown into. The way Doc saw it, he had just a few options. The first was to go ahead and snatch one of his candidates. Sepp and Chicken wouldn't go for that because it would mean that an unwilling person would have to be smuggled along. The second plan was to use what little time he had to prepare and scope another med student north of the border. Sepp would probably meet this with approval, but it would mean that he wouldn't have the time that he would like to prepare for the operation itself. Doc knew that he wasn't just medical support; he was also another needed gun barrel. Just like his time on active duty, his Military Occupational Specialty (MOS) was 68 Whiskey, a Combat medic. But he was also expected to fulfill the role of an 11 Bravo (a line infantryman) if needed. This was his dilemma. *Fucked if he does, and fucked if he doesn't.*

Doc struggled with his problem for his allotted three hours until he had to head back into the beehive of motion that was the cabin. A Zodiac boat and another similar one cluttered the entrance with Sal and Dognut working furiously on the motors. They were welding something to the exhaust ports. Matt and Killer were equally busy with all the weapons save the .50 cal, which was already in British Columbia. Doc headed to the wall map to talk with Sepp.

"What ya got?" it was impolitic, but they were all the words the team leader reckoned he had time for.

"We need to talk," Doc said as he maneuvered his way between his boss and his boss's work. Sepp then knew that he needed to pay attention, and so he did.

"Talk to me," Sepp ordered. He did not use words like "shoot" when asking a question. Nor did he use phrases like "lock and load," in normal conversation. He used those terms when he wanted rounds chambered and triggers pulled.

"OK, well, it's just gonna be me on this one. We still have the staff from Seattle, but we'll have to come to them if there's a problem I can't handle." Doc spoke calmly, trying to persuade himself and Sepp that he was up to this unknown challenge. It did not work.

"Look, Doc, it ain't cause I don't think that you can do the job," although that was Sepp's exact concern. "It's just that we have to have more than one medic going into this situation. We can't just hope that all goes well and no one takes a hit. You're correct to think that we can't take someone in with us, and you might be right to suppose that we may not be able to make it back down here to Seattle. If you think you don't have time to get a Doc up there and do your rehearsals for the hit, then so be it. But we need a medical doctor up there. I don't care what you have to do to make this happen, just make it happen. I got to move all this," Sepp said as he gestured to a long list of equipment. "All the fucking way to Canada without being seen by our Federal government or theirs, so do me a fucking favor and make it fucking happen." And that was, as they say, that. Doc dejectedly went to work on a plan that he hoped would satisfy the team and its leader.

It has been said that the amateurs talk strategy and the professionals talk logistics, which is true. The logistics alone were considerable for this mission. But at least a few things were moving along nicely. Miller Creek Valley on the north side of the Olympic Peninsula, would serve as their ad hoc embarkment point. On a clear day, you can see Victoria across the twenty-some mile span of water.

The Valley would provide enough space and cover for the team's move. It was heavily forested, prone to morning fog, and easily accessible via old logging roads. Getting the team there and back wouldn't present a problem as backcountry passes would allow the vehicles to remain there a night or two without arousing suspicion. Every vehicle already had an extra set of credible plates to attach, and the boats would be brought in with a rental truck.

Getting across the Strait of Juan de Fuca posed a bit of a problem, but Joe and Dognut would pilot the boats. Sepp trusted their capabilities. All he had to know was that it was possible to go there and come back without being detected by any radar or shore patrols, which he had already done. Matt had an old friend in the Coast Guard who would get the necessary timetables to him. Obtaining it was a risk they needed to take. That intel was expected to arrive tonight.

The real business at hand was intelligence on the objective and its inhabitants. Eric had provided a lot, but there were still logistical queries to be made and literal ground to cover. Chuck was in place, but just outside of Objective Hotel, as the letter "H" is pronounced by the military. Good intel was still expected from Chicken, which was due to arrive at any minute. Once the encrypted transmission arrived, Sepp had hoped to be able to issue an Operations Order (OPORD). This is supposed to be an exacting and comprehensive breakdown of the impending Op, but the situation couldn't allow for that. The team had to move, and move fast, so it had to be a Fragmentation Order, more commonly referred to as a FRAGO. It would describe what the current situation demands. A FRAGO is a down and dirty method employed by commanders to get the intent of the mission out to the men. Broad strokes are all that is needed with these orders. Once Chicken gave his private briefing to the leader, Sepp informed the team of its mission objectives.

"Gentlemen, what we have here is a fast-fucking way to make a shit-pot of cash. It is extremely dangerous, but it can and *will* be done if we decide to do it." Sepp did not add any bullshit. *Some of them may not make it back.* That much the team fully knew.

"We are going waterborne, as you know," he gestured with his knife to the map, "from here," he indicated Siebert Creek, "to here," another tap of the blade on the topographical where the letter "H" was written in yellow highlighter over a cluster of buildings. Sepp learned long ago that fingers are never to be used when pointing at a map. The index finger alone takes up a 500-meter square area on the typical 1:50,000 scale military map. The point of a knife greatly reduces any confusion concerning the exact place being referred to.

Sepp then pressed the point of his Randal blade into the center of the objective. The steel gouged into the plywood support. "This is the abode of one Harry Liu; as you can see, it is four klicks from the landing point. Chicken can get us from the landing to the objective if that is necessary at the time. METT-TC will dictate." The acronym was for Mission, Equipment, Terrain, Troops available, Time and Civilians. It was merely a catch-all acronym for "mission dependent." All the factors that a ground commander must take into account when hasty decisions must be made.

He continued, "Otherwise, we hump from the boats to the OBJ. The terrain is a steady grade up, with thick wet vegetation." Sepp did not need to tell the men that this meant a slow, but very quiet approach to the OBJ. "Cover is good from the reports that Chuck is sending. He says we can approach from here." The knife point went to a private golf course. "And from here." A wooded area to the west of the OBJ.

65

"We have a New Moon and lots of cloud cover, so there will be practically no ambient light. Our night vision goggles give us the decisive advantage."

Before any operation, the team took one last look at a plan before a decision was made.

"Let's get to it," Killer blurted. Everyone got up and moved toward their combat gear.

The Victoria hit was a go.

The team began to disassemble the operations room immediately. The map and map board were the last to hit the fire. All the gear was made ready and driven up the Olympic Peninsula and staged in the dense woods along Siebert Creek. The creek flows north into the Strait of Juan de Fuca. From there, the team would cross the straits, kill some men, steal their dope and cash, and return. How hard could it be?

Not twenty-four hours had passed, and everyone except the Kentucky twins were ready. They had left to drop off the rental truck that had carried the boats. The tents and fire circle were all staged well, so the team milled about waiting for their three friends: Sal, Dognut and darkness.

During the interim, Sepp reminded the team that in the event gunfire had to be returned during the waterborne phase of the movement, the only people to fire were the SAW gunners. They had removable barrels that could be tossed over the side to prevent them from melting the rubber Zodiac boats.

Their entrance into the straits was cloaked by fog. The surrounding mist absorbed what little noise they made. Although they had modified the outboard motors, the team left the continental United States under the power of their own arms. They had even wrapped the oar blades with old brown Army T-shirts to dampen the noise of their paddle strokes. Once a quarter mile off the coast, Dognut, Boat #1's coxswain, engaged the motors. He had done a great job cloaking the exhaust noise of the motors. Even a random sea otter was taken by surprise at the team's passing. Killer pointed to the startled sea mammal. The men shared a silent smile at the wonders of nature.

Most GPS systems won't identify military watercraft, but Chicken didn't have civilian equipment. The device was showing that the Canadian coast was fast approaching. Sepp made the hand signal for the team to abandon the luxury of motorized transport and again to take up the oar. The night was cold. Paddling warmed the team. Joints cracked and muscles ached in response to the exercise.

Once they had the boats hidden on the rocky shore, Sepp had the men place an infrared or "IR" beacon to the watercraft so they could easily find it with their night vision goggles. He then checked the strip map and moved his team toward the target house. An old adage in the military goes something like this: find the most difficult route between A and B, and take it. No one will be guarding this path. Patrols will not be manning this route. Sentries will not be checking the most obstructed places. Soldiers know this because they know themselves. A man on guard duty will not put himself through unnecessary discomfort unless he's highly trained. Most men relegated to guard duty are not. Sepp was counting on this principle to prove itself true. It almost always is.

The team moved by foot toward the objective. The target house lay to the west of the actual golf course, even though the team considered the two to be the same. Four hundred feet of elevation had to be overcome as well. At approximately 02:00 hours, there was no visible activity on the golf course except for the blinking of another IR strobe light that Chicken set to activate at a quarter of every hour for a one-minute interval. He knew the timing of their advance and activated these accordingly. The ground team paused as it positioned for the main assault, a collective inhalation before the task at hand.

The Victoria Golf Club isn't exactly known for its challenging links. The club is a hangout for jet setters of the world. More than one celebrity has been photographed by the paparazzi playing golf after a few too many drinks or smoke. British Columbia has the most lax laws pertaining to marijuana in North America. Celebrities searching for a legal high can forgo a flight to Amsterdam and instead hop a quick flight up the California coast to smoke up in a Victoria, B.C. coffee shoppe. Sometimes they end up in the tabloids, but never in jail.

Five minutes prior to mission execution, within the cramped confines of his van, Chicken activated the team's jamming package. For thousands of dollars less than the commercial version, Chicken had constructed several book-sized boxes that he had placed around the objective. Inside each was a tiny transmitter that broadcasts on the same frequencies the cell phone companies used. All the cell phones operating between 1930 and 1990 MHz started to proclaim NO SERVICE AVAILABLE to their owners. By using four of these devices, Chicken had interlocked an area that extended for a hundred meters in every direction from the objective. Coupled with a powerful transmitter, all radio and cellular phone frequencies were now effectively blocked by the tremendous output radiating from the van.

Jamming local communications means overloading the entire electromagnetic communications spectrum with your own white noise. In addition to radiating conventional frequencies, Chicken was also overloading the immediate airways usually reserved for the police and the military. It is not commonly known that most federal governments hold in reserve for themselves a much larger band of the electromagnetic spectrum than is allocated for commercial interest. It would take a dial the length of a dashboard to tune into the breadth of Chicken's transmissions.

Atop the roof of the maintenance shed that overlooks the third tee box, Chuck depressed the trigger on his rifle. The two-and-a-half-pound pull resulted in a facial shot. The guard had the entirety of his cranium taken off by the round's impact. All that remained of what could loosely be referred to as a head lay beneath the mandible. The jawbone, with its incisors jutting upward, began to stutter as the half-head succumbed to gravity's pull. Chuck moved to his second target. That man's wound proved no less ghastly, and no less fatal than the first.

Chuck keyed the handset on his radio twice but the team was already moving on its own accord. Sal and Dognut straight murdered the two men just inside the target house. The interior guards were slacking in their duties, confident that the men pulling exterior guard would alert them to any danger. They paid for that oversight with their lives.

Killer found himself running over the open ground, closing his distance between the sand trap and the objective. His body armor, the weight of his weapon, and the Kevlar helmet all conspired against his being swift. He felt like he was in one of those nightmares where you can never run as fast as the situation demands. It was a singularly dreadful sensation, which had Killingsworth reevaluating his decision to partake in such activities. And as always, the answer came to him in a moment of despair; his chosen profession is like living in a dream. *Row, row, row, your boat.*

Killer steeled himself just in time to let fly a seven-round burst of .45 caliber projectiles at this enemy of the day. The backlit vision of a man's torso dropped from the window. It would not count as another confirmed kill in his Army record, but his official personnel file had enough of those documented within it already. He was a bad man, knew it, and was pleased with his response to yet another eminent danger.

Immediately afterward, a controlled volley of fire erupted from within the home. This had happened to the team on the ill-fated Atlanta hit. It was not a welcome turn of events. The element of surprise had been blown. It was an advantage that all military minded men seek to gain, and to keep, for as long as possible. Every suppressor and silencer that the team had manufactured went toward that end. Sepp contemplated washing the entire mission once this shift occurred. But he could not, and he did not. Instead, Sepp allowed the team to work its own particular brand of magic. Battle is the art of improvisation and in this field, Sepp had confidence in his men's ability to prevail. He concentrated his efforts on the here and now, not on *would have, should have.*

After the men left the security of the woods nearest to the second hole, aptly named "Calamity" by the club members, Sal and Dognut were now pinned down. Caught in a dark space near the base of the stairs, they were too low to shoot at the threat, and too far from the tree line to retreat. It would be up to the others to crack this nut. Both men elevated their weapons to counter any threat from the windows directly above their position and hoped to God that the enemy had no hand grenades. Dognut wanted to rush the stairway, but Sal convinced him to let Sepp handle the problem for them. Chuck knew instinctively what needed to be done.

Warfare is an unscrupulous teacher, and it has been said that leadership is the ability to act in the absence of orders. Chuck possessed that type of leadership at critical moments. He set aside the H&K and hoisted the Barrett .50 caliber toward himself. Positioned twenty feet off the ground, Chuck's "deer stand" vantage afforded him an almost unhindered view of the objective. He was looking at the house from the South as the team's eastern assault was stalling out. Chuck pumped rounds into the walls the enemy was hiding behind. The structure had fared well against the 5.56mm and 7.62 rounds, but nothing in their composition

70

could stop the sabot rounds exiting from the maw of his rifle. The sabot round looks like any other, but the comparatively soft projectile houses a small cylinder of spent uranium. That little cylinder does not stop when the bulk of the round is halted. The kinetic energy is transferred to the tightly packed core. Being far denser than steel, and traveling at roughly 3,200 feet per second, the small core easily punches through ballistic armor.

The walls that the Asian men had positioned themselves behind proved to be no match whatsoever to the lethality of Chuck's weapon. The masonry that was providing cover began to explode. The disintegrating walls themselves began to kill the security element. Small, hardened bits of plaster and stone were turned into mortal fragments. Sepp gave the audible, "Go." Both ground teams knew exactly what their leader meant.

Within the objective building, the concept of Feng Shui wasn't working out so well. The geomancy of the Asians was powerless against the steel of the assaulting element. An interior design that was supposed to bring peace, harmony, and wealth to its occupants was being torn asunder by both incoming fire and outgoing small arms fire. Immaculate gardens and ancient vases were violated in every conceivable manner as chaos and desperation gripped the manicured home. A mirror placed on the exterior of a door was splintered by a round, its shards falling haphazardly to the floor, thus allowing all manner of evil to enter the home.

From the support by fire position that augmented Chuck's heavy weapons fire, Matt and Joe hosed the second floor of the objective with automatic weapons fire. They both noted that the team's movement was stifled at the basement entrance to the residence. Sal and Dognut were in a bad way. They now knew something had to be done to help the team and that had to be a forceful, violent, and unwelcome rear entrance.

Sal could hear the air above his head ripping apart, and knew that only Matt could be so precise with fire. It was

71

all the motivation he needed. Not knowing that Dognut was behind him, but he was, Dognut hit the top of the wooden stairs and pivoted on his right foot into the structure. He was at crotch level, and so the shots fired at him passed only inches over his head. He saw the man that had fired at him a scant few feet away. **Pop. Pop.** It seemed to him that he and his adversary had fired at each other simultaneously.

Released from the fearful cringe and fighting off the deafness it had borne, Dognut saw that it was Sal firing, not some unseen enemy. Sal had saved his ass once again, striking a man that he had failed to. The defeated enemy had been hit directly in the center of the pelvis. The thick stream of blood found its way around every finger that he clenched around the fatal groin wound. Death was in a holding pattern around the man. It was slowly, deliberately sponging the life from its prey.

"Time now," Sepp blared over his mini headset. It was the signal to tell the team that the police, or constables as they are known in Canada, could be expected. It was a shock to all that could still hear. Five minutes had already passed and they were in no way close to their actual objective. Such are the vagaries of combat.

It was here, at such a moment, that the team found itself ill-prepared for things to turn on them. Unknown to the team, the main security element for the Syndicate players were just a few houses away. Only a fraction of their powers were in place. Two vans full of armed and angry men ran headlong into a pitched battle with an enemy that they did not know anything about. The team had prepared for an eventuality of this nature, of course. Chuck had noted their presence and reported it to Sepp. Chicken planned a similar welcoming present that he would have offered to the police.

He had been the one to place the Claymore mines in the trees. A nasty, indiscriminate anti-personnel weapon, the Claymore mine consists of a two-pound base of C4 plastic explosive. Steel ball bearings are embedded within the front of the explosive and then encapsulated within a hard-plastic housing. The Claymore is violence in stasis. When discharged, the explosive force is enough to kill those in close proximity to the actual detonation. For those a little further out, the ball bearings typically do the rest. And when placed in a tree line, well, slivers of knotted wood and such accompany the steel balls. Wood itself is not what one would call a technologically advanced killer of men, but when traveling at thousands of feet per second, it is deadly. Only when Chicken felt a particularly foul mood upon his soul, a canister of pepper spray was taped to the front of the charge. But tonight, Chicken was in no such mood, and so only lethal methods were employed; his cruelty had mostly been spent in Baghdad.

Starting already within the perimeter that Chicken had cordoned off north on Newport Avenue and west on Beach Drive with Road Fang Spike Strips, the van had the drop on Chicken, but he was able to let Chuck know of the threat in a timely manner. Chuck took his mind off the firefight and concentrated on timing out the explosion. As any of the team could attest, taking out a vehicle with an explosive is tough. The many roadside bombs in Iraq and Afghanistan had mostly failed to kill because of poor timing methods employed by Haji.

The simplest way to destroy an enemy vehicle entering your Area of Operations is to funnel that car into a choke point, like what happened with JFK's motorcade in Dallas. *Slow is good, but better yet bring the vehicle to a halt.* It was at such a point where Chuck clicked the clacker in rapid succession. The electrical current produced by the small generator traveled down the electrical wire like a telegraph signal. On the other end, a small cylinder of the blasting cap answered the call with a death knell of its own. The rippled explosion traveled down the length of the ladyfinger-sized charge. The explosion was then forced to jump mediums into the larger body of the plastic explosive. Within the blink of an eye, a high-order explosion occurred. Its shockwave traveling faster than the speed of sound.

A US military Claymore mine has the words FRONT TOWARD ENEMY written on it. The face of the charge with the all too clear instructions came off first. The single layer of hardened plastic was swept away by force, heat, and the steel ball bearings that erupted from beneath it.

Sepp watched as the trees lining the driveway shook and swayed. Thousands of green leaves fell long before Autumn could have its way. Both vans were showered with ball bearings mixed with twisted wood. For all their martial artistry and devotion to their masters, the hapless lives within the two vans never made it past the mailbox.

The force of the detonation advertised the team's presence far more effectively than any call to the police could possibly have.

Sepp gave info to the entirety of the team. "Two Mikes!" meant that they had a collective one hundred and twenty seconds to secure the cash and get the hell out of Dodge. That might seem like a very restricted amount of time to deal with, but is an eternity when viewed through the right lens.

Matt and Killer had caught up with Sal and Dognut at just the right time. Killer slid across the waxed floor and joined the stack. Sal thundered through the doorway and shot the first man he saw. Dognut did likewise. Shots were returned before either man could even consider where the shots had originated. Sal was hit squarely in the chest with a shotgun blast, but before it could register, the long burp of the belt-fed weapon drowned out all other noise within the room.

"Man down!" The expostulation seized everyone's heart, because from here on, the operation was a goatfuck. The only variables would be how many goats would be in attendance and how much humping they could take. Battles don't end when someone gets hurt. They just become more intense. Matt's barrage of rounds caught the man with the shotgun and physically picked him up. The force of the bullets initially propped him up and the next ten rounds held him there as their invisible force ripped through his body. After the tenth round, there was little left to hold the man upright. The eviscerated corpse collapsed to the floor like a *scarecrow with all the hay pulled out*. Matt never let up on the trigger; he simply moved the barrel toward the other men. His SAW became a scythe as the six other men fell to the sweeping motion of his cutting tool. They danced a macabre jig before being released from the weapon's grip and succumbed to gravity's pull. It brought to Matt's mind the cheesy 1980s band *Spandau Ballet*, which took its name from the ballet performed by men caught in a hail of bullets discharged from the Nazi machine gun, the Spandau.

Tactical lights flooded the room, and again Chuck breathed easy. Sal, however, did not. He was gasping for any breath he could get. The titanium breastplate that he had special ordered had served him well. While the rest of the team wore the ceramic plate, he had the foresight to invest in the best protection. There was even a 1-800 number that he was supposed to call to report how well the plate had performed. It was a salesman's dream that would have to go unactualized. Dognut bent over the twisted and contorted body of his friend and ripped open the Velcro closure that held the armor in place. The effect was immediate. Sal's lungs could finally expand, and as they did the stress on his ribs became unbearable. Sal's back arched in response to the pain, his chin extending as if willing Dognut in his task.

Dognut's fist struck hard and the consequence was expected. Matt handed off the SAW to Dognut and then used his considerable strength to hoist the now unconscious man to a fireman's carry.

"Bring him here!" he yelled as he removed his Med Pack and retrieved a collapsible stretcher known as an Israeli Litter. Without waiting for further instruction, Matt took one side and Doc hurried to the other. They turned and made their way toward Chicken and the van. In their absence, the ordered chaos continued.

The lacquered furniture of the home was splintered and broken throughout. Rice paper walls bore the faint marks of powder burns and splattered blood, but surprisingly, most remained upright. Sepp, in his quest, began to tear them down. Row after row of the partitions fell. He was looking upon the inner sanctum at the halted drug deal. Two dead men lay alongside large metal cases. Each case was attached to its deceased owner by handcuffs. Sepp drew his Buckmaster survival knife from his web gear and proceeded to hack off the first man's hand. The knife was heavy and beyond razor sharp, but it still took several strikes to sever. Bone and tendon are most resilient. The first case would be Dognut's and the second one Sepp took out himself. There was no time to check the contents, only enough time to get away with their lives.

Sepp was forced to divide his team because the situation demanded it. He would take the healthy men to the water and complete the planned exfiltration. Sal and Matt would have to go with Chicken and Doc. Chicken would already have an escape route mapped out in his head. Doc would have to get Sal to the doctor alive. Matt would provide security for the element and ensure they made it back across the border. Sepp's task was to take what was left of the team back to the water and over to the Olympic Peninsula. The Royal Canadian Mounted Police were sure to be on the way, so haste was the watchword.

"Dognut, grab the other case. We are un-assing this AO A-SAP," his message was short, but his eyes conveyed every nuance that he intended. This would be a race to the water that if it went poorly, would end in a firefight with a force they could not surmount.

Like specters in the mist, Sepp's half of the team moved noiselessly over the well-groomed grass of the 5th fairway. The wailing of sirens could be heard approaching.

"Roll, man, roll!" was all that Matt had to say as he jumped into the van. Doc and his patient were already in. The medical attention had begun. Even without the full illumination that he needed, Doc could already tell that Sal was in a bad way. The man needed help that he was ill-equipped to give. While the titanium plate had surely saved his life, The bruise that was forming was immense. It spanned the length of the tunic that Doc was presently shearing off with medical scissors. Every breath that Sal took was an eternity of pain, and yet Doc could not in good conscience give the patient morphine. Internal injuries were not his specialty and Doc did not want to kill the patient in order to alleviate the pain.

In the back of the van, Matt found the thick stack of dossiers collected by the Private Investigator. He scanned through those, looking for a candidate close to the I-5 corridor. Brian Gaddy, *yeah, he will do.*

"It's gonna be about an hour thirty minutes, Doc!" Matt yelled at the sleeping medic. *What the fuck?* His shouted words jarred Doc from his sleep. *Holy Shit, I can't be sleeping now!* Doc slapped himself for his transgression and began again the treatment of his wounded comrade.

Chicken was busy evading the R.C.M.P. Any official border crossing was a no-go. They could never get across at Blaine, Washington. or any other large crossing, this Chicken knew. His mind raced to solve the problem,

Chicken drove down the dirt and gravel road, pulled over. "Matt, you got to drive." He had never let anyone else drive before. From the back, Chicken gave him navigational instructions. At a "T" in the road, Chicken told him to take a right. Matt was sure that the crossing was going to go off without a hitch, and then the bright lights hit the van. Some serious military wannabes were running the Minuteman checkpoint. Matt almost laughed when the fat man with the goatee asked him the purpose of his visit to America. Using a heavy Georgia accent, Matt told the man that he was driving around and got lost. He hoped the stereotype of the slow Southern man would work in his favor. What helped the most was old-fashioned white privilege. The fat man ended up giving Matt directions back to the fatherland. Down the road a few miles, Chicken was back in the driver's seat.

"Pretty smooth, dude," was all that Chicken had to say. Having the big white guy drive was a masterstroke. An hour and a half later, the van pulled up alongside a weary man. He had just worked for twenty hours, but he was going to have to work some more.

"Get in," Matt said from the passenger's side window, his face covered in a ski mask way that a balaclava fits. Dr. Gaddy was too smart to refuse. In the rear of the van, he found two similarly masked men. The wounded man was not that seriously injured, but was in terrific pain. His ribs were bruised and his spine had compressed around a nerve. With all the gear in the van, it was obvious to Dr. Gaddy that he had been shot. For his own safety, he didn't inquire as to the cause of the massive bruising. Instead, he focused on the patient. The man who was acting as a medic kept dozing off. *Narcolepsy?*

Sal had received as much aid as could be given. Matt told Chicken to drive up a logging road in the Cascades. He had Doc and Sal get out and wait. The road was going to be rough, and Matt knew he would hurt Sal more if he went along. Returning to the van, he blindfolded Gaddy and told Chicken to get the doctor lost. He drove like hell for about fifteen minutes. At the terminus of the road, the blindfold was removed, and the good doctor was released. Matt held the dossier up to Gaddy's face.

"Not a fucking word," was all Matt said to him. He would talk. Matt knew this, but Victoria was a long way away. "Go, go while you can."

78

Matt would never have killed this man. He only killed when it was necessary. Sal and Dognut would have done it without hesitation, but not Matt or Chicken. Perhaps they should have, though, but Matt could not have known about the shortcut that Chuck had made in finding the doctor, or that he lived in the same town as O'Brien P.I. *Morality can be a real bitch.*

After retrieving Sal and Doc, the van hauled ass back to Yelm. It would be hours before Dr. Gaddy reached civilization; a few hours was all Matt needed. Once back at the cabin, he hurried to its rear. The timer on the demolition device next to the propane tank had only fifty minutes until it expired. When that happened, all the physical evidence of the team's presence at the cabin would have been wiped clean from the face of the earth. The propane tank was full and there was a full stick of C4 attached to its top. Little would have been left of the cabin had someone not stopped the timer. The team had always done this. If something went wrong, they had to completely un-ass the AO, so the cops had even less to go off of. It was a standard operating procedure.

R & R

*"And therefore, since I cannot prove myself
a lover, I am determined to prove a villain."*
-Shakespeare

When the time comes and one's service term is finally
ending, you're compelled to have a sit down with the in-
house recruiter. The reenlistment Non-Commissioned
Officer's job is to convince the soldier that he/she can't and
won't make it in the real world, and that the only sane action
is to re-enlist. The non-commissioned all have this day, and
Sepp was no different than anyone else.

Sitting with a Sergeant First Class in one of the out-
processing buildings at Fort Benning's WWII era Splinter
Village, Sepp was a bit of a different case. A combat veteran
with the 3rd Ranger Battalion, Sepp stood decidedly apart
from most soldiers. Rangers have a well-deserved reputation
as being cocky, arrogant bastards. In this, Sepp was typical.
He had moved the metal folding chair away from the others,
and had sat down with a scowl on his face. Sepp was pissed
that he was being lumped in with the rank and file of the
Army, and was generally pissed at the world. But Sepp was
not angry with the other soldiers, the Army, or even the
President. Many soldiers were exiting the military because
of all the extra work the war carried. An endless string of
overseas tours is not for everyone. But Sepp was not one of
those soldiers. He wanted to safeguard his nation. He liked
the long absences. He liked not having to call home all the
time and being able to take his military leave as he pleased.
Interesting times, he called them.

No, Sepp did not mind the war. On the contrary, Sepp
thought that the War on Terror should be expanded. He felt

the nation was pussyfooting the whole thing by not prosecuting it thoroughly enough. Why America had not yet gone to a serious war footing was beyond his comprehension. *We need to mobilize!* Sepp had seen firsthand the men and women who were in a death struggle with America. They frightened him; well, their determination frightened him. *The regular Haji's were not the problem, but that rare breed of suicide bomber or the serious Wahhabis certainly was.* Those bastards were fearlessly undeterred in their hatred for America. *How could the Iraqis not be when the real enemy was hiding in nations deemed friendly by our government?* As a soldier, Sepp knew he should be apolitical, but it was his life on the line. No, war did not scare Sepp, but getting killed as a speed bump to the inevitable next attack certainly did. And there were other things, too.

Sepp had made a combat jump into Afghanistan and earned another Combat Scroll in Iraq. He was tired of the asinine restrictions placed on his conduct overseas. *No alcohol? No hookers?* Seriously. *And forget about having a shotgun sent to you. Fuck that shit!* Of course, Sepp had scored booze and had friends in the States send him porno. It was just that serving in Iraq and Afghanistan was nothing like those two great Vietnam movies *Coming Home in a Body Bag* and *Body Bags II.* Those guys got laid, got drunk and killed indiscriminately. *This* war had too many rules imposed on it to be fought effectively.

"What the hell do you think you're gonna do in the real world? The Sergeant First Class said. "You got no skills that they need; all you guys know is the gun, and son, there just ain't no need for no 11 Bravo, Hell, an infantryman in the real world. I've seen it a hundred times. Guys like you who are gonna get a job as a security guard, try to make some police force, work as a bouncer." He had worked out his spiel pretty well and with the exception of Sepp's military occupational specialty being a 13 Fox, Fire Support Specialist, not an infantryman, and the bouncer gig, he had

Sepp's plan well anticipated. It had the young sergeant thinking about what he really was going to do on the outside.

"I mean, you Rangers don't know shit except how to kill folks and live off the land. What the hell you thinking? A man like you on the outside is gonna be a cop or a criminal. You need to stay here and be a lifer." Both terms *outside* and *lifer* are from the penal system; they made Sepp feel that he was in a prison, one that he desperately wanted to escape. A crystal seed took form in his mind. The retention NCO was right; Sepp only knew the violent arts. Besides two years of college, half of that on academic probation, Sepp had little else marketable. Being a cop was no different than being in the Army and Sepp was tired of that. Being a criminal was not what he thought he wanted to do, but if there was a way he could do it right and make a lot of money. Maybe this idea had promise.

The notion of the team solidified during that meeting. If Sepp could find a few men like himself, then it could be done. Of this, he was sure. A good reality is far superior to the best of dreams. Sepp suddenly felt cocky.

"I wouldn't stay in this fucking Army one more damn second if I didn't have to. All due respect, Sarn't." He had used a pejorative term for Sarge that is never used in the Rangers. Sepp looked down at his own uniform: his combat Ranger scroll, his Ranger Tab, and his Airborne Wings with the mustard stain that denoted a combat jump. The only reason he didn't wear the Combat Infantryman's Badge was because he was a Forward Observer. He had served alongside the 11 Bravos every step of the way, but like the Medics and Commo geeks, was rightfully denied the Combat Infantry Badge. Sepp felt that this was altogether fitting and proper; he took pride in the fact that he was *not* an Infantryman. "You there sitting behind this desk, a goddamn Chair-borne Ranger."

Sepp glanced down at the Black Beret next to its owner's award for paper pushing. Sepp had *earned* that complicated piece of headgear. He didn't really mind that the general population of the Army received the coveted black beret. It was just that they wore them all fucked up. The Sergeant's chewed up, unshaven, un-shaped beret sent Sepp into insubordination. "You REMF leg, I don't even think that you are in *my* goddamn Army." It was too much to say, even though the Sergeant First Class was a Rear Echelon Mother Fucker *and* a non-Airborne qualified leg.

SFC Melvin Jefferson dismissed the young Sergeant by telling him he had to stand in a line that he was going to have to stand in anyway, but one which was particularly long at the moment. SFC Jefferson, or Big Sarge as he was called by his staff, was dealing with guys like the young Ranger far too often these days. *They are too quick to anger.* Although a laid-back man, the Big Sarge was also a damn big black man. He might not have killed no one, or jumped out of no airplanes, but Big Sarge got lots of soldiers to and from the theater of combat. There was honor in his job, too. He did not smoke or drink and Jesus was a personal friend. A good Christian in his own estimation, and teaching his young ones the same; SFC Jefferson did not feel he had much to fear. But with that young killer that he had just dealt with, and more than a few like him. Those men scared Big Sarge. He was frightened not just for his personal safety, which he was, but scared for everybody around these guys. *Too young, too violent in thought.* The Army needs to keep these men in, keep them safe from themselves. *It is my task*; he chided himself for the thousandth time. There were just too many of those boys to deal with these days.

Sepp thought it was the REMF's feeble way of chastising him, but it was not. SFC Jefferson had just sent him on his way. Sepp walked out of the office knowing that he had done wrong, but too damn pissed to atone for it. He sat beside a big black soldier who lacked a unit insignia on his left soldier. This usually denotes a boot camp failure, but on closer inspection Sepp noted the airborne wings and the un-faded patch of uniform where a Ranger Scroll had been. Immediately recognizing the shadow scroll, the place where

84

the patch had been for multiple washings, Sepp then wondered why the soldier had left the Rangers. *Was he RFS'd?* Released For Standards was a catchall discharge for a member of the 75th Rangers, but left a question as to why one left those formations on Peden Field. Sepp decided to check out his first potential recruit. The man looked even more pissed than he was. Sepp leaned toward him and began a recruitment of his own. The guy's name was Clarence "Chicken" Pandy, and he seemed quite interested in Sepp's sales pitch.

At his office in the FBI's J. Edgar Hoover Building, Agent Adam Britton wore an amazed look on his face as he listened to the attractive female detective tell her tale.

"So, let me see if I got this right, Ms.?" the F.B.I. man let the question mark float in the water, hoping for a bite on its hook. He was sure that it was Penning, but genuinely did not want to chew it up. She was, after all, very attractive.

"Penning, Jenna Penning," she stated simply, but intentionally added her Christian name for a touch of familiarity. Jenna knew how far that went with men.

"You're telling me, *you* think that all these unsolved, and some of these solved crimes, are in actuality part of an ongoing crime spree being perpetrated by a gang of cops, soldiers, or a hybrid of the two?" he said waving his thick bear-like hands over the stack of files that Detective Jenna Penning had compiled.

"That is exactly what I think, Agent Britain," she smiled. "Britton," he corrected, her feminine wiles evaporating while his professionalism assumed its rightful place in his mind. She was cute, but she was also twenty-five years his junior.

"And what exactly makes you think this? Some of these cases have been solved," he pointed to the black magic marker lines through the proverbial red tape that ran across the tabs of the file folders.

"Solved?" she sat up straight in her chair as she clutched at one of the case files. "This one, Memphis of last year, was attributed to a gangland retaliation, but there were no leads, no real investigation; it was simply written off. This case was never solved, and any greenhorn rookie who takes the time to read them could tell you that." Her air was indignant; her body language began to cut him off.

"You're right, you're right," Special Agent Britton began to feel as though he was arguing with his ex-wife and wisely gave in, but just enough to keep the exchange open.

"I never read them, or needed to, but you did. Why?" Britton asked.

Detective Penning reached for the coffee cup he had offered at the beginning of her appointment. She drank from it and began.

"Five weeks ago, there was an incident in Orlando. Big bore weapon used to initiate, explosives used in conjunction with water bags, at least a six-man hit-team rode through my town. They killed all the players, then took the cash and the drugs. My men were responding to a four-alarm arson fire on the other side of the district. No one saw anything. There wasn't even a shell casing found. I wrote the whole damn mess off as a drug related gangland hit because the captain wouldn't listen to my theory. I had a few weeks of vacation piling up, so I called Dan at the Miami Field office and he gave me your number."

Agent Britton shook his head at that one. Dan Berquist was an old friend, close to retirement as well. He was not surprised that Dan had sent this young woman his way. Dan was not lazy; it was just his style to point people in the right direction.

Jenna leaned toward Britton. "Nothing pisses me off more than knowing that I fouled something up. And when I went to set it straight, I found all of *this* hiding in the database," she waved her hand over the stack of files. "These guys angled me there and others too. We have some very serious, very professional, and very dangerous men running around the nation, and until today, they had a free ticket. That is why I am here."

Special Agent Britton cocked his head, looked down at the files and finally into her eyes. "Are they all like this?"

"Yes, with minor variances, they all follow the same pattern. But the connection was hidden because some of them were solved," she said, using hand quotes around solved. He looked uncomfortable with this. She made a mental note not to do it again. *Some people simply don't like hand quotes.*

"The programs did not pick them up. I don't have the foggiest notion of the military, but these guys are badges or soldiers. I'd stake my reputation on it."

"You came to the right person. I just might be able to help you here," he turned a photo on his desk toward her. It showed Agent Britton embracing a young camouflage clad man. Even with his face painted, it was hard to tell whose smile was larger, the father's or the boy's.

"That's my son, Max, at his Air Force Pararescue School graduation. He messed his back up something fierce on a jump a couple months back and now he works at the Pentagon. Let's go see his Boss."

Detective Penning was impressed. She had a great deal of authority where she was from, but she didn't have the clout to just *run over to the Pentagon.*

But the Air Force? Jenna knew that she did not know much about the military, but she was convinced that an Air Force guy would not be the right person to ask about what she was sure was a group of Marines or Army men. Jenna *was* right about one thing; she did not know anything about the military.

Deep within the Pentagon, in a windowless room connected to many other windowless rooms, Master Sergeant Maxwell Britton was shining a seat with his ass, but as his father entered the room he stood up straight away. The father noted the son's physical discomfort in standing and quickly gestured for him to sit. His son ignored the invitation, preferring to suffer lest he be something less than a gentleman to the woman who followed his father into the office.

Some men can wear the Class B uniform and look good doing it, but Max looked as though he needed his camouflage uniform to be at ease. He was a tall man, even with his slouch toward the cane. The left side of his pressed shirt was dotted with many metallic insignia that Jenna could not discern. Agent Britton could, though, HALO Wings, Jump Master Wings, and a SCUBA insignia that Max had told him were referred to as a "Bubble." He had been to every graduation. The medals were another story. Few people can decode the various service medals found at the Pentagon and the senior Britton was not among them.

The father and son shared a firm handshake. "Max, this is Miss, err... Detective Penning. She'll need some help with these files and has some questions about the Special Operations community. I told her that you were the man to see."

"You staying, Dad?" Max asked.

"No. I got to run a second analysis on some of the data that Miss Penning has brought to our attention, but tell you what, I will pick you both up for dinner. Call me." The father was deft and left the situation open for his bachelor son. And with that, Agent Britton left the two with the task at hand.

"My name is Max, ma'am," he stored his cane behind the desk and offered his right hand to her.

"Jenna, from the FBI Orlando Field Office." His demeanor and his medals impressed her. There were five rows of them below the shiny emblems.

"Dad told me the gist of your problem, but can I hear it from you, Ma'am?" Military men always use ma'am.

"Okie Dokie," she began, immediately embarrassed by her provincial quip. Recovering with the help of his smile, she continued, "I think that we have some ex-Special Forces guys running around putting holes into a bunch of dealers, and I need your help."

"What's the problem?" Max said rhetorically. Drugs are the bane of the command and control of the Armed Forces. Good Soldiers, Sailors, Marines, and Airmen throw away their careers and the taxpayer's money every day of the year due to the stuff. Max made no effort to conceal his indifference to the death of a few dealers. He made his way to his chair to ease the pain.

"Sergeant, this is not some joke. People are being killed and it is my job to stop them." She didn't know or care enough to consider that he had not been addressed as a simple sergeant for a decade.

"You're right, of course. How can I be of service to you?" Master Sergeant Britton asked, placing his hands flat on the desktop. Detective Penning noted the absence of a wedding ring, diverted her eyes, and then ran her theory past him.

Obviously, Miss Penning was a woman driven. His primal urges had begun to stoke the fires of his professional instincts. As with most men, Master Sergeant Britton was fueled by a desire to impress Detective Jenna Penning. She had taken note of this in the past, and had never been displeased by it. If her tits and ass could help solve a crime, then so be it.

Near the end of her briefing, he looked at her incredulously, "And this is how you spend your vacations?"

"It's no trip to Paris, but this is important."

"Well, then I'm glad to help. There are a few things that you need to be aware of. I'll start with the whole Rambo theory. This is not the work of any Vietnam vets. They are too darn old for this stuff. Their weapons and techniques

89

have gone the way of the Dodo. And this isn't three or four men, this sounds like a squad plus."

She had never before thought in the terms of modern day soldiers being a threat to the public at large. *Those guys are heroes.* She had a faded yellow ribbon and a torn American Flag decal on her SUV for Christ's sake.

Britton cleared his throat "At any time you are unclear about what I am saying, please speak up. It is a lot like algebra. You can't fake knowledge about the service. You either know it or you do not. I can see that all of this is critical info so let's do it right."

Jenna nodded in consent and he continued. "A squad is a five to six-man element; the plus is when other outside men are in the unit. From what you told me, they probably have a sniper. He is a "plus," and if there is a sniper, then there is probably a medic. Maybe some others. I have worked with the best in the business. DELTA, Rangers, Force Recon, the SEALS, and some OGA's," he saw the blank look of confusion on her face and expanded on the acronym, "Other Governmental Agencies, and believe me, from what you have told me—" He was cut off by a look of grave concern on Jenna's face.

"You think other agencies are behind this?" Jenna asked.

"I think that if they were, then you and I would not be having this conversation." The gravity of the situation brought a chilling silence. Britton scribbled on a notepad and passed it over.

We should go someplace… more private.

The beauty and horror of Applebee's is that they are all the same. You know what you're going to get every time you walk into one. Max had changed into his civilian attire. Jenna had taken that time to apply some makeup, so when they walked in together, they looked like any couple in any Applebee's. The waitress noted the desperate sense of privacy that they both wanted. She did not entirely misread the situation. She promptly retrieved a tall pilsner, for the handsome man, and an Absolute and tonic, for the dismissive bitch with him.

"What the hell have I gotten into?" Jenna pleaded with her tone and stunning blue eyes.

"I don't think that it is an OGA, but my office is not the best place to have a conversation about anything that might even concern them," Max held his hands up, palms forward in an unconsciously defensive posture. "I think we have a group of guys who were discharged from the Service. What was the city where the first of these happened?"

"Atlanta."

"Yeah, I'd say three months prior to the Atlanta crime scene, the last of these guys got his discharge. Anyone discharged under terms that were less than honorable during that time frame are prime suspects."

"I don't know. It seems to me that this is a complete team. These guys know each other, and have worked together for a long time. I think that we're looking at a Special Forces unit gone awry." Jenna had the force of conviction in her voice, but Max was not convinced.

"Look here, Miss, there is no A-Team. That was a TV show, not real life. Special Forces and Special Operations are not the same. These guys *have* worked together for a long time. Seven possible combat situations, by *your* count!" Jenna's eyes retreated inward. She had not thought of it in that manner. "Mercenaries are a different breed. They usually take their ranks from the Rangers, not the guys from Regiment, the short tabbers, ya know? And the Force Recon boys. DELTA doesn't operate like this. Your men are in it for the money, not the Flag. The only thing that can command the very best is the Flag. Some of the others can be bought and sold to the highest bidder, but not the D-Boys. Which brings us to two possibilities: some rogue Rangers or maybe Force Recon guys, maybe even some regular Army guys that are real good. Unless we got us a bunch of Tom Clancy's."

"Tom Clancy?" Jenna was confused by the reference.

"You know the guy that wrote all of those great military books, Clancy? Ring any bells?"

"Yeah, of course, but he was a Navy man, or something, wasn't he?" her voice was filled with doubt. She had seen a few of the movies and was pretty sure that the author would have to have been in the Navy or CIA at least.

"No, not one day in the Service. Well, some Rot-C time. He's just a hell of a smart guy. Wrote all those books by reading about and interviewing real soldiers. My point is that even a layman can grip on this military stuff. I can find a flaw here and there. As I said, you can't fake it, but you can write entertaining novels about it. I just hope that these guys are professionals. As Murphy's Law of War states; quote, Professionals are predictable, but the world is full of amateurs, unquote."

Like father like son, Britton used verbal, not hand quotes.

"We do know that they have a sniper," Jenna stated. She tried to continue, but the dashing smile and the subtle shaking of Maxwell's head cut her off.

"You have a great deal to learn about the Service, Miss Jenna." Britton explained that Snipers are not solitary creatures. There are two per team. The strain on the eye and the nerves forces one to lose focus after around thirty minutes, so the spotter and the sniper change out. The sniper takes up the task of looking through the field glasses and the spotter handles the rifle.

"Now that doesn't necessarily mean that there has to be a spotter. With a short enough mission, some men can do the job alone. I just want you to be aware that there are some guiding principles that the military follows, this is just an example," Max was hedging his bet here. There are no certainties where the military is concerned, and he was seasoned enough to know it.

The drinks were starting to loosen Max's words a little more than he wanted to admit, and he considered calling it a night until Jenna went ahead and ordered another round for them while he was in the bathroom. She was herself a bit flush, slightly intoxicated as well as being truly enthralled in the hunt. The thrill had her eager to learn more about her perspective quarry. She was a woman on a guided tour through the inner sanctum of the manliest of the male arts, and she was being ushered through that world by a dashing and proven master of the subject. She had to admit that Max carried himself with an air of confidence that she rarely, if ever, found in her colleagues. He *was* a tough guy; he did not need to act like one. "Master" was even part of his rank.

"What sort of bastards are we dealing with here?" Jenna asked in wonder of the magnitude that had just presented itself.

"The worst sort of bastards. The trained sort," Britton replied.

"So, I was thinking," Jenna drew a sip of vodka and tonic from her straw, "that we should get together with your father and run all this through the database." They both smiled at that. Max was drunk enough to want to get together with Miss Jenna, but not with his father present. Jenna saw the look in his eyes and laughed out loud.

"Tomorrow, then," she said coyly, not agreeing with his smile and then again, not disagreeing either.

Sal and Dognut were high. Both had over two grams in them and had plenty left. Hell, they had enough dope to overdose an elephant. And that was just the cocaine; the heroin was still waiting to be sold. They knew that Sepp thought they were selling the drugs, which was true. But it was deeper than that. The men had taken a shine to the stuff. It had started as recreational. You could drink all damn night and then go snort some of the white stuff into your nose, and you were better than sober. Uninhibited and wide awake. *You can get drunk enough to hit on any chick and high enough to bang her for hours.* There is a good reason for cocaine's popularity and high price.

It was all under control, of course. That is until the sniffling grew out of hand. Cocaine makes the mucus membranes in the nose work overtime while consuming it; this causes the nose to run. This is obvious to other people, and to an anti-dope fiend like Sepp Lokken it was as dangerous as flagging your weapon around a corner. They knew that he would kill them for it, and so they sought out measures to ensure that he would not know of their usage. Halting their cocaine intake was not one of the precautions they pursued. A buyer had told them that smoking the coke was the best way to avoid the runny nose and that it produced a better high as well.

Well, these country boys weren't about to smoke crack cocaine, so their associate had to educate them concerning the various ways that one can smoke it without actually calling it smoking crack. The process is quite simple. Pour out about a half gram of cocaine onto the dull side of a sheet of aluminum foil. Add approximately one-third of the coke's weight in baking soda, then apply a few drops of water to the powders. The actual amount of water is a subject of controversy in the doper's world. There is a variety of acceptable methods to yardstick this sort of thing. You need just enough water to make a light paste. This is spread into a fine sheen around the foil in a circular pattern. When you're done, make sure to rub the tips of your fingers across your gums for the numbing sensation.

Allow to dry for as long as the fiend in you can wait. That's it. Now you can get high. Break out a butane lighter. Zippos and matches are unacceptable in this situation. Apply the heat of the flame to the underside of the foil and capture the resulting smoke with a straw. Contrary to movie fiction $100 bills are quick to expand and are not preferred here. But since the cops are probably not watching, it's more of a guideline than a rule. Heady stuff the smoking of cocaine is.

It turned out that the Kentucky Twins were not impervious to the powerful effect that dope can exert on even the strongest of men. They both became such raving coke addicts they were not even aware of the corrosive effect that it had upon them. They could not see the forest for the trees. And so, it turned out that they had a conversation late one night that would alter the course of their lives in ways that neither could fathom. Downing beer after beer in an attempt to calm down, they still could not resist the call of the wild. They got drunker, and they got higher, and then they got what they called smarter.

The dope was too good to waste setting up the next hit. It was too good not to sell. It was too good to share with the rest of the team. It never dawned on them that the rest of the team had no interest in the stuff. The two then had an epiphany, a clear view of what needed to be done. They would double-cross Sepp and take all of the dope from the next hit for themselves. He would never know, and if he did, they would kill him.

When people make asinine assertions, there is a good reason that others ask, 'Are you high?' In their right minds, both men knew that to cross Sepp was to face him in a fight to the death. Both men also knew that Sepp was their better. He was superior to them on the field, and off. But dope makes a man think in funny ways, and in this respect the two men embarked on a course of action that would lead their interest in a contrary direction to that of Sepp. "Fuck Sepp!" Sal said with a *c'est la guerre* attitude.

"Yeah, man, fuck him," Dognut interjected. "Let's go score us some pussy."

Patty sang along with a *Foreigner* tune belting from the radio. She and Linda Lu were as close as sisters, perhaps closer. The road trip they had embarked on three days ago was bound to draw them closer still. The endless road between LA and Miami was a blur in the rearview mirror. What these twenty-year-old girls needed was, in their words, "Some cock and beer." Not having either, the prospects were dim, but these two ladies were not without their own devices. A road sign advertising a military school caught Patty's eye, and she conveyed its message to Linda Lu, who was relieving herself of some sexual frustration by discreetly pleasuring herself in the back seat.

"It said *what*?" Linda Lu irritably bitched. She had been having a good fantasy concerning herself and two firemen and was none too pleased about having it interrupted.

"A fucking military school, girl! Get those fingers out of your pussy and get ready to do yer patriotic duty."

"America. Fuck yeah!" Linda quoted their mantra of the day as she exited herself and re-buttoned her jeans. The two had already thanked a policeman and a fire marshal, and looked forward to sending a soldier or two off with a smile. They made no distinction between a cadet at a military prep school and a deploying soldier. *A man in uniform is a man in uniform.*

The closest no-tell-hotel to the *R.M. Cash School for Wayward Boys* was the Neptune Motel, and it even had a pool. As Patty booked room #161, Linda Lu went to check out the accommodations. Rounding the fenced off swimming area, she ran smack dab into Sal, spilling his ice cold beer all over both of them in the process.

"Oh, Fuck!" she squealed, laughing as she did so. Her nipples tightened by the frosty heat.

"That's alright, little lady." Sal smiled at the saucy little minx. "I got plenty more."

"Can I have one?" She was busy tying her T-shirt into a breast-accentuating, belly baring knot. Linda Lu was a tawny, raven-haired beauty and knew it. She had a small Treasure Trail of hair that extended up to her belly button. It was just a hint of what lay beneath her Daisy Dukes, and Sal definitely got the hint.

"You Fri'king know it," Sal replied. He was too enticed by her essence to even consider her age. This, Linda Lu noted with pleasure and a deep want. This hard man had booze and was in damn good shape, even though he had a nasty bruise on his chest. She immediately knew that this man was going to give her a full service fucking, and soon.

When Patty finally linked back up with Linda Lu everything was looking just fine. Sal's hunky friend had a weird name, which she initially thought was Donut, but *damn if he weren't hot.* Toting a cooler of cold beers down to the pool, Patty noted that Dognut's arms were extremely muscular and covered in cool looking military tattoos.

"What does this one mean?" Patty asked as her finger traced the Arabic script on Dognut's left arm.

"White Infidel from the West" he replied with a smile. "That's what they called us over there, and Dognut kind of liked it" his third person could tell that Patty kind of liked it too. *Dognut gonna get laid tonight.*

Because they had no swimsuits, Patty and Linda Lu had to swim in their bras and panties. The men had no trouble with that, and neither did anyone else. This was because there would be no one else. The fuck-off looks they gave the few patrons wanting to use the pool solved that problem. No one that hot day had the balls to even enter the chain link fence that sectioned off the pool.

The two couples had a fun day of getting to know one another. Sal and Linda Lu were a natural fit, as were Dognut and Patty. Soon it was obvious that the men were no longer soldiers, but by then it didn't matter. They had really good coke and a cool red '67 Mustang convertible. It was a dusty old car, but there was something sexy about it. And all the guns in room #731 added a level of danger. *Does my gun make you horny, Baby? Yes, yes, it does.*

Sal and Dognut did copious amounts of cocaine, but they did not smoke it around the girls. That, they thought, would have been too much. And it would have been. Patty and Linda Lu had never done coke; they just faked their way through the whole powdering the nose thing. They had seen movies. Around midnight they split off into proper couples and retired to separate rooms. Patty had objected to the split, but Sal gave a quick command of "Quiet Vagina!" She went silent. He wouldn't have said it if he knew she wanted a foursome.

In the sober light of day, Sal and Dognut found themselves still attracted to the young women. To their surprise, the girls felt the same way. The men had plenty of cash and liked to spend it on them. When Sal handed Linda Lu a wad of $100 bills, he asked her to meet them at the Bluegrass Festival in Owensboro a week later. Sal and Dognut had some shit to do, but wanted to make sure that the womenfolk would be there too.

Patty and Linda Lu were on summer vacation and had nothing better to do, so they accepted. Hold onto a briefcase full of dope and make their way to a kickass music festival; it was a no-brainer for the girls. Instead of following the band around, they would follow Sal and Dognut. It was a cooler gig, and a paying one. The starting salary was five grand a month, a shit load of coke and two men that were more gangster than anything else. Patty and Linda Lu felt like they were in a movie or something.

Sergent Colt was not referred to as Sergeant here. In the present company, it was Daddy that he answered to. As with most of his father-son outings, this one involved the outdoors. They were going to float the rivers of the Missouri's Ozark Mountains. Calling them mountains is kind of pushing it, they're more jagged hills.

The Current River is nice and calm. At most there are Class I rapids at certain points. It was there that the father decided to teach his adopted son how to be a man. The good people at Fort Ozarks Canoe Rental and Historic Preservation Society were known to give more than a fair shake to members of the law enforcement community. *A twenty percent discount. Not everyone does that.*

As they entered the Fort, Colt was filled with trepidation. This would have come as a surprise to his wife, but it had nothing to do with the family outing. Colt had the nagging feeling that something was off. The Guard's towers were first on his list of discomforts. No matter where he was within the compound, he could see the towers, and he knew that anyone in those towers could see him as well. Colt could feel it; *the place was militant and harsh.* It left him unsettled.

"Compound" was the word he had chosen out of the many that floated in his mind. Compound denoted a military air to Colt, and he had made a conscious effort to disassociate himself from that time in his life. This might seem incongruous to a civilian, but you never clock out of a police job and there are no such devices as timecards in the military. Colt wished that Ross was there to bounce his ideas off of, but Ross's divorce had been messy and Colt took measures not to rub his own good fortune in his partner's face.

Little Drew broke free from the grip of his father and ran toward the cotton candy vendor.

Colt lost his train of thought long enough for him to realize that this trip was about the boy and male bonding, not his past. The vendor shook his head as to say "not necessary" at Colt as he proffered the cash, and so Colt smiled and took the unconcerned hand of the child. At the river's edge, the canoe was waiting. Men wearing the grey cap of the

Confederacy were busy loading the watercraft as the two Colt males approached.

This was as unusual as it was unexpected. Colt took pride in his river skills and had hoped to teach his son a lesson in balancing a canoe's load. But Colt noted that the canoe was being packed well, and that Drew was obviously proud that the men were so helpful to his father, and the beer in his hand was cold. *Being a State trooper does have its advantages.*

Colt kindly accepted the push off from the gravel bank and asked little Drew to keep an eye out for rocks. It was an important job, Drew was told. The safety of the entire boat was in his hands. Drew clambered a bit too far to the bow for Colt's comfort, fully expecting to avert disaster and save the day. Colt watched with proud approval, cracked open another beer, and gently guided the watercraft into the middle of the river. With the exception of a lone man drifting in his canoe, the river was theirs. Colt noted the man; he never paddled, but was intent on watching his chronometer. Every so often he would scribble something down on a note pad and then return to steering only, never paddling.

Strange, thought Colt, but not so odd as to arouse any real inquiry in him; Drew announced that rapids were ahead, and all was right with the world. And so, it was that for the second time that day, Colt ignored something that was to have a lasting and real impact on his future.

Agent Britton and Detective Penning were busy compiling a detailed list of commonalities from all the suspected crimes. The list proved some of Jenna's assertions to be true. Agent Britton was becoming increasingly convinced that he needed to assemble a task force to deal with this emerging threat. There was a cursory knock on his office door as his son let himself into the room. The uniformed man did not bother to drag a chair over to the worktable. Instead, he leaned his cane against it and pulled out a file from his attaché case, laying its contents out in front of Detective Penning.

"We got a couple of matches for your profile, Miss Penning," Max said as Jenna moved as sultry as she could without drawing too much attention. Unfortunately, she drew none from him. But at least he was being professional. *If she only knew how hot I think she is,* Max pined.

"OK, shoot," she replied, her tone all business.

"Well, we have a few people that fit your criteria regarding dates of service and military specialty." They were interrupted by the ringing of the telephone. Max's father grabbed the line. Max and Jenna averted their attention from each other, and directed it to the elder Britton, who was furiously scribbling down notes in his day planner.

The receiver was not yet in its cradle when the Special Agent began to convey the phone call. "It seems that your boys have done some damage in British Columbia. We're strap-hanging on a flight over there with INTERPOL. The bird takes off in ninety minutes." He looked at Detective Penning, "Pack your bags. We are gonna make that flight." He was grabbing his jacket and checking his firearm as he spoke. His son being in the US military could not accompany him to foreign soil. Even if it was just Canada.

On board the helicopter to the Ronald Reagan International Airport, Detective Penning realized she wasn't carrying her passport. Special Agent Britton assured her that they wouldn't need any documentation. Aboard the flight, it was made clear to Detective Penning that she was only an observer. However, once on the scene, her intimate knowledge of the suspected perpetrators impressed the female Commander of the Royal Canadian Mounted Police enough that she was given a brevet authority over the golf course side of the crime scene.

When Jenna found one of the jamming devices left by the retreating hit squad, her acumen was truly acknowledged by the rank and file Canadians. The mention of her name in the official INTERPOL report was likewise sufficient to warrant a phone call from the FBI Director of Operations to the Mayor of Orlando. Agent Britton was pleased to inform Jenna that she had been temporarily assigned to his new Task Force Vigilante. *That is what everyone was calling it anyway.* Her first assignment was to liaise with the Pentagon and come up with a profile on the crew. This was exactly what she had been doing, but agent Britton wanted to make it clear that she now answered to him.

Agent Britton had to treat her that way. He hoped that she understood. It was the only way to bring what she had to the table. He was sure that it would be her insight, her vehemence, which would knock this crew to its knees. Britton had been around long enough to know how cases went. This one was in *her* veins. Either she was going to solve it, or because she was involved, it was going to be solved. Britton could not put this idea into words; he purely felt it to be true. And history had been kind to his intuition. He trusted himself; it was a gift that age had given to him.

MR. GATLING'S TERRIBLE MARVEL

"Death was mechanized. Human beings were interchangeable, just as were the parts in other new machines.

-J. Keller

"What are the production figures looking like today?" Douglas asked his right-hand man as he fastened a belt around his ample belly. It pained him to see his reflection. His stomach was out of control, and his head nearly bald, such a contrast to his vigorous youth. But Douglas reckoned that he deserved to live well. He let go of the image in his Italian floor mirror and turned to his underling, focusing on what really mattered.

"Boss, it's better than the last time you asked," Dan Brewer replied. It was an understatement. Fort Ozarks was a cash cow. Dan sometimes wondered how his job could be more lucrative. He then always answered himself with the admonition that his job was both dangerous and illegal. *There but by the grace of God go I.* Despite his vocation, Dan Brewer took his oaths, both to his boss and to his God, quite seriously.

"That is welcome news indeed," Douglas nodded his ample chin with satisfaction. He then gazed out his bedroom's ten-foot-high picture window. The expanse of Fort Ozarks lay before him. His home stood on the banks of the Current River, nestled in the backwoods of the eponymous Mountains. It was here that kith and kin had protected the Younger-James Gang from the federal government and its Pinkerton detective agency. Here, any law enforcement beyond the local sheriff is still known as a *Revenuer*, and even the National Park Rangers are treated with unspoken suspicion.

A native son who had done well for himself, Douglas Nelson was safe here. Indeed, some would go further and declare that he was the 'King of the Ozarks' and that the rivers and valleys were but his fiefdom. There was no one who would not alert him of danger, not in the Missouri State House and not in these hills. Sheriff Caldwell was little more than a puppet on a string. Caldwell and his men knew that in the event of trouble, the whole of Poplar Bluff, Missouri would burn before Fort Ozark was abandoned.

"Please have a car brought around, Dan. I want to dine with the mistress this evening." Douglas made the order sound like a simple request. It was just his style.

Dan didn't care for the current gold-digging flavor *du jour*. He winced at the directive but followed it to the letter. Mr. Nelson was Boss, and the Boss made the rules, not him. Dan passed the request to an underling and thus gave the go-ahead for the woman to be summoned. It was always like that. Douglas ordered, but Dan approved. With him the lone responsibility for the Boss resided. Dan had authority over everyone except the few women that Douglas enjoyed. It was just how things worked at Fort Ozarks.

A servant brought a glass of fine Iberian port to Mr. Nelson. He took the crystal glass from the platter and sipped lightly. The port was from the Douro Valley and was exceptional. Douglas downed its entirety. The distilled wine warmed his blood, but that was all. He drew the line at insobriety, but he learned all about intoxicants in a little place he forever after called Viet-*Fucking*-Nam.

Southern by birth, and by the grace of God, Douglas had no interest in drugs then or now. The moonshine distilled by his kinfolk was as far as he had ever wanted to go. But over there, so many years ago, Douglas had learned the lengths *other* men would go for their next high. Master Sergeant Douglas Nelson, 2nd Special Forces Group, only had to be told once of the enormous profits to be made trafficking heroin. MSG Nelson knew that scoring "H" in the Golden Triangle was easier than getting the clap from one of the local whores. The problem, he soon learned, was not in getting the dope; it was in getting the dope back to the world without getting caught. The world is what soldiers called home. Damned few men were in such a position as Douglas on this score, what with all his secret comings and goings between the JFK School of Special Forces and Viet-*Fucking*-Nam. It had started with a couple of kilos in his carry-on bags, but that small amount only served to whet his appetite.

The tonnage of material going back to America from Indochina during the late 1960's reached staggering proportions. And to make things even better for Douglas, none of the returning men or their cargo were subject to any serious scrutiny from Customs. A soldier of sufficient rank could board a plane in Southeast Asia, sign in his cargo, and after the obligatory stopovers, drive a U-Haul loaded with government-transported heroin right out of Andrews Air Force Base without so much as a pat down from his brothers in arms. It was out of this circumstance that Douglas concocted his scheme meant to transform him from Green Beret to Drug Lord.

There was no enthusiastic Airman greeting listeners with "Good morning, Vietnam!" on Master Sergeant Nelson's radio. Instead, was the mellow, pot-addled voice of Radio First Termer's DJ Dave Rabbit. He was the voice of the underground pirate radio station "69-69 Saigon, Republic of Vietnam." MSG Nelson tuned in for humor and some hard Acid Rock.

"There is a Korean pushing some bad H, I say again, there is a Korean pushing some bad H, down at the China

Lounge." the radio was informing the first-termers that a dealer was pushing bad heroin and of an impending vice raid, "and if any of you motherfuckers wanna doubt what it is that my main man has to say, then I wanna let you know that Captain Zeep is the nose that knows, if you can dig what it *is* that I am saying."

MSG Nelson laughed at the thought of it. If you really had to listen to a rogue radio station like Dave Rabbit's for that sort of thing then it was best, in Nelson's estimation, that you were busted. He hated users, which was ironic, seeing that he was single-handedly responsible for shipping tons of heroin back home. He laughed, rubbed his freshly shaved chin, and tucked his brown T-shirt into his olive drab trousers before walking out into the intense light of the tropical morning. Only a tiger-striped boonie cap shielded his eyes from the sun. Douglas had seen what sunglasses could do to the eyeball when incoming ordinance shattered them, and so only wore the soft cap. He never wore his green beret in the field, even though it was authorized. There was something ostentatious about that particular piece of headgear. Adjusting the boonie, Douglas made his way to the team awaiting instruction. He, the Master Sergeant, was ready to issue them. No need for officers here. Nelson had operated without one for seven months and was pleased with it.

"Hey Doug, how about a snort?" his corporal asked about the bottle of booze. Ever since the dope running got out of hand, the corporal figured he had some leeway, and he really did.

"Fuck off, you," was Nelson's sole reply to his booze-addled underling.

The operations order was getting ready to begin and there was the usual milling about of his ten-man element. The corporal was the lowest ranking member, so there was an assortment of E5's and E6's to be dealt with, sergeants and staff sergeants. Everyone knew their place and with the exception of a Mormon E5, they were all in on the scheme.

And since the Mormon was going to get whacked on this mission anyway, it was to be a relatively truthful operations order.

In the broadest of strokes, this was a simple assassination. A personality of a certain interest to the organization." It went unsaid that Central Intelligence was the creator of this mission. *They all were these days.* It also went without saying that a side mission was to be neatly folded into this one. Master Sergeant Nelson would be heading home soon, and everyone knew he was fattening up the cattle before he left. They all had a job in Missouri when their terms of service were up, so they had decided to keep the pipeline open until they were discharged. Well, all except the corporal. He was an insubordinate drunk and was to be fragged by the last man in the country.

After the disturbing mission, Douglas found himself listening to Radio First Termer yet again. "And here is one from the latrine walls. Only fifteen more days until I can go home and picket and protest this fucking waste that lifers and politicians call a war."

He was composing a letter to the Mormon's family in Salt Lake City. They would expect one and Nelson would have to write it. He did not relish this part. *If only that dumb bastard could have let his religious shit go, he would be richer instead of deader.*

Douglas saw the drug trade as a huge gamble where the stakes were mastery or death. It was an all or nothing venture that consumed his life. Shipping crates, personal mail, and ammo cans all went home to the Ozark Plateau. They were laden with heroin, and all were shipped at the expense of the American taxpayer. Eventually, even the fallen soldiers themselves were used as mules to feed the addictions of St. Louis, Chicago, and New Orleans. After their ultimate sacrifice, Douglas and his ever-growing concern would pervert the soldier's deaths so that their own corpses would facilitate the poisoning of that for which they had laid down their singular lives. The dirty hippies snorting

107

and shooting up the shit never thought twice about their part in the conflict over there in Viet-*Fucking*-Nam.

Moral implications did not apply to Master Sergeant Nelson. His addiction was to the money, and to the power that the other addiction had over men. He was in his third tour when the money took a turn to the serious. It would prove to be his last hitch with the military. Killing Charlie had lost its luster. The coffee cans of cash in his far away storm cellar had slowly become his master. There were never enough of those cans, and they were never full enough. Corrosion is a slow process. One seldom sees it on the horizon. Doug Nelson's connections in Vietnam were still obedient to his will. Although he lost some money by returning to the States, more and more was funneling into the Ozark Mountain retreat he called home. When it was his turn to out process at Splinter Village, Douglas told the retention NCO to go dry hump his own leg and walked out of Splinter Village.

Once back in the Ozarks, Doug Nelson proved an entrepreneur to the hilt. He had seen the changes sweeping the nation after the last helicopters from the Hanoi embassy were shoved off the side of the aircraft carrier. Marijuana looked to be the drug of choice in the United States, and so pot became his craft. Just as he had mastered jungle warfare, Douglas and his crew set out to master the intricacies of dealing marijuana. And master it, they did. Douglas found himself working and competing with some astoundingly unprofessional people. Damned few Harvard grads traffic in pot, and fewer still sell metric tons of it. This fact was not lost on Douglas. His few competitors were not killed in drive-bys, or in Italian restaurants; no, they were killed in single vehicle auto accidents or they simply vanished. People tended to disappear when their interest ran contrary to Mr. Nelson, but no one really thought he and his crew of ex-Green Berets were even involved with narcotics, much less that they were high end dealers engaged in the systematic killing off *all* the competition.

No one thought that this could be true because Douglas Nelson surrounded himself with like-minded men. He employed those with formal advanced military training: the kind of knowledge that makes one's actions deceptive, seemingly innocuous, and ultimately lethal. In the Green Berets, it never paid to advertise, and this translated well into the world of dealing pot. A quality product advertises and sells itself. Street smarts are so goddamn easy because the people of the street only get one chance to jack things up before they die. And when they do die, no one seems to notice. *It's a fate to be avoided.*

Douglas and his team had certain acumen where covert operations were concerned. They were not going to be killed off. No, they were going to prosper. In the early 80s the new drug sensation was cocaine and Douglas was one of the first on the scene. He invested in airplanes and small plots of land near the border. The local tough guys happened to be bikers. Douglas began using them as his couriers. Due to the money, he generated for the Southern Missouri Chapter of the Hell's Angels they agreed to become a licensed subsidiary of Nelson Enterprise. Bikers now formed the core of his drug delivery network. The toughest, meanest men in the land had joined forces with Mr. Nelson. The venture proved profitable for both sides. In those heady days, Douglas transformed his growing concern into a full-bore empire.

When an up and coming young attorney named Bancroft came to him for a contribution, Douglas was all too happy to help the politician get dirty on the way up; he still had the 8mm film to prove it. It had been copied to VHS and then to DVD over the years, but he still had that 8mm in its original form in the wall safe. As that young attorney grew into an older State Attorney General, Douglas' conglomerate grew beneath an umbrella of legal protection. This fertilized

109

the tree of Douglas Nelson's criminal enterprise until he solidly controlled the entire county within which he operated. Not as large an empire as some men would be satisfied with, but more than enough for Mr. Nelson.

In the late 80s, Reagan's War on Drugs was going strong. Cocaine was now enemy number one. The Federal Government passed laws that could send fine, upstanding men like Douglas Nelson to the electric chair. So, when the rules of engagement changed, Douglas changed with them. He and his interstate crime syndicate transformed Poplar Bluff, Missouri into the capital of the drug future. His biker gangs began to deal methamphetamine instead of cocaine. It was not illegal for Douglas to be dealing methamphetamine, because it was still so new that the laws hadn't caught up. The brave new world of the drug culture was afoot. Designer drugs like ecstasy were still in the legal realm, and therefore within one's right to possess and distribute it. The biker gang Douglas controlled now began to push his new goods. Meth became the cornerstone of the castle he forged in the Ozarks.

The Fort Ozarks Historical Preservation Society and Canoe Rental was Doug's joke on the world. A kitsch frontier-styled outpost, the fort was both a beautifully and a cleverly designed emplacement. It was every man's dream: a home and a castle. Fort Ozarks also fronted as a legitimate place of business. Rough-hewn logs with sharpened tips reminded parents they were showing their children how the old West really looked, and the look also served Doug's interest, as it was also a truly defensible emplacement. Lines of sight were taken into account, guard towers erected, and the place even had its own water source and electrical power plant. Douglas was set up to defend this place for a long time.

Only a single hardball route served as access to the Fort, and if he really needed to use it, the river itself could hurry him away from uninvited company. That physical security, coupled with the squads of men he had working in shifts, replete in period costumes, had always proved him secure.

110

Tourists even had their pictures taken with the guards for family albums. The Buckeyes and Hoosiers never imagined that once back in their towers, those nice young men would lay down their fully serviceable muzzleloaders and take up semi-automatic assault rifles. Little kids who thought they were posing with soldiers from the eighteenth century were, in reality, being photographed with mercenary men from the early twenty-first. *A man's home is his castle.*

The wisest decision Douglas had made to insulate himself from the vagaries of life was to hire a man named Dan Brewer. The self-deprecating man would never proclaim to be the keystone of the entire operation, but he was. It was a job fitting for a man with a steadfast nature. Although he had no formal military training, Dan had learned the hard way how to conduct armed operations. An incredibly normal upbringing had somehow produced a man able to lead a growing concern through the rigors of drug distribution and territorial acquisition. It still amazed Douglas that Dan had at one time been so bland as to actually sell insurance. But at twenty-seven, Dan had inexplicably bought a Harley-Davidson Fat Boy and subsequently joined the local biker gang. He rapidly molted his weak past and began a new life in earnest.

Earning his stripes as a dealer of exceptional merit, Dan soon found himself working for one of the surprisingly few gangs that leased its services to a certain Nelson Enterprises. One day his refusal to get high was about to brand him a cop infiltrator and get Dan killed. But as fate would have it, Douglas asked to see him. When pressed on the reason for his refusal, Dan said that it was "not good business" to be high. What raised the ire in others was seen as intelligence by the Boss. Brewer was taken under his wing and groomed for higher purposes.

In Dan Brewer, Douglas saw much that others had missed. Dan only had to be told how to do something once; he understood what intent was. That is to say, Dan instinctively knew what the end-state of an operation was for

111

Douglas. And by truly knowing what his Boss wanted, Dan was able to draw up his plan to fulfill that intent. Douglas more than once lamented that he didn't have more men like Dan with him in Viet-Fucking-Nam. He raged over the fact that he was the lone survivor from those days. Now in his mid-sixties, Douglas's old buddies from the war were fewer and farther between. The drug trade, like the war trade, does not easily give its participants longevity.

It was Dan's suggestion that Fort Ozarks had become a fortress in more than just name. Douglas had been talking about how good the ground was at that bend in the river for a defensive position, and how he would have liked to build a true fort on it. Dan had not asked why? He asked, why not? And so, it came to pass that a fortress was constructed in the wild, and with it, a methamphetamine distribution center had sprung up in the foothills of the weatherworn Ozarks. Instead of bikers moving relatively small amounts, select people would rent a canoe and leave with kilos hidden in the fore and aft ballast compartments. The addition of the parapets and embrasures had likewise been Brewer's brainchild; even the hokey guards had been his idea. The cotton candy booth and the old stone igloo-style oven were Douglas's later contributions.

Dan Brewer was also the brain behind the county's only legally owned, fully automatic machine gun. Keeping in line with Douglas's demand that the façade of Fort Ozarks be fully legal, Dan had purchased a genuine reproduction Gatling gun. For twenty-three thousand dollars, the Dixie Arsenal had created the ultimate machine gun for Fort Ozarks. Because it was hand-cranked, it was godfathered into the legal realm. And because it was a .45 caliber weapon with 70 grains behind it, it could strike from hundreds of yards. A .45 caliber bullet isn't known these days as a long-range weapon, but in the last century they used a higher grain count behind the bullet, effectively making a Gatling gun a fully automatic, buffalo-killing gun. The only problem faced by the Fort's armorer was the fact that no one in the world made tracer rounds for such a caliber, and Dan Brewer had specified that a full one fifth of the Fort's ten thousand rounds had to be red tracers. Legality was not the problem. Practicality was. Buying the supplies to make tracer rounds was perfectly legal, but making all two thousand rounds took two full months. In the end, Douglas wasn't so sure about the expense and man-hours taken, but Dan Brewer again stood like a rock on the soundness of his idea.

At the seat of his power, Douglas needed to maintain control. His satellite communications system enabled him to seek out those who owed him allegiance, as well as those who owed even more. There were those who questioned his keeping a meth lab of industrial size on location, but to Douglas, this was obvious. He had the power to depose one of the most powerful men in the state's law enforcement department. The tape was withheld from the news media at his whim. Douglas did not even like the "sum-bitch" Bancroft, and had even considered releasing the tape on general principle, but always-cooler thinking prevailed. Bancroft was, as Douglas always bragged, "In the words of Franklin Delano Roosevelt, 'he might be a son-of-a-bitch, but he is *our* sum-bitch'." Roosevelt had been speaking of Anastasio Somoza, Nicaragua's dictator in the 1940s.

When Troopers Colt and Ross and the other members of the law enforcement community wanted to enjoy the Ozark National Scenic Riverways, they knew that a discount was offered to all "Badges" at Fort Ozarks. Even their kids would be given a special gift from the souvenir stand. They never got one of the special canoes, though. *Certainly not.* Those canoes had removable nose plates where the dealers found the meth and then left the cash. This kept business transactions safely off site.

Douglas was upset that he had to let a man go today. He was a driver for his canoe rental business and had been cited by the local sheriff for driving under the influence. The idiot was so drunk that there was no getting around the ticket, and that was a good thing, too. Douglas had no time for a man dumb enough to get caught by the police. He also had no time for a drunk; it was the same problem with that corporal all those years ago.

Like the Captain on some 17th-century navy vessel, Douglas had several men present for what he called *instructional purposes.* Six Jon boats collected over the deep pool of water Douglas had picked for this lesson. Stanley McCormack was neither bound nor gagged; he simply had a small cord tied to a single ankle. He knew that to resist would cause his wife to suffer an even worse death.

"Do it!" Douglas said callously to Dan. The assembled men looked at Dan, knowing he was being given some authority over the matter. This pleased the men greatly. Dan was the future of Nelson Enterprises. Douglas was getting too long of tooth and new blood was needed. It pleased them to follow Dan's order and push the large rock into the water. The rope that was attached to the rock quickly began to uncoil. The man attached to the other end of the rope was quickly pulled overboard. Stanley's fingertips were a scant few inches below the clear water. Arms flailing and a look of absolute terror on his face, it took over a minute before death calmed the body. The water became mirror-like again, placid.

"This is what happens to slackers here in this outfit," Dan stated the obvious, but it needed stating nonetheless. The boat motors were cranked back on and the assembled men left white rooster tails and a single dead man in their collective wakes. *Crawdads have to eat, too.*

114

"So what we have here are some Green Berets, Rangers, or whatever." Jenna inferred from their prior meeting. She had met Max in a cigar club this time. The dim lighting and the earthy smell of tobacco mellowed the mood. They were relaxing in deep leather chairs. Patrons of this establishment were given their upmost privacy. Jenna sipped her neat scotch, desiring one of Max's cigars but lacking the spirit to ask for one. He would have happily offered, but there is something too phallic about a cigar. Damn if it wasn't unprofessional to offer. *There's something especially sexy about a woman smoking a cigar.*

Max spoke with an economy of words. "We have a damn good lead. When I combined my father's data with my own, I found that I have a few things yet to learn about our boys in the service. We're looking for a personality with Special Ops training. Someone who trained not only in the art of violence, but also in the coordination of violence. We started looking at Commissioned Officers, but Uncle Sam keeps pretty good track of those guys, and they tend not to drop off the map. It was when we looked for discharged men that we got a hit that matched your criteria. An Army Ranger, combat proven, and all that. But when he was given a chance to *go Mustang*, OCS, Officer Candidate School, he refused."

Max saw the look of *Yes, I understand*, but he knew that she did not.

"It's a way we keep the trained killers in the service. They don't always make it on the outside. I hope I'm not feeding the reputation that enlisted men are morons who had to join the army because there was no other option. Don't feel bad if you did. My Pop felt the same way when I enlisted. It's the stigma that we live with," he explained. *And true in my case*, he failed to add.

"You'll be happy to know I don't think that about you at all." She offered a warm smile. "So if this man isn't an officer, how does he know how to run a platoon or company of men?" She took a manly pull from her Glenlivet and pushed her head forward, awaiting the inevitable answer. Max obviously liked to hear himself speak, and Jenna was growing fond of hearing him do it.

"The Company Commander, the XO, the Platoon leaders, maybe the Fires Officer… yes, he's Field Artillery but he is an officer, then the First Sergeant, and the Platoon Sergeants are in charge, in that order. These men are prepared to take charge if circumstances dictate. Well, it turns out no one fit the time frame that you gave us. So, I looked a little deeper. In the event all those guys are dead, the only people left with the tactical knowledge to actually lead the entire element are the Squad Leaders, the RTOs and the FO," Max detailed.

"Enough with the acronyms," she said a little more bluntly than she meant to. "Will you please tell me what you are saying?" She was clearly exasperated but remained truthful and direct. To Max, she had never before been as beautiful as she was now. He wanted her, and his smile conveyed just that. *OK, tell her what you know.*

"When the Platoon Sergeant is dead. Who knows what is going on? His Radioman. Who else? The fucking Forward Observer." Britton was fired up and his language went to the extreme. He had used the F-word in front of her and he had not even noticed it. "He is the only other man that has been to the battalion level Operations Order, and is listening to the radio traffic and knows what the hell is going on with a mission. It was when looking at FO's that we struck gold. One of the Special Ops guys that was discharged in your window is unaccounted for. The man isn't drawing his GI Bill, or using any Veterans Affairs disability, and when we phoned his home, his dad, a Judge, told us that he was still in the Service. But he isn't, of course. We have him here and there, with long periods of untraceable activity. Couple this with the Private Dick's statement and the Coastie. We got him, baby, we got him, a damn buck

116

sergeant, even!" Max let his enthusiasm get the better of him, and he affectionately grasped Jenna's hand. She did not retract her hand. They shared a moment of unguarded mutual affection.

Going home was always a pain in the ass for Sepp—so many questions about where he had been and what he was doing. At least there was technically a war on, and everyone knew he could not answer questions officially. He always had the photos and the supporting documentation. Sepp *had* been in the Army. He had the medals to prove it now. He could come and go as he pleased, but there was always something false about his absences now. He had more money and more free time than was expected from him, and sometimes, he felt as if it showed. It did not, but his self-doubt did, especially around his father.

"I still work for the government Dad, just not the same as before." It was like a lie he had often told women during his days on active duty. *I work for the Department of Defense*, he would say. It was technically true, but far more glamorous than saying, "I am in the Army."

The Judge was skeptical; something was not right about the call from the Pentagon, but the Master Sergeant had not said that anything was wrong with his son.

"Dad, why the hell does that shit-bag Douglas Nelson get to peddle dope all over our fair state, and not a single finger is lifted?" The question would take his Dad's mind off the awkward subject at hand but also was a good segue into Sepp's desired topic.

Sepp's father had drunk beer for two hours while he was barbequing and had eaten more than his fair share of the proceeds. Alcohol added with the unexpected arrival of his son, made Judge Lokken loose of the tongue. Senator Bancroft had defeated one of the Judge's old political allies last year with significant financial backing from an anonymous donor from the Ozarks. Judge Lokken knew that something was rotten in Denmark when it came to Bancroft, though he could not prove it. His gut told him Nelson was behind the political move. "Where do I begin?"

After a few days, Sepp was tired of hanging out with his family, so he rented a car and drove to St. Louis to visit some old friends. He had a warm reception initially, but as soon as the drinks piled up poisonous words flowed from his friend Arnold Berkowitz's mouth. Arnie as Sepp called him.

"Why have you become such a tight-assed prick, Sepp?" Few men on the earth had a pass to speak to him that way, but Arnie did. "I used to know who you were, and now I don't even give a fuck." Arnie didn't mean what he said. He was just drunk. *Maybe he did mean it.*

"Dude, I have been freaking busy, unless of course you don't read the freaking papers," Sepp mixed the word freaking with the F-word dependent on his audience, and Arnie was a friend, after all.

"Why the fuck you decided to fight that goddamn war will always be a mystery to me, man. To think that all of those sand-niggers are more important to you than us is plenty fucked up." Arnie's choice of words proved as poor as his knowledge of current events.

"Don't use that word." It was not a polite request. Sepp called all Muslims Haji's and not out of respect for the journey to Mecca. Chicken would have objected to the N-word. Sepp felt it would be a betrayal for him to not push back.

"OK, man, it's just that all the plans that we made are now straight fucked 'cause you're a war on terror... A warrior." It sounded horrible and was terrifically slurred, but the truth sometimes comes out that way. There was irony in his friend's words.

"Arnie, you know that I was a soldier well before this damn shit started. What the fuck was I supposed to do? Just leave?" Sepp did not like this part of the conversation. The eventuality of it was one of the reasons he didn't show up much anymore. Sepp knew that he had effectively abandoned his past in a terrible gamble for his future. Sepp knew in the event any hit went bad, that he would either be dead or have to flee the country. He had placed cash all over the globe in case that problem ever presented itself. But still in the recesses of his mind, Sepp did not fully grasp the ramifications of his chosen profession. It was not until that day that he realized he may never see his childhood friends again.

When he was in the Army, the possibility of coming home in a body bag was ever present, especially after the war had begun. Sepp had no trouble with that. If he were to be killed on the dusty ground in some shit-hole of a country, then so be it. His mother and father would be presented with a finely folded flag, and that would be that. Here Lies a Soldier, and all that entailed. It wouldn't be pretty, but there was honesty and a dignity that went with it. But if he were killed as a mercenary, his entire secret life would be let loose on those he loved. That part he did not like so much.

"Man, I don't mean anything by this." Arnie said. "You ever get tired of all that Hooah Army bullshit, and I'll move to the Caribbean with you and we'll have our damn bar."

Sepp knew Arnie was drunk now. He liked to say Hooah when he was. It belittled his friend's high-handed vocabulary. Sepp didn't mind. Hooah was a stupid, non-word to Sepp, but he used it regardless. Everyone in the Army does. He also knew this was all just drunk talk. There was no way Arnie would leave his high-paying investment banking gig, add to that a rumor that his friend was about to propose to the girlfriend. High school had been a long time ago. Arnie and the others had normal lives. Sepp's choices were foreign to them. But that went both ways. *Who the hell wants a wife* and *kids?*

He decided to humor him. "All right, Arnie, it's a deal. When my enlistment is up, I'll move to the Caribbean. I got some money saved up. I'll even buy the damn property. You just make sure that you get your ass on down there when I do. I have nine months left." Sepp played that one loose. He knew that if he were killed it wouldn't make much difference. But he figured that if he could pull off the plan that his Dad had inadvertently given him, then nine months would be just about right.

"It's a deal, Buddy," Arnie said. The two drunks shook on it, but there was a lie in both their hearts. Sepp didn't know if he could pull it off or even be alive, and Arnie had concerns about his fiancée's approval.

Sepp left the bar shortly after the handshake and stumbled into his hotel room. Unable to sleep that night, Sepp decided that if he lived through this last Op, he actually would open that crazy bar he and Arnie had conceived one spring break. They were on psychedelic mushrooms at the time, but the idea was quite sound. He would invite Arnie on down to help run it or watch it for him while he took his vacations. *Yes, the crazy ski lodge bar in the tropics idea.* Sepp never thought of it in terms of *retiring*. He thought about *working* at his own bar. A normal person can't live a vacation; you have to be born rich for that sort of thing.

LEADER'S RECON

"It cannot be called virtue to kill one's fellow citizens, betray one's friends, be without faith, without pity, and without religion; by these methods one can indeed gain power, but not glory."

-Niccolo Machiavelli

Like all the movements made by the team, the transition to the rugged hills of the Ozark Plateau was staggered. The team never moved as a whole unless it was absolutely mission dependent, and even then, only with serious reservations. Sepp and Chuck customarily went prior to the rest of the team in a leader's reconnaissance. The two men were to establish a forward position and ensure that it was safe for the rest of the team to rally onsite. They were also tasked with some of the more rudimentary aspects of establishing a base of operations.

Sepp had used the Internet to rent out a riverfront cabin to stage the team's Operation. A genuine bank account under an assumed identity had already paid the bill for a month long stay. The anonymity of the World Wide Web was a new concept for Sepp. He did not trust it, so he integrated its use on missions with extreme caution. Chuck, who was several years the younger, often rubbed him about Sepp's sometimes-antiquated ways. The difference in their ages was a scant few years, but it really made a difference. Sepp owned a laptop and a cell phone; Chuck was just more adept regarding their usage.

As Sepp and Chuck pulled their vehicles into the small area between the surface road and the fenced in gravel easement that lead to the property, they both mentally

121

assessed the terrain. A long road strewn with rock and gravel disappeared into the forest of green foliage; there would be no visitors that just happened to drop by. Sepp set a combination lock on the gate regardless and mentally played out defensive scenarios as his Toyota Land Cruiser ate up the quarter mile to the riverfront. Sepp was a man who had read his history, and well. *In Peace, there is no better endeavor than the preparation for war.* There *is* a next war. There is *always* a next war.

At the terminus of the road, hidden in the dense green of the trees, a small cabin lay with its riverside front on short stilts. Its porch overlooked a deep pool surrounded by a solid rock walkway accessing the water. Shade trees surrounded the rear of the cabin, providing plenty of cover for the numerous tents that would be erected behind their succor. The slope of the terrain here was gentle to the water, not abrupt like other places on the river. This place was definitely within parameters for the Op to be run with a nominal expectation for success. The broad requirements had been met, but now it was a matter of checking the specifics. *The Devil is in the details.*

Sepp and Chuck had parked their vehicles in full view of the river. They wanted to be able to watch the random canoes and kayaks that silently glided by and to use the rigs to shield the encampment from view. Sepp proceeded to pull the canoe off his Land Cruiser. Chuck meanwhile opened the cabin's doors and windows. It was hot and stuffy inside, with a slight mildew smell that reminded Chuck of his old Army tent. Sepp turned the valve on the huge propane system that, after four tugs of its cord, began to provide electrical power to the property.

Inside the cabin, the refrigerator immediately shook to life. Its rumbling startled Chuck. He felt cajoled into cleaning its exterior and when that task was accomplished, he felt further compelled to open it. Chuck immediately regretted taking the initiative.

"Man, fuck Sepp, this here titty-fucking fridge is a shit-hole." A heavy application of bleach water would be only the first of many tasks involved in the cleaning out of the icebox. Chuck knew that Sepp was not going to do anything to help. No landlord was going to be called either, so Chuck found himself doing what he deemed to be women's work.

Once the cabin was on its way toward livability, the two men decided to go for a diverting excursion up the river. It was a good excuse not to clean the damn cabin and a great way to wash the stink off them. After a quick swim, the two men took to the canoe. The water was smooth on that stretch of river. Only the occasional ripple belied the massive rocks beneath the water's surface. With both men digging deep with their oar blades, the journey up river was quick work. Nearly a half-mile upstream lay a small unoccupied gravel bar that could serve as a good place for a tent or two and a fire. There was even a close root wad from which to draw firewood. Chuck and Sepp got out of their canoe, walked over the deep, wet gravel and tossed the wood into the stream. They did not want anyone to even think about camping so close to their cabin.

They climbed back into the aluminum canoe and continued paddling up the river. It was harder now. Their progress was slower than before. An eighth of a mile further Chuck dug his plasticine blade into the soft gravel bottom of the shallows. The canoe's front end slowly turned to the south, downstream. A second pass confirmed that there were no obscured cabins nor were there any other good places for people to camp out nearby. Returning to their portage, Chuck was again pissed at the prospect of having to deal with that damn refrigerator.

It was agreed that although the cabin had no running water, a sketchy electrical supply, and a genuine outhouse, it was paradise found for this gang of miscreants to plot their evil. The quiet of the river was intermittently disturbed by the rumble of the diesel powered secondary generator, but

123

then was soothed by a Hank Williams tune Chuck was playing on his Jeep's stereo system. Periodically, a canoe or two would pass by, the occupants of each passing silently with a friendly wave or with a hoot and a beer can raise.

Sepp spent the remainder of the daylight hours continuing with improvements so as to establish a more suitable base camp from which to assault Fort Ozarks. Several simple tasks had to be performed to accommodate a prolonged stay. The radio-telephone was transmitting and receiving well with the help of a field expedient antenna. The inner workings of an antenna are a mystery to most humans, but with ground soldiers, it has become an art form. Even the most learned technicians know that "theory" is the best way to describe how an antenna operates. The team's current field expedient antenna employed half a spool of commo wire and seven copper nails. Chuck was sure that the contraption would not work, but Sepp was able to call Sal, who was over a hundred miles away. Sepp insisted that no cell phones or satellite communications be used in this operation. The Federal government listens in on all communications, he insisted. Forget the NSA and their wiretapping, the government's *Echelon Project* has been eavesdropping on civilian and commercial communications for decades. When the weather satellites or antenna arrays picked keywords and phrases out of the ether, phrases like "kill the president," "I am a terrorist" or "we are going to kill these drug dealers." It will automatically flag a transmission for further scrutiny. This type of government interference is what Sepp wished to avoid. Geography and the rural nature of the Ozarks played in Sepp's favor. Neither he nor Chuck had cell reception in the Ozarks. All Sepp had to worry about was one of those clunky sat-phones.

The four-digit combination to the lock and the ten-digit grid coordinates were transmitted to Sal. He re-secured the information and then passed it along to the rest of the team. Sepp then placed maps of the river, the county, and the state on every conceivable bare wall, even the inside door of

124

the outhouse. Knowledge of the terrain was vital, and Sepp wanted to ensure that all team members became intimately familiar with it. This was not the Victoria Hit to be conducted on the fly or an Atlanta Op to be jacked up. They had time for this one, and time, even in the course of a routine bodily function, was to be consumed with training up for the operation. Upon exiting the shitter, duct tape still in hand, Sepp paused to soak up the beautiful river view. The pure, clean, and deep waters that ran past Sepp's toil mocked the true intent of his actions. Disengaging himself from the vista, Sepp fetched the permethrin bug killer and applied a liberal dosage to the outhouse. *Killing is natural, no?*

In the morning hours of the following day, the entire infrastructure was more or less up and running, so Sepp and Chuck decided to take the canoe out again. Downstream this time, for a more intimate look at the objective. The Current River is a slow lumbering waterway after joining the Jack's Fork tributary. It seldom shows the white part of its nature after the joining, but when it does, one best be on the lookout. But at midsummer this is unlikely. Sepp had picked a good time of year. They needed the river calm.

Chuck called that *other* the local canoe rental and set up a pick-up place and time before joining Sepp at the water's edge. A case of Pabst Blue Ribbon was thrown in the cooler, along with all the snacks that seemed to facilitate a good river drunk. Chuck pushed the rear of the canoe off the well-worn stone as Sepp cracked the first beer of the day. He raised his can and saluted D.H. Lawrence, as Jack Nicholson had done in *Easy Rider*.

Beer drinking is a must for a lazy canoe ride. The summer sun proved too much at times, and they would slip into the river or rest a bit in the shade. The deep pools of spring-fed water that hallmark the Ozarks stun the senses and encourage more beer drinking. Those swim breaks also preempt the drunken from standing up in the canoe to relieve themselves. No one wants to get hurt before a mission or worse, draw attention.

Around noon, the two men hauled their canoe onto the gravel bar that served as Fort Ozarks Historical Preservation Society and Canoe Rental portage. They were obviously drunk and, therefore, not in any way different from any of the other groups of men at the pullout. This was yet another of Sepp's plans coming together. The two interlopers were exactly what they wanted to be: drunken men taking a break from the river to buy beer and ice. Sepp was genuinely hungry and staggered into the Fort's complex to get himself a frankfurter. On his way out, he took note of the rock face of a bluff that lay about a klick, or kilometer, to the west. The line of site was just as the map recon had suggested it would be.

"It's perfect," Sepp said to himself as he chowed down the last of the frankfurter.

"Hey buddy, get a picture of this," he yelled to Chuck. He acted as if he were snapping pictures, but his digital camera was taking a continuous video of the Fort.

After a few too many looks from concerned parents and the men in the frontier costumes, Sepp said in a voice a little too loud, "Let's get the fuck out of here."

The two drunks returned to the shore and fell backward into the water to take a piss. After polishing off another beer, they resumed their voyage. By the time they noticed that they were a scant few hundred meters from their real pull out point, the two men opted to beach the canoe early to down the remaining beers. They didn't want to lug around a heavy cooler.

"This is gonna be a doozy, ain't it, Sepp?" Chuck asked with the truth of drink in his words.

"In Vino Veritas, Chuck, don't you think? In a drunk there is truth, that is. You *know* that this is gonna be a big tough bitch to fuck. But you guys, all of you, want to do this. You want big money, and you all seem to want it yesterday. Well, I prefer the slow and steady, and that is how I have been running things. But no more. Sal, Dognut, and the rest of you all's greed is gonna run this one," Sepp sensed that

126

even with the alcohol he had said too much. He paused and waited for Chuck to agree or disagree. But even in his inebriated state, Chuck was far too wise to speak what was on his mind. Sepp let the uneasiness pass, alighted the canoe, and then headed to the site where Eminence Canoe Rental was planned to porter their canoe.

They were dropped off at the head of the road leading to the cabin. Sepp immediately noted that they had company. After the canoe rental van pulled away, the two men hauled the canoe to the wood line and withdrew the side arms that they always kept concealed on their persons. Small fanny packs are an excellent way to both carry and conceal a pistol. The long rifles were concealed within the chassis of their rigs, still parked at the cabin site, but these men were always armed. Chuck camouflaged the empty cooler in the wood line as Sepp did the same for the canoe. The two men then went through the woods, down the hill toward the cabin. They moved tactically in a bounding over-watch, sober now. The scenarios that Sepp had been playing in his mind on the first drive into the cabin began to resurface in his mind, and rightly so. Defense is an unending process.

About a hundred meters from the cabin the pistols were again placed inside the fanny packs and some hollering began. Reunions of this sort require a lot of drinking and a seriously big fire. Killer was offloading a pile of firewood from the bed of his truck, and Doc was busy retrieving the tap for a keg he had brought. Even Joe was slugging back a fifth of Maker's Mark as he worked on a sand table of the objective. Sepp helped tap the keg. It took him three pours before his cup wasn't all foam. He ambled over to have a look at Joe's miniature.

Sand tables are a staple tool of the infantry. They're miniature models of the objective area. They can comprise of simple sticks and strings or, in this case, be incredibly intricate. Joe's sand table was a little out of proportion, but a damn good reproduction nonetheless. He had fenced off a small flat area with twine and then had erected a north-

127

seeking arrow to provide a reference for any observer to work from. True north on the model was also true north in reality. Joe had used his lensatic compass to ensure it. On the southwest corner a swath of blue spray paint on the sand denoted the Current River; plastic trees purloined from a model train set were placed around a wall of Lincoln Logs vertically set into the sculpted earth. There was a large empty space within the wall, and Sepp noted two lollipop stick houses in Joe's kit box that would fit nicely into the center. Sepp knew that when he gave the actual operations order that this little model would come in damn handy.

"Great job, Joe," the team leader spoke quietly.

"It ain't done yet," was the only reply. Sepp used the awkward silence to move on and help Killer with the fire, leaving Joe to be alone and content with his task and his bottle. He and Joe once had been close, but Sepp knew this would go unsaid in front of the rest of the men. It was deemed to be unprofessional.

Doc was busy messing with the engineer tape and wooden stakes that went with constructing a Glass House. When coupled with schematics of the objective, the heavy engineer's tape and surveyors post were used to build a layout of Fort Ozarks. Like with a terrain model, Doc's scale was understandably minimized, but the crucial lines of sight were preserved. Later, his construct would be used in the rehearsal phase of operations. Grown men would later pretend that the strands of tape were walls and that the sticks were weapons within this house. As childish as it might seem to outsiders, in reality, it was yet another serious technique employed by highly trained soldiers.

By mid-afternoon, it was generally agreed that work could wait, and beer drinking could not. Chuck climbed his lanky frame high into a tree leaning over a deep pool in the river and hung a length of knotted rappelling cord from its height. He shimmied down the rope, lopping branches with a razor-sharp combat machete until he had cleared a way for a nice drop.

"Hey Killer, think fast," he blurted as the machete whirled through the air landing blade deep in the earth a safe distance from his friend. Chuck laughed as he let go of the rope, cannonballing into the limestone-blued waters below. Everyone but Sal played on the rope swing. His chest was still too sore for the drop. The body armor had saved his life, but months later the pain still lingered. Pain pills were out. He had to stay sharp for the mission.

Swimming, rope swinging, and generally drunken horseplay ensued. It was a good release for the men. The Victoria mission was hard on the group as a whole. They needed the camaraderie.

In a few hours the sun was setting on the cabin. Sal grew bored and left the group to set up a nice bed of coals for the steaks. Everyone was drunk and hungry for a solid meal.

"Where the fuck is Matt?" Killer asked.

"He'll be here tomorrow," Sepp replied from the water's edge. "He has some work to do." He grunted as he let loose a stream of piss into the darkening water.

Matt was in charge of a key element in the Hit. It was his task to acquire the topographical maps that the government uses. He stopped at a local library, and within minutes of flashing false law enforcement credentials, Matt was online downloading satellite images and real-time data concerning the Ozarks region of northern Arkansas and southern Missouri. The last website Matt visited was an obscure link from the US Coast Guard. There were a couple of areas he was interested in looking at but didn't have the time before.

Matt closed the link and cleared the history. He thanked the kind, yet unattractive, schoolmarm and headed on the long drive to the cabin.

When the USCG link had been established, Jenna's squad on *Vigilante* felt the tug on a carefully laid line. The fact that the Victoria hit deftly slipped past the Coasties had not been overlooked. Someone from the inside had to have giving the night's schedule in the Straits of San Juan De Fuca but they hadn't been able to track down who. They hoped a seaman had shown up for duty in a fancy new truck they couldn't afford but no such luck. And now, months later they found that detailed military sat-photos and operational schedules for the Coast Guard's inland river patrols were accessed. The area extended from Baton Rouge, Louisiana, to New Madrid, Missouri two miles away.

Salem, Missouri was where the recent access had originated, and that was where Special Agent Britton had chosen for them to start. The name that the librarian had sent them was fake, and her description was vague. She had been focused on putting books back in their place. All she said was he is a hulk of a man. *That's not a sailor*. This was one of their suspects.

Britton was in D.C. trying to get more than the twelve men that he had been assigned. There were roughly forty drug dealers of any real size within the map area accessed via the Coast Guard's site. But the Ozark National Riverways were home to only three possible targets that Jenna and her team could realistically expect their quarry to strike. Jenna immediately dispatched a liaison to the area. She made the necessary preparations to move the command cell to a shabby motel on the outskirts of the small river town of Eminence, Missouri. By the end of July 4th weekend she would be prepared.

If anything happened in the area, *Vigilante* would be able to strike within twenty-four hours. In the interim Jenna dispatched her assigned driver to blanket all the Private Investigators in the region. A certain PI named O'Brien had contacted the Chief of Station for the Seattle FBI and told them of a lanky man who had requested a thorough dossier on interns at the local hospitals. He was watching a news segment about the bloodbath in Victoria when they mentioned that a medical intern had called in anonymously about being forced to help a wounded man. This was all the intern had said before hanging up. O'Brien would have let it go if there hadn't been the mention of an FBI's cash reward. He walked away with a chunk of cash and the FBI had the list of Interns.

Jenna's driver was busy searching for local PI's to see if more intern data had been requested, but it was too little too late. She would not have those few precious hours of research to aid her cause. Sepp was moving far faster than she could have anticipated. As the FBI's traveling circus broke camp, Sepp's was poised to strike.

As with all men, idle time breeds idle banter. The team was close-knit, and as such, they liked picking at each other's perceived deficiencies. In some strange way it made them closer, and regardless, men do it all the time.

That night, with full bellies and a nice fire, a few of the team decided it was time to see if they could get a rise out of Chicken. As the driver, he had the easiest gig of the operation. He was due a little ribbing.

"Hey Chicken, why the hell do you think that so many guys in the Rangers and Special Forces are white, and so damn few are darkies?" There was nothing politically correct about Sal as he made his inquiry. Chicken took a deep breath and considered his response. He had been in this situation before and knew that he had to tread lightly on this ground. The fact is that the Special Operations Community and the infantry in general are indeed heavy with white boys and light on "people of color."

"Might have something to do with the swim test at the beginning of each phase, man. We don't grow up swimming in dirt ponds like you hillbillies." His response had teeth. Sal didn't want to admit it, but his family was a generation removed from hillbillies.

"Yeah, well, I got a theory on that too," Dognut chimed in. "I think it's because of all of that hard, hard work that wearing those fancy little tan and green berets seems to come with." Chicken felt the stinging barbs of his teammate's comment.

"Come on man. You know recruiters don't use the tough sell when they're talking to gangsters. The soft stuff sells, like cooking and—"

He was cut off by Sal's old-timey southern Negro accent, "clean'n and driv'n them trucks. You fuckers are all the damn same, don't want no hard ass work, just wanna go from welfare check to another government teat." Sal knew that this was not true. The man in front of him was living proof of that. But Sal and Dognut were out to rile him.

Chicken had never let them get under his skin and he wasn't about to now. Still, the veins that coursed blood beneath the Black Panther tattoo on his forearm had begun to swell. Chicken's mind was relatively calm, but his body was preparing to fight.

"What you two cracker ass mother-fuckers should be thinking on is why so many brothers are kept from serving in elite Army units? Like that damn swim test at the beginning of Ranger Indoctrination. What the fuck is that about? When in the damn regiment did you ever have to swim?" he asked the entire group.

"During the quarterly swim test," Chuck spoke the truth, bringing at least some reason to the heated exchange.

"Damn straight, never in the field, never, not once. Yeah, it is a good thing to know how to do, but the only reason that we ever did it was to reinforce in those white-ass minds of yours that swimming is essential and to keep out people like me."

"Bullshit, Negro!" Matt slammed his keg cup down so hard it crinkled beneath his force, spilling beer onto one of the many schematics that Sepp kept putting every-fucking-where. The racial epithet had to be taken in context. Matt indeed intended to offend Chicken, but only mildly so. Among men who have been in combat there is a level of rubbing that they can breach without offense being taken. Being called a "Black Bastard" was a term of affection, not derision. But "Negro" was designed to let Chicken know that blood was heating up, and Matt was the physically largest of the team. "Nigger" would only be used to initiate a serious fistfight. Chicken awaited the rest of what his bulky friend had to say. They were all armed, so a certain brand of tact needed to be deployed.

"The reason that whites constitute the majority of personnel in the Special Operations Community is that first, we are the ethnic majority in the country from which join the Army. Secondly, southern white people have a tradition of military service that dates back to the slaveholding times where the males of a family had to be soldiers in the event of a slave revolt." Matt was drunk but felt he was articulate and well-reasoned. He had the group's undivided attention.

"And thirdly," he let his lucidity pervade the audience, "negroes can't swim." The boys laughed so hard half of them fell on the ground. Matt smiled at Chicken, letting him know he was cool. His friend tossed back a welcome smile.

"Hey Matt, you big ass vanilla gorilla, did you know that the Marines are a department of the Navy?" Chicken asked. He had to get the big man on something.

"Yeah," Matt smiled, "the *men's* department." Everyone had a good laugh at that one. Matt was the only former Marine on the team and took his fair share of lumps for being an outsider

"Y'all want something to argue about? I will give you something to argue about," Sepp said after the laughter had subsided. All heads looked to him as he began his diatribe.

"These effing bullets," he was holding red-tipped tracers that he was loading into an empty magazine, "are about to become scarce as hell if congress gets its way. What the H are we gonna do then? Make our own?" He looked to Killer whom he knew was against any such labor-intensive idea. As he knew that such a chore would be his. Killer rolled his eyes in a don't-look-at-me sort of way.

Sal jumped in. "These goddamn crazy gun laws passed by all those fucking liberals out east are gonna put hard working Americans, such as us, out of business," he said mockingly.

Dognut had to follow. "What we got to do in this country is realize that your average gun owner ain't the problem. The problem is that all those Tec-9 owning gang-bangers that shoot up their own fucking streets, killing their own freaking people," Dognut said all the while looking straight at Chicken.

"Fuck you, Redneck!" Chicken retorted. "Ain't no gun factories in my neighborhood. White industrialists be making shit-pots of money selling them to me and my brothers, just praying that we will kill each other. And further mo,' you Wonder Bread look'n Sister-Fucking asshats, there ain't no crack trees in Brown Town neither."

"Well, in Kansas," Chuck tried to interject, but was interrupted by Matt's bluster.

"Fuck Kansas. Fuck everyone in Kansas. Fuck people with friends in Kansas!" He saw Chuck's blood was ready to boil and stopped his rant to laugh with the rest of the team.

"As I was saying before I began having visions of Matt in my scope. In Kansas, we don't need anyone telling us what guns we can or cannot own. The Second Amendment guarantees me the right to keep and bear arms."

"No, it doesn't," Killer said, adding his two cents worth. "The Second Amendment reads, and I quote, 'A well-

134

regulated militia, being necessary to the security of a free state, the right of the people to keep and bear arms shall not be infringed', unquote." These men did not use hand quotes for any reason whatsoever. It could mean an ass whipping, that sort of thing.

"Well, we certainly are a militia," Joe added sardonically. Laughs were had at that one.

"But are we well regulated?" asked Dognut as he jabbed a thumb in Sepp's direction. More smiles.

"OK, people." Killer once again took on an academic air. "Suppose that Congress can't pass a law eliminating those vicious Tec-9s. What option is left to actually safeguard the national security?"

Everyone knew that since Killingsworth made his bread and butter in the gun trade, he was probably headed somewhere with this, so they let him say his piece. "Well, I have an idea here if you gentlemen will allow it. I propose that Congress pass a tax on ammunition, a really high one, say ten bucks a shot. That would allow the decent law-abiding gun owner to keep his arms, and deny the dumb-ass his ability to shoot the damn things."

There were hoots and hollers, just the type one would expect in Congress. Some thought the idea to be brilliant, others that it was fascist. The argument went on well into the night, with no real consensus being reached. Such are the politics of gun control.

In the days before the Op, when all the sand tables had been studied and the Glass House walked through *ad nauseam*, Sal and Dognut wanted to check out the actual objective one more time. They convinced Chicken to pick them up down the river. They loaded a canoe with supplies and pushed off from the rocky outcropping that gave the cabin river access.

Sal flat out admitted that he didn't trust Sepp any longer. "The guy's acting too skittish for my liking." It was a funny thing for a cokehead to say, but it was already out. "Sepp's never conducted an operation this big. Shouldn't he be involved more? Why's he so reluctant to take part in the team's training? He's always off on his own for this train-up."

Action had to be taken. They were high enough to believe that they were making competent decisions about their future. The only way that the Op was going to go off in their favor was to make damn sure that it was done right.

To hell with Sepp, the two men concluded. The Op was not going to turn out well for them if they allowed it to go off according to Sepp's plan. What the two did not fully realize was how correct they really were.

As they sat in a backwater hidden from river view, they began to speak about the opportunity that now presented itself. Sal took a large hit off the aluminum foil and passed it on to Dognut's greedy hands, and then he began to articulate his views on the upcoming operation.

Although Sepp had set up the Hit, Sal knew that the real goldmine was in the drugs, not the cash. There would be more dope than cash, anyway. Dealers of this caliber have safes for money, and safes are hard to break into. For the drugs, there will just be guards. Ones that can be killed easily, as both Sal and Dognut knew. Sal proposed that they disregard the cash. Sepp was going to go into the residence of the Fort and find himself quite alone. Sal and Dognut would be making their way into the structure's basement. There, they would find the lab itself. Each man figured he could haul twenty-five kilos out. That would be over a hundred pounds of meth.

Not a few thousand each, but a few *hundred thousand* each. And that is if everyone else got out alive. The Op would be tough; they knew that Sepp was being honest about this part of the Warning Order. Sepp would surely die without any backup. Chuck would be left to get out on his own and if Chicken gave them any shit, then they would *kill his black ass.* Sal had quickly forgotten how Chicken had saved the entire team. His drug addiction held such sway over his mind that the past had begun to be rewritten in accordance with his present views.

"Fuck yeah," Dognut said as he exhaled a couple cubic liters of cocaine smoke. Sal did not know if he was agreeing or simply getting high. It made no difference; Sal pulled out another of their premade foils and then gestured for the lighter and rolled up twenty-dollar bill. It wasn't going to work as well as the plastic straw he accidentally threw away but it would do. In another few seconds, all that Sal could really say was that he was pretty fucking high.

When Agent Brown, Detective Penning, and the rest of the Task Force arrived at the *Paddle on Inn*, they found out something that should not have surprised them. All the rooms had been rented out and *no dang revenuer with his fancy ass badge was going to do a dang thing about it.* It wasn't just this place. All the campsites for fifty miles were filled up. Jenna wanted to reason with the man, but Brown had ordered her not to. They were both starting to grate on each other. A helpful local did, however, direct her and her crew to a large field on the other side of the river. The bridge was only a few miles upstream and the road, though a gravel and dirt one, should accommodate their triple-axle box truck.

"You'll be right down from Fort Ozark. Hell of a fireworks display they put on," the man added.

They thanked the man. He just smiled, knowing they were FBI or something. But the old man did nothing to alert the sheriff. He was certain those agents were positioning themselves around Fort Ozark. He hated Douglas Nelson and his ilk with all his law-abiding and God-fearing heart. *Let it burn.*

At 20 Hundred hours or 8 p.m., Troopers Ross and Colt began their shift. Colt's time with his son had been too short. Driving out of Highway Patrol Substation F, the two men decided to head south. They had a patrol schedule, but had their own ideas about how law enforcement should work. Their Captain had been too long behind a desk. Following I-44 South to Springfield, they knew that they would be busy tonight. The 4th of July did not fall on a weekend this year, nor was there a full moon, but none of that would deter the drunks from getting behind the wheel. DWIs were the focus. He hated drunk drivers more than anything. They would pay double for him having to work this holiday weekend. What good is bonding with your son when you can't even spend the 4th with him?

THE BATTLE OF FORT OZARKS

*"If bitten by a Cobra, find a nice tree, lay
down next to it and die like a Man."*

Advice given to the 13th Hussars, 1874
Imperial India.

Dawn's early light was already warming up. The morning's
cool fog was rapidly converting into stifling humidity. It was
to be a hot one, this 4th of July. Most of the team remained in
their racks long after sunrise. It was not because they had
partied the night before, for the team had done nothing of the
sort. On the day before this mission they hydrated, went over
the plan, and went over it again. Then they slept as much as
their individual nerves would allow. The men had followed
a nocturnal routine for the last three days; it was mission
essential behavior. A man's rhythms run best in daylight, but
this weakness can be overcome with training and discipline.
Although the team's training was receding into the past, their
discipline was still of an iron constitution.

The Hit was to be coordinated with the evening's
fireworks display to provide a veneer of tactical cover. Sepp
knew the subterfuge would not last long, but in this sort of
operation, a single second can make the difference between
life and death. *One must play all the cards in one's hand.* It
was risky conducting such a task on one of law
enforcement's busiest nights of the year. More than once
Killer had argued that it would be wiser to attack the Fort
another day. It might be sexier to do it on a holiday, he
reasoned, but it was not necessarily the best time for an

operation. More cops are on duty, he argued, and the river would be filled with weekend revelers. Also, Killer did not want to accidentally kill any women or children. He was adamant about this.

The team had collectively considered moving up the date because of the potential for collateral damage. Police refer to evenings like Independence Day as a night of a thousand stars because of the number of badges that are on duty. Chicken argued that his distraction at the lumberyard would reduce the number of cops. That was pivotal. There would be no shootout with the law tonight. Sepp and the rest of the team liked the aesthetic more than they feared the risk to others. Killer was uncomfortable but he went along with the team anyway. *What is life but a series of cost/benefit analyses?*

Killer was awake watching a DVD on his laptop, headphones on, but the majority of the team had racked out. Sepp tried to quietly enter the cabin. He was dripping wet and noisy in his movements. Though the rest of the men were snoring deeply, Sal was also still awake, hunched over a table intently studying a graphic representation of the objective area as seen from above.

"What'cha been doing?" he asked Sepp without looking up.

"Just a swim," Sepp assured. But he had omitted something and it was obvious that he had done so. Sepp pretended to be overly quiet and exited the cabin quickly.

Outside, Sepp could feel the action in the air. There had been days like this for him before. Over in the land of Allah he had experienced days when he just knew it was going to be interesting. Violence has a way of transcending the normal. It can be felt on the beaches of Normandy many years later, and it could be felt along that stretch of river even though it had yet to happen. Men were going to die today. This he knew. They all knew it. Most figured it would be someone else, and privately a few knew that they might be the ones to depart the Earth on this day. As with all

140

premonitions, some of their prophecies would prove to be self-fulfilling.

After the sun had reached its zenith, the team collectively awoke and set out about their preparatory tasks. Chicken has a system of checks that he was performing on his vehicle while the others cleaned and prepared their weapons for battle. Since time of old, raw recruits have seen the cleaning of their weapons as the most absurd of practices. To take a perfectly clean weapon and then to clean and oil it again is seen as some sort of bizarre punishment by the uninitiated. But to those who have seen combat, cleaning and maintaining their weapons is akin to love. Shots would be fired today. It was not an *if* situation but a *when* kind of day. And on days like this, it is best to have a loud popping noise follow the pulling of a trigger. The worst noise imaginable on the battlefield is the impotent click of a non-functioning weapon.

Doc had a sickening sense rattling in his head when he got out of his rack. It was a feeling of utter despair, permeating his soul. *Doom.* A vision of himself with his head crushed in pervaded his thoughts. It was like on those hasty, poorly thought out missions in Afghanistan. Doc was sure that this day was his last, and so he did something that disconcerted the others. He had broken with convention and used his sat-phone to contact his woman. It was a simple call; *he loves her and all that.* The thing is, no one had ever done anything like that before.

While waiting for the outhouse, Killer overheard the call and told the normally reserved Joe. He was not friendly to the news. Using any unsecured communications was a breach of security, not to mention the damning effect it was bound to have on the team's morale. Joe could overlook a technicality, but not a dagger to *esprit de corps.* He saw it as

141

a harbinger of failure, and so he begrudgingly told Sepp of the incident. Bullshit of that nature could not be allowed to stand, and so an *ad hoc* meeting was called inside the literal and figurative pressure cooker of the shoddy cabin.

Sepp waited until all the team had taken their place on the provided chairs and windowsills before he took up the small platform that had been used to explain the mission. He was, of course, carrying his weapons. *All the world is but a stage.* His Glock .45 was on his hip in a hard-plastic holster, and his M4 rifle hung about his neck. The jungle sling ensured that his rifle was slanted tightly over his chest. Any trepidation that he had earlier felt around Sal was gone now, replaced by a pure sense of purpose. The overall effect was to project the visage of a man ready for battle and inured to its hardships. Sepp was ready to kill a man, and he looked like it.

"Look here fuckers," Sepp was in his command mode, poking his gloved fingers at the collected men, "I know that it is gonna be a long day, maybe one of our last, but we don't need this harbinger of horseshit!" He shot a look of death toward Doc.

The team of infantrymen didn't collectively know what "harbinger" meant, but they knew the tone and by proxy, the meaning. Sepp did that a lot. *He is a teacher of men*, Chuck mused, sitting too closely to Joe at the cabin's single picture window. It was the only place for the team's cigarette smokers. Sweat trickled down his chin, staining his tunic. It was already a hot one, and it was going to get hotter still. Chuck returned his concentration to the message.

"Focus, men, focus on the future. We fucking own this situation. The men down there don't even know to be deathly afraid. They should be. If they knew that we were coming, they would be locking and loading right fucking now. But they don't know. This gives us the edge. Yeah, they are fortified. Yeah, they got guns. But this is about what *we* know. We have more knowledge and firepower in this room to take the fucking Kremlin," he butchered the

142

language, but no one in the room took note of it. Sepp was charging the air with confidence. That was his job, and he was doing it well.

"There's over a million dollars in drugs and cash just a few klicks from here. I for one, am gonna take all that there is to take. You fuckers wanted this, and now you have it. Our destinies are in our hands, and right fucking here," Sepp man slapped the M4 rifle that he had slung over his chest.

"And as for this shit," he held aloft Doc's thousand-dollar satellite telephone. Everyone was sure they knew what would come next. Sepp slammed the phone onto the table so hard it shattered into a thousand pieces. That settled that. "Anyone tries to come up against me on this, you're gonna fucking break, not me."

Sepp walked past the men and out the door of the cabin, making his way to the cool of the shade trees. He needed to calm himself down. A dip of fresh Copenhagen between his cheek and gums would help. Joe approached Sepp and discreetly informed him that walking around outside in his battle rattle was probably not a bright thing to do. Sepp was still hot under the collar, but agreed to display some discretion in the matter.

Each man on the team made his way to Sepp to let him know that what he had done was right. Not everyone agreed to the destruction of the phone, *that fucker was expensive*, but they understood that the ship had to be righted, and that Sepp had done just that. Doc eventually approached his boss and gave a silent nod. Everything was right again. No one was fixing the blame; these men were fixing the problem. No words were needed after the fact; rather there was a *silence is consent* attitude to the way things were shaping up. In the military, this is a crucial point of fact. It is a largely unwritten rule that when one makes a request of a superior in a time of

143

battle and no answer is given in the positive or negative then that silence becomes consent. Most standard operating procedures require the junior to ask three times over for the rule to be validated. There was a rumor going around after Mogadishu that Randy Shughart and Gary Gordon of Delta Force were required to ask three times before leaving their airborne sniper platform to save downed Blackhawk pilot Mike Durant, but that no one had the balls to send them. It was just a rumor, but it helps to illustrate the point. The silence in and around the cabin had that same sort of weight. *Unless you fail in doing it, then everything is all right. It is your life at risk.*

FBI Special Agent Adam Britton was in route to the Ozarks. It was the Fourth, making it difficult to get a flight out of Reagan International Airport. Delaying him further, his flight had landed late afternoon in Memphis. He was headed northwest as fast as the local field office sedan could carry him. The many one-horse towns that he passed through slowed his progress considerably. The occasional family wagon filled with children necessitates a cautious speed when navigating the serpentine roads of the Missouri boot heel. Agent Britton knew he would be late, but he also knew that even if Brown was not a competent field leader then Detective Penning was there as a backup. He slowed down to allow a box truck to ascend the hill ahead of him and cursed the delay.

Combat is a damn dirty business, one mostly shunned by polite society these days. But there are a few men, from *all* socioeconomic backgrounds, that like the action of it. It is out of these few that the proficient warriors draw their ranks.

To be weighed on the scales of combat and to be found not wanting is a rare feat in our day and age. Military service is a calling that few hear, especially during war. A competent veteran of well-conducted missions can be a great asset to the nation when, and only when, he is under the control of that nation. But these nine men, each government trained and battle hardened, were setting out to wage a little war of their own devising.

After the matter had been settled, the men gradually toted their collective kit into the woods behind the cabin. The shade of the trees was cool, preferable to the cabin that had become a stifling reminder of regret. With the exception of Joe, they were dressed in their fluff-and-buff attire. Old woodland BDU's and even older boots from their days on active duty were the uniform, though most wore the more expensive T-shirts and socks that the Army does not provide nor condone. Out back, and out of view of the river, they checked each other's kit. Sepp took the time to stop at each man to ascertain his mental state. It was just the way that Sepp did business. *Parts to be checked and then rechecked.* He ended with Matt who was affixing the shape charge to the cabin's propane tank. The two men spoke as the timer was set. Matt made haste after their words were exchanged, but Sepp lingered. Only when the sun began to set did Sepp begin his own final gear check. He was a smart soldier and had performed his initial gear check in the cool of the morning.

Chuck had left the cabin hours prior to Sepp's departure. He had the longest way to go and the slowest mode of transport. After several miles, his thighs were burning as he hefted the Barret .50 cal. up and over the last rocky outcropping. He took a moment to enjoy the view. The diminutive ribbon of the Current River was golden with the sun's reflection, surrounded by the deep green of the forest. Stone spires jutted up from the emerald sea of trees. In the distance, at about a thousand meters, Chuck eyed the wooden castle that was Fort Ozark. It appeared four inches wide now. A small place, easily dominated from his position. After setting up his fighting stance Chuck peered again at the objective. It was huge now, as the Leupold scope revealed more of the Fort's actual scale. Individual men were easily discernable at their postings. Chuck could even tell that one of them smoked Marlboro cigarettes. The red and white package was hard to miss through the magnified lens.

Closer to him and without the aid of the weapon's sight, Chuck could see the minutiae of Ozark beauty. An immense coarse stone would serve as cover for his weapon. Lichens and the surrounding flora added concealment from prying eyes to comprise a naturally made fighting position. All that was needed was to clip a single errant branch and perfection was achieved. Chuck quickly made the necessary preparations for the night's festivities. When finished, he settled beneath a mental quilt, one woven of quiet and a sniper's patience.

Three hours after Chuck made his way into the woods; Sepp said his goodbyes to the rest of the team as he headed down to the water with Chicken helping him carry some of the equipment. In the water the burden could easily be borne, but without the assistance of buoyancy, Sepp needed help toting it.

"Now, Chicken, if this doesn't go off well, I want you to get the fuck out of Dodge. I know that you and your woman can get by for a long time on what you got saved up, so don't be no damn fool and un-ass this place if we ain't there in time." Chicken looked doubtful; he had a lot of confidence in Sepp.

"Promise me you will 'pop smoke' if it gets to be time," Sepp demanded. Popping smoke was a reference to using a smoke grenade to guide a chopper in to exfiltrate. *Un-Ass the AO*. Soldiers thus use the term interchangeably with leaving. Reluctantly, and for the first time that Chicken had really contemplated Sepp could fail him, he agreed. The two men shook hands and Sepp disappeared beneath his mask as he sank into the shade-darkened river. Chicken then made his way to Joe, who also seemed to want a final word with him.

As dusk settled and the fireflies began their luminescent communication, small pops could be heard. Then, joining in the fireworks game, roman candles could be seen lunging through the humid air. And when the children had had their fun, the grown-ups began their version of the game. Larger displays of pyrotechnics jetted up into the Ozark sky. Chuck could see that almost every campsite was in on the fun. He also knew that he could safely sneak a smoke. Igniting his Zippo, he knew that Chicken's pyro display was getting ready to begin. Chuck checked his watch and realized that in a minute and twenty seconds the really big kids would join in.

Joe waited until dusk arrived before donning his balaclava. He walked around to let everyone know it was time to move out. The trip for the bulk of the team was to be covered by ground pounding the distance between the cabin and Fort Ozarks. Sal and Dognut were sleeping on top of their assault packs. They cradled their weapons in their arms and had all their gear on despite the heat. It was a classic picture of an infantryman's rucksack flop. *Sleep is a weapon*. They looked

147

no different than any soldier who has a few minutes to sleep before moving out on a road march. Joe took great pleasure in kicking them both in the soles of their boots. *Time to go, boys.*

With the exception of Joe, clad only in black, the ground assault team was dressed in their cammies and had their faces painted green and black. They were collectively happy to be out of the urban environment. The thought of moving tactically, meaning slowly and quietly, through the dense woods of the Ozarks was exhilarating to these men. Sal and Dognut felt at home in the Kentucky backwoods and the trees of Missouri were not that different. Killer had grown up mere miles from their present location. Matt McCall was a good old boy from Athens, Georgia, so he too found himself at home in the sticks, although he missed the red clay of the true southland.

Even Doc was a white-boy from Arkansas. These men had joined the military because they had grown up in the woods and liked the thought of being paid to continue doing so. Not a man among them was a Johnny Come Lately to the military after 9/11. Joe smiled as he made the hand signal for them to move out in two wedges in a bounding over watch to the OBJ. Joe's element took point. Matt's followed to the left rear. The whole trip to Fort Ozarks went off without a hitch. Only Killer lagged behind, and that was because of the unwieldy rocket propelled grenade launcher that he toted. Just like with mortar rounds on active duty, the projectiles for it were spread out amongst the rest of the ground team. This made sure that no one man had to carry a load that was meant to help the entire team. Killer was not begrudged for his slowness.

It should have been a well-prosecuted affair. The invaders had constructed a coherent plan of attack, and the defenders had years of preparation behind their embattlements. Both sides of the equation had chosen this terrain to fight upon. The former through careful selection and the latter through a more abbreviated process, but both had picked this place to fight. *It should have been a well-prosecuted affair.* But combat is not a theoretical venture, and when the two schemes clashed, utter chaos ensued. Battles are a goat-fuck of the first order, for that is the way of all warfare, from our first recorded battle on the slope of Megiddo to our present martial concerns. If the past is any indication of the future, then Armageddon itself is bound to be a cluster-fuck too.

It was Sepp's honor to initiate the Op. Normally an operation, like an ambush *writ large*, begins with the most devastating weapon in the assaulting force's arsenal. This axiom held here as well, but with a twist. The most effective weapon in this operation was a piece of simple army gear. It was Killer's woodland camouflage poncho from his days on active duty. That poncho had served him well over the years. It kept him dry on training missions in Panama, Puerto Rico, and Thailand. In Iraq, it had stopped sunlight rather than rain. That poncho had done Killer right, and so he parted with said poncho with great reluctance. And using his poncho-liner or "woobie" was out of the question. No one on the team would have willingly parted with his own woobie, so no one would ever suggest that another man give his up. The woobie is the only soft warm thing that an infantryman possesses. It is near and dear to his heart, and not to be trifled with.

Sepp swam down the now wine-dark Current River. Once he navigated to the proper coordinates, he attached himself to a massive rock in the middle of the river, placing his feet on the base and leaning his bulk toward the current. The pressure of the water held him suspended. Sepp hovered beneath the surface, waiting for the time to pass. The water beyond his dive mask distorted his view of the fireworks overhead, but it was beautiful nonetheless. Streaks of diluted flames arced back and forth over his head. Their fire kaleidoscoped into a mild hallucination when viewed through the rough water above him. He waited patiently for total nightfall before creeping slowly up to the Fort's rough-hewn walls. There, Sepp traced his way around the outer wall to the rear of the compound. The poncho was placed over a small air intake vent leading to the fort.

The intake had been overlooked by the planners of Fort Ozark because of the steady stream of electricity that the county's power co-op provided to it. Located near the base of a large oak tree, the vent should have had its own wall, and that was denied in order to cut costs for a man that wanted "no expense spared." Some contractor had lined his pockets with the proceeds of that little oversight and neither Douglas nor Daniel had caught it. During any normal circumstance the poncho would have had no effect whatsoever. It was only after Chicken detonated a small, yet effective little bastard of an explosive at the regional transformer that the poncho took on a new importance. Cut off from the main power line running in from town, the Fort's own diesel generator kicked on. Those within the Fort were aware of the power failure. Dan Brewer saw to it that the generator was powering the compound before he inquired about the cause of the disruption. Satisfied that a transformer had simply failed on an extremely hot day, Dan made the first mistake of the evening. He went about his duties, indifferent to the Fort's electrical supply so long as it was there. It took only ten minutes with a blocked air intake before the temperature of the generator slowly began to rise above functional parameters.

By the time that Sepp was at his breach point and the rest of the team was in position, the generator had become so inefficient that it was creating a brownout. The slowly dimming lights and reduced power to all systems was lost on Douglas Nelson and his crew because of its creeping nature and due to the extravagant pyrotechnic display that held their attention.

At the County Lumber & Supply, behind five rows of 2x4s, the ice that separated the contacts on the charge melted through. It was a primitive, yet no less effective timing mechanism that Sepp had learned from Haji. The fuses within two incendiary grenades then began much shorter countdowns of their own. Two popping sounds occurred so closely together in time that they appeared to be simultaneous to the few rats that happened to be in close proximity.

It was about ten o'clock, so the night guard was still sober enough to recognize that his workplace was aflame. He dialed 9-1-1 and then ran in an attempt to put out a four-alarm fire with but a single fire extinguisher. His call went through to the dispatcher and she put the word out onto the net. And as it happened Detective Penning's assigned driver had just acquired the local frequencies. Penning was immediately suspicious. She made her way to the Agent in Charge's plain white panel truck. Agent Brown was relishing his temporary command while Special Agent Britton was in transit. He admitted her out of courtesy, but had no real intention to listen to that female cop from Orlando.

"Agent Brown, sir, this is their Modus Operandi. They did this in Orlando and they're doing it again." She had no idea that the target of the team's hit was just across the river and up the bend.

"Ma'am, we don't know for certain that we are even in the right place, and further ma'am it is in all likelihood simply a fire. They happen here all the time. On top of that it's the 4th and everyone's shooting off fireworks," Brown responded tersely.

That much, Jenna had to admit was true. The Ozarks were especially hot this year and all the woods seemed to be a tinderbox just waiting for a match. But that was not enough to dissuade her from what she knew to be evidence of an imminent move by the men she was pursuing.

"Sir, this is how they operate! They burn up some old warehouse or something that lures all available units away from their target and then they strike. It is going down now. It fits the M.O." She was adamant in her plea for action, but Brown was unconvinced.

"Did they do this in British Columbia?" He asked knowingly.

"No," she was forced to answer. "But that target was hastily picked. We know from the Private Dick. All the people that they planned to grab were in and around Seattle. The hit in Victoria was a lark," the last word was inopportune and she knew it. *A real deal breaker.*

"Ma'am as long as I am in tactical command, we sit still. If the situation evolves, then we will move. Now if there isn't anything further, I need to get some shuteye." And that, as they say, was that. Agent Brown turned back to the console and began to act as though he was going to work instead of sleep. Frustrated but with no real recourse, Jenna made her way out of the large panel truck.

"Shit!" It was all that she could muster. Jenna stood by the truck looking out over the Current River hoping that its placidity would calm her, but she knew that it could not.

"Detective?" It was a man's voice from behind her. She turned to see FBI Agent Chester Mabe. She had seen the agent in Victoria on the second day. He was quiet and reserved then, following the lead of others, a real polite man.

"Yes," Jenna responded.

152

"Detective, I seem to remember that you were pretty sharp about the goings on up in Canada. What are you thinking?" It was just what she needed to hear. Jenna quickly began to verbalize what she was thinking. Agent Mabe and a cohort were quickly brought in line. Preparations were made so that they could move out fast.

Sepp had affixed his charge to the wall and was now settled behind a tree watching it. There was little else to do. It crossed his mind that he was staring at what some would call a petard. A French word that literally means a fart, the word petard was also used to denote a black powder explosive attached to a stonewall in the age of castles. The men would place it on the outer wall, light the fuse and then try to run away from the device before it went off. Sometimes the men were lucky, and sometimes they were not. And when they were not, the phrase went that they were *hoisted by their own petard*. It's where the phrase "destroyed by their own devices" originates. Sepp smiled at his internal history lesson and then found himself hoping that he was not about to shoot himself in the foot, so to speak.

During one of the more expensive, and therefore explosive, pyrotechnic displays put on by Nelson Enterprises, Sepp clicked the M-60 detonation element that was attached via a thin filament to his petard. The rough-hewn wall of the Fort was reinforced with rebar, but not even that could withstand the incredible force of the shape charge. A five-foot wide and ten-foot-high section of the wall was caved in by the blast. Although it coincided with the large airburst of fireworks, the ruse fooled no one. Panic stricken men, women and children screamed in terror, fleeing the parking lot in search of safety from what they believed to be a fireworks display gone awry.

Sepp's men anticipated the explosion, so they began to dispatch the few guards who were awestruck by it and had failed to seek immediate cover. This did not last long, as Dan Brewer quickly rallied his men to face the multiple threats that now presented themselves. The hole in the outer defense was plugged first, although that action had been too late. For Sepp had secreted himself inside the walls of Fort Ozark while the smoke and fires of his explosive were still fresh. There was an enemy within, and Dan was completely unaware of it.

Not to fault him, though, for Dan had many responsibilities at present and he was ably handling all but one of them. The crowd had vanished, but the fireworks show was still in full swing. The pyro technicians were like artillerymen in a gunfight. What they saw and heard was nothing out of the ordinary and as such they continued to send mortar rounds high into the night sky. The technicians had ear protection on and couldn't hear him yelling. Dan didn't have time for this. He shot them, bringing an end to what amounted to illumination flares being fired over his Fort.

The hole in the defensive wall was covered, but men within the compound were continuing to be shot. Dan scanned the area but couldn't place where the fire was coming from. Another explosion shook the fort's walls. Killer had fired an RPG into the parking lot side of the building, devastating a huge section of it as well as a guard tower in the process. The damage was horrendous to both men and material. Two guards were ripped into chunks of man-flesh and were strewn about as if by a careless giant intent on crushing bones for his bread.

Douglas Nelson was deep within his woman when he heard the first explosion. It had been a long time, but Douglas knew the sound of battle. He pulled out of the woman and armed himself with his SPAS-12 semi-automatic twelve-gauge shotgun. He called the Sheriff who was busy at a lumberyard fire. He was promised that the entire force would disengage and be in route within one minute. Douglas also received premature assurances that all would be well. He dismissed this promise as soon as it was made. While trying to deflate his Viagra engorged member, he used the walkie-talkie mode on his cell phone to contact Dan Brewer. The reply was short and terse and then terminated by Dan.

This was not proper military procedure. The junior never "outs" the senior man, but Douglas knew better than to be angry with Dan. The subordinate did not know anything, and Douglas was wasting what little time Dan had to figure out the situation. Douglas knew that he would be told what was going on as soon as that was ascertained, and so he dressed, and took his woman to refuge within his walk-in gun closet and waited to be updated. Such is the nature of great field commanders. The ability of a commander to let his men do their jobs is a rare one indeed. But Douglas knew that Dan was both competent in his job and that he had a full understanding of the true hierarchy of importance for what was happening. The Fort could fall, all the henchmen killed, but Douglas had to be evacuated from the situation just as soon as possible. Douglas was comforted in his expectations of Dan when two armed men arrived to safeguard the Boss. Aware of his sustained erection and the resulting bulge in his trousers, Douglas dispatched them to the security node of the residence. He then tried to calm his woman.

When Matt connected the copper wire to the 9-volt battery, the current ran down the wire at the speed of electricity. At the terminus lay a pre-positioned blasting cap. The explosive power of the blast converted itself, with some magnification, to the body of plastique. Explosions happen in a ripple, not at once. The ripple moves from the point of origin outward in all directions. Only where there is resistance does the explosion channel itself. Just as a man chooses the path of least resistance, so goes a rapidly expanding mass. Ordinarily, solid to gas transformation has no guidance, but when human hands come into play, extraordinary things are possible. If one shapes the charge (hence the term shape-charge) in the appropriate manner, then one can force an explosion to collapse upon itself. Those ripples start to interact on each other to form something that scientists call instability. A normal man would term it *really fucking cool*.

The charge's collapse focused the kinetic energy of the explosion. Charges of this nature are framed and given a small standoff distance from their target. The plasma jet formed at the collapse of the explosive ripple packs anywhere between three and four million pounds per square inch of pressure and burns at around 20 to 30 thousand degrees Fahrenheit. *Plasma jet, oh yeah*. It is that jet that does the cutting. Heat and pressure combine to strip the electrons off molecules. When a High Explosive Anti-Tank (HEAT) round is fired, a shape charge in the nose cone forms this exact same sort of plasma jet, allowing even hardened armor to be breached. Few things on the earth can withstand this type of precision assault and the inner wall of Fort Ozark was not among them.

Matt and Killer were moving to the inner wall as the linear shape charge exploded. In its fiery aftermath, they made it into the interior of the Fort's main structure. As one man moved, the other provided covering fire for the man in motion. The two men were tasked with the gathering of the cash, and so they moved in a bounding over-watch into the main structure that lay within the walls of Ft Ozark. Much fire was directed toward them in doing so, but the two men escaped serious harm with their swift entrance through the Fort Ozark souvenir shop.

Sepp made his way up the plush stairs of the Fort's residential wing. He knew that he was close when the doors were made of mahogany instead of metal. He found it interesting that a man such as Douglas Nelson would sacrifice security to gain an aesthetic decorative look. He had been told by his father that Nelson had once been a formidable man, but that the years of success had softened him up. Sepp believed his father and trusted his judgment on this one, but there was a strength here too, one that bespoke younger blood. During his preliminary research of the compound and its inhabitants, Sepp had learned that a man named Dan Brewer was the compound's real director of operations. That Dan was an ex-biker was all that Sepp knew of him, but from what he had seen thus far Sepp was convinced that he was ex-military.

Sepp crouched low to open the door. He knew that the rounds fired at the door would most likely be fired at a typical center mass height. Low crawling along the floor, Sepp mitigated that risk. The massive wood door opened smoothly, quietly. There was no one waiting in the anteroom. Sepp rose to a low crouch and made his way silently along the thick shag carpeting. He came to a corner, crouched, and paused for a listen. There were muffled voices coming from the darkness. Sepp figured that they were probably not the voices of a welcome wagon so he tossed a flash-bang grenade around the corner. Sepp quickly covered his night vision lens with his gloved hand and awaited the detonation. As soon as it happened, he pivoted around the corner and dropped the temporarily deaf and blind guards that stood dumbfounded and bewildered in the smoky haze.

He had to adjust the focus dial on his NODs to compensate for the close quarters. The green/black vision of dead guards was washed out by a dim, intermittently blinking illumination. Sepp pulled off his head mount and

157

visually acquired the light source. It was a bank of plasma screens that sat atop a security console. Sepp looked around and smiled. He was at the nerve center of Fort Ozarks security. Some of the flat screens were distorted by the flash-bang and all had a layer of residue on them, but they told an incredible story in real time.

Sal and Dognut were slated to go in next, but the barrage of fire coming forth from the towers proved too much of a risk. "Chuck, a little help," Sal whispered calmly into his headset, as if he needed a basketball retrieved or something equally as mundane. Chuck took a few seconds to identify their infrared strobe signature and then provided the requested aid.

A .50 caliber bullet does nasty, unspeakable things to men when it impacts their bodies, but Chuck was not encumbered by such visions. He was placed a little more than nine hundred meters away, and even with the benefit of his scope, the carnage that he created was blurry and black to him instead of the stark and messy red it was to the men on the objective.

As Sal and Dognut moved Dan Brewer noticed where their cover was coming from. *A sniper, goddamn it!* And all the long-range weapons were out of his reach. He had a thirty cal., 1906 model more commonly known as a .30 "ought" six in the bunker, but needed to remain on site to coordinate the defense. Dan asked himself, *why didn't I cover the bluff?* But it was too late for that. Action, not regret, was the one thing that could alter the situation.

The only other weapon in the Fort's arsenal capable of hitting the sniper was the Gatling gun, but the interior catwalk and the guard tower between him and it had been destroyed by the RPG. If he was going to reach the Gatling gun he would have to go around the entire Fort or go through the killing ground that his enemy was now traversing. There was no choice in the matter, he had to take the long way. It was either that or let the sniper kill them all.

During his movement to the Gatling gun the import of the sniper hit him. *This is a coordinated assault*, and that means that there was an objective trying to be reached. There were many possibilities. The first that crossed his mind was a hit on his Boss. Douglas Nelson had killed many a man, and that tends to create a certain level of animosity. The second was that the men attacking the Fort were cops. That eventuality could not be prevented. If the cops want in, well, they were coming in. No one has the resources to fend off the Feds. The last contingency that raced through Dan's mind was that they were being robbed. As insane as it was for him to contemplate, it made a certain sense to his mind.

The Road Fangs that Chicken had placed over the pavement had just paid off. Three of the county's finest sheriff's deputies had just incapacitated their own vehicles by running them over the spikes placed along the only axis of advance afforded them to the OBJ. Now there were only four ways in or out of the OBJ area, and three of them had similar booby traps placed on them. All of them were obscure dirt roads, only one was clear, and only the team knew which of them it was.

Chuck noted the incoming, but discounted it. The little dust devils that popped up every time a bullet struck the earth were still not even close. Even with the Fort using tracers, Chuck was killing at will. Their only long-range weapon was incapable of reaching him effectively. In contrast, when Chuck moved his weapon's barrel, a few scant lateral inches expanded his killing zone by hundreds of feet. A man dropped. Chuck paused, swatted and killed an insect that was trying to feed on him. *The Ozarks are rife with them.* A moment later, Chuck felled another man, then one more.

Dan was losing men fast and knew how to stop it. He stepped over the body of a fallen man, and took up the .45 caliber magazine fed Gatling gun mounted on a tripod. *The angle is too high.* There are damn few men alive that can hit anything by super-elevating a weapon and trying to guess where the rounds are landing. *Just try to hit a barn door without pointing at it*; you need either a physics degree or Special Operations training. Dan was not among the people with either qualification, but he did not need to be.

He had requested a tracer round in every fifth spot in the two-foot-long magazine of ammo. At the time it had seemed a bit unimportant to those placed in his charge, but this endeavor would prove to have consequences. Churning the crank, Dan noted that his shots were wide left and well short of the target area. Adjusting, he watched 1/5th of his bullets get closer and closer to his quarry, fully knowing that rounds 2, 3, 4 and 5 followed invisibly behind the marker round, ever toward the blip of menacing light that bespoke the .50 caliber threat.

It's hard to miss tracers being fired at you. Chuck took note of the renewed incoming fire but dismissed it as the last-ditch attempt of an amateur. He felled another man. Chuck then scanned for more to kill, his attention rapt on the seeking out of targets. This changed with great rapidity when Chuck noted the discharge of tracer rounds. They were no longer to the left and right, but being shot straight at him, but they were all too short.

Not even suddenly, but with a smooth transition, Chuck was inexplicably at home. The summer breeze carried the enticing aroma of apples and cinnamon. His mother's pies were cooling on the windowsill. It's pleasant here. Chuck feels almost weightless like he's slipped into a warm, easy bath. He never wants to leave.

The .50 cal rifle began to cool down in the night wind. Residual smoke rolled out of the weapon's massive barrel. Curious insects bite and eat at the flesh that had so recently been swiping them away.

With the threat of the sniper resolved, Dan Brewer directed his resources toward the present dangers that surrounded him.

Sepp had watched on the monitor as the man on the Gatling gun stopped cranking its handle. The tremendous arc of light that had been spewing forth from the antiquated weapon was quelled. The man was pointing inward, back into the Fort's walls. The multiple barrels of the weapon were red hot, appearing white on the monitor. The battle had stoked the fires of his military professionalism. Never since the Middle East had it done so. Sepp found himself wishing that he had some Little Bird gunships to direct onto targets. Sepp also felt the absence of his sniper. He felt the pain of the loss but put it away inside him. It would do him no good here. If he lived, then he would have the rest of his life to ponder the death of his only real friend. It was not the time for that, and as a matter of plain fact, it simplified his exit strategy considerably. On the monitor, the white-hot barrels slowly faded to black as Sepp realized that his brown out had eased into a total blackout. *Time to move.*

Doc was using the cover of a tree to watch the fight. His job was to scan his sector and be ready for an immediate medical response should someone get hit. The role was an easy one, relatively speaking. Should everything go smoothly, Doc wouldn't have to fire a single round. The view of his sector somehow darkened, and then it disappeared altogether. It was replaced by a warm, fuzzy, dreamlike vision. The barrel of his weapon came off its rest and began to flag itself as the weight of his slumbering head forced the buttstock to the ground. A man in a Confederate uniform on the Fort's parapet took note of the moving barrel and double-tapped the man behind it, *just to be sure.* Doc's narcolepsy had just become permanent.

Matt and Killer bore the brunt of Dan Brewer's reallocation of manpower in response to the absence of a sniper threat. They were out in the open and had been living under the umbrella of protection afforded them by their man in "overwatch." All the guns that had been directed at Chuck were now focused on *their* ill-fated position near the old-time kiln. At least the thickness of the stone igloo would provide *some* cover. Fire converged on them, and they stood back to back with each other in response to the imminent danger. Emptied magazines began to pile up in the gravel at their feet. Spent casings mixed with the small stones at irregular angles.

"Last Mag!" Killer declared. Matt had the same ammunition status, but did not bother with any exclamation. Both of their weapons began to spew red tracers. Five are always loaded first into the magazines. This is done so that when one sees a continuous stream of red coming out of the barrel, it means that one is running out of rounds. Matt and Killer knew it was time to reload, but there was nothing left.

They went into that dark night well, men such as they always do. Killer took a round to the back and was thrust into the open where multiple rifles engaged him. Matt took a round in the neck; his last vision was one of a winged horse swooping down on him with a beautiful maiden riding atop it. He had led a good Viking life and was sure he was being ushered to the great beer hall of Valhalla.

Salvador and Dognut had disregarded their directive to seek out the money, instead focusing on the drugs. Once they had secured two duffels full of meth, the two men began their egress from Fort Ozarks. All they had to do was to make it to Chicken and his *black ass* would ferry them to safety. They were prescient of the .50 cal.'s silence. From inside the canoe rental area, they witnessed the torrent of gunfire that was killing their friends. Like Sepp, they saw the opportunity placed before them. Chuck was dead, Matt and Killer too. That meant there would be more dope and cash for them. The guards had shifted fire from the outside of the Fort to the inside of it. They decided to make a run for it, guns ablaze.

What they were attempting took real courage and faith in each other. The gantlet that they intended to run was brutal. Three elevated positions on each side would open up on them. But it was the only way out, and so they ran it. When the towers took note of them, they kept on running and gunning. Bullets broke the sound barrier as well as the earth at their feet. Sal took a round in the back plate of his body armor and almost fell, but regained his traction and kept moving. Dognut reloaded on the fly. He was not only laying down suppressive fire, but actually scoring some hits. Even the men firing at them had to hold some admiration for their courage. One does not expect to see men so bravely face death. But their training and experience had ensured that

Sal and Dognut were not average men. Hundreds of bullets had been expended in their direction and although one had left a nasty bruise, both men were free of leaks. The rally point was right around the corner, but Chicken's van was gone when they got there. Sal checked his watch. *Damn, we're late!* It was one of those grim moments when plans fail and hope only lingers. Not a word was wasted in exasperation. The two men turned back toward the fight and scanned for new ways out of the AO. And there it was: an entire parking lot full of potential escape vehicles.

It was GO time, a place where these two men loved to be. All hell had gone to shit, and they responded with enthusiasm. Turning to shoot some more, Sal chimed in with a "Get some!" quote from a movie that he was too busy to cite. Bullets were still coming at them, but there must have been something more important to shoot at than them because the fire shifted away. This pleased them greatly.

There was a nice-looking VW van in the first row of vehicles. It attracted both of them. The progression toward the van was as smooth as the path of least resistance. Unlocked! *Some people are just trusting bastards.* Sal did the hot wiring, and within seconds they were accelerating toward the main road. Chicken had blocked all routes in and out with those damn road spikes of his, but they were too amped up to remember which one was free and clear. After only one misstep, they remembered and fled down a narrow dirt trail that seemed to follow a creek on the left-hand side. Sal swore he saw the team's van turn to the right as they crested a hill. They continued forward.

The team was no more, and only by creating as much distance as possible between Chicken and themselves could The Kentucky Twins expect to escape with the dope and their lives. Sepp and Joe would have to manage alone.

Dan Brewer was the first to recognize the new threat. Black uniforms moved slowly across the river's ford downstream. They were not shooting yet, but Dan knew this would change rapidly.

Detective Penning had told them over and over not to start shooting until the whole team had made it across the river. But Agent Brown had deemed her just another dumb skirt, and had admonished his men to do the same. Brown engaged the enemy just as soon as he could.

When walking across the relatively shallow, yet swift river, the legs must work hard just to provide motion. The upper body must shift and adjust to remain upright, and this does not provide the most stable of gun platforms. It was in just such a predicament that Agent Brown found himself. He would lose his footing every few steps and then struggle to regain it. During such an episode, he realized he was being shot at. Not believing it at first, Agent Brown thought only of the burning in his legs as they moved him closer to the shore. But then small-whitened jets of water began multiplying around him.

Jesus Fucking Christ! They are shooting at Me! Agent Brown joined the fight, holding his weapon over extended and sideways gangster-style. Brown let fly a burst from his HK MP5. The results were predictable: lots of noise and a threat more to friend than foe.

"Stop that Shit, Injun," a subordinate ahead of him, crouched behind the shingle of gravel bar, yelled. Some of his fellow Agents called him "Injun" because of his Casino-American heritage; *no one is immune from a rubbing.* Agent Brown fought through the rest of the water and took up a position near the man who had chastised him. He began to lay down more effective fire, wishing he had brought a weapon with a better range. Quickly traversing his weapon to the right, his 9mm bullets hit a large rock that lay a scant few feet from him. Rock and bullet shattered in all directions, *"Oh Fuck, I'm hit."*

Sepp had loitered in the kill zone for too long and knew it. He left the surveillance room to seek out his real target, and soon found himself in the master bedroom. At the far end of the massive room, Sepp noted a moving light escaping the doors of a walk-in closet. He walked to it and then thundered its doors in with a powerful kick. Douglas was there with a shotgun in hand. A blonde behind him held a shaking flashlight.

"I'm in," Sepp spoke into a non-functional headset. It was a bluff. He had killed his radio early on but felt the ruse would work. It did.

Douglas did not pull the trigger. Instead, he slowly lowered the weapon. The flashlight dropped to the thickly carpeted floor. Sepp's night vision had a small IR light attached to it, so even without the flashlight, he had a clear view of both man and woman. Douglas was a shivering wreck. Fat, old, and bald, this quivering mass of flesh was no drug lord, at least not any longer. Without his henchmen, Douglas was just another man about to turn seventy, and with a pathetic hard-on, Sepp wanted to laugh at the man who had once instilled so much fear. Douglas was a small, trembling wreck.

"The money, give it to me." Sepp let the muzzle of his weapon provide the emphasis to his command.

"I don't know what you're talking about," stammered Douglas.

Sepp made sure that the closet door was shut behind him before he flipped open the IR cover on his tac-light and turned it on. The closet was a large walk-in with a marble dais in the middle. The whole thing spoke of incredible wealth. Armani suits were lined in rows opposite a stunning array of weapons.

"The fucking money or your fucking life, old man!" Sepp raged through the words. His face wore a mask of deranged anger. Douglas was in more of a mood to protect the woman than he was to fight for what little cash there was in his safe. Rightly, he dropped the shotgun to the floor and indicated with his hands that the thing he wanted was just to the right of him. "Open it," Sepp demanded as he toned down the theatrics.

Behind a horrible still life painting of orchids was a rather large wall safe. It had a spinning dial combination lock that only required three turns, like a junior high locker. Inside were fat stacks of US Dollars and what appeared to be Euros. Sepp used his left hand to release the snaps of his watertight backpack and let it fall to the floor. He then carefully backed up and indicated to the woman that she should retrieve it from the floor. Douglas tried to help, but was rebuffed for his effort. This caused him much embarrassment, Sepp could tell.

The money was loaded into the thick rubber bag. Sepp noticed that three items remained in the steel safe.

"What are those?"

"Nothing. Keepsakes, a family video." Douglas was trying desperately to be dismissive of the black rectangles.

"Put them in the bag," Sepp ordered.

As Douglas turned to do so, Sepp put a single 5.56 round into the man's lower back. The woman shrieked loudly in his ear. He used Doug's writhing body as a stepping-stone to the safe. Douglas let out a terrific groan as both the air and the life slipped from him. Sepp loaded his arms with the additional loot and turned to the dumbstruck woman. The look in her eyes said that she was both frightened and intrigued. Sepp dismissed her starry eyes, bent down and filled his bag to the point where closing it was no assurance that it would remain watertight. He then stood erect, donned the bag, and gave a look of contempt to the doe-eyed girl who clearly wanted to leave with the new Alpha male.

S.E.R.E.
(Survival. Evasion. Resistance. Escape.)

"A Boy needs to learn to shoot and take orders, less he is no more useful in the next war than an old woman."
       -Lord Robert Baden-Powell

Despite his moniker, Chicken had remained on station far longer than he knew to be wise. He was no rookie fool, having been there for Ops that went well and ones that went down poorly. And to his trained ear, the sound of this one signaled that it was a goat-rope. Chicken checked his watch yet again. The Op should have been completed by now. He knew that he had specific directives from Sepp and Sal not to linger beyond the approved time. That time had already passed. It was then and there that the thought hit him. Chicken, in the blink of an eye, figured out something very important. The titans of team leadership had both told him not to stay any longer than the Op order stat. He thought it odd at the time, but now he found it quite telling. Both leadership elements were warning him that they may not be coming back, or if they were, then they would not need his help. *The team is fighting more than the enemy out there. They are fighting each other.*

  For seven minutes the radio speaker amplified static. It also became apparent that the Barret .50 cal. would speak not again. Chicken put the van into reverse and slowly exfiltrated the AO. The main weapon was lost, and with it, the team's primary advantage. It was time to make a hasty exit.

  Chicken had seen a van in his rear-view mirror and had taken evasive action to lose it. But what he had not

169

counted on was to end up on the same damn road that he was trying hard to avoid. But, as there was no turning back and no going toward the scene of the crime, he proceeded at a slow and steady pace. That lasted only a minute until the shrill sound of a siren and the flash of roller lights blasted his diastolic pressure through the roof. Chicken gunned the van and jammed all the cop's communications. The cop had the benefits of knowing the terrain and having an engine with a souped-up cooling system built for high speeds, but Chicken was not without his own advantages. Coming up on a stretch of the road that had no right-hand barrier and a steep grade, Chicken hook-tossed a paper sack out the driver's side window. The bag hit the road and popped open in response to the pressure. Ten caltrops were let loose onto the road. Caltrops are pyramid-shaped spikes that, by design, always land correctly. Chicken wished he had a button or something sexier to deploy them, but the paper bag did just fine. Deputy Billy-Bob Zarzecki had been bred to think of this stretch of road as Tater Hill, because *if you lost it here, then you were tatered,* as in mashed potatoes. He never really thought much of it before, but he did now. After his tires were punctured by the caltrops, his squad car seemed to have a mind of its own. In reality the vehicle was simply obeying the laws of physics. His eighty-mile-an-hour chase ended when Patrol Car 67 hit a massive pine tree.

Chicken was not gunning, he was running. Shooting draws attention, and Chicken was in no mood for that. After relieving himself of the lone pursuant, he simply drove away from the incident, not so fast as to garner attention, and not too slow either. Over hill and over dale, Chicken kept a steady pace of twenty-five MPH. More than once, he could discern the lights of emergency vehicles headed in the opposite direction. He had made it about fifty miles over back roads and the occasional field when the first signs of civilization became apparent.

The team van was devoid of any distinguishing marks, so he didn't have to worry about that, but Chicken wasn't about to take any chances. Although the team technically owned it, Chicken held the van's title, so he was ultimately responsible for it. He knew how to run and how to hide, having done that just to grow up, but history was cold comfort at the present. Once on the outskirts of the small town called Salem, which had a minuscule amount of residents according to its population sign, Chicken lowered his speed and began to think instead of run. It would be a hard row to hoe. St. Louis, the anonymity of the big city, was more than a hundred miles off.

Either take the interstate or the blue highways. Those were the choices. Chicken decided to head directly home, and that meant the back roads. He would have to run, and he would have to hide. There would be no financial reward for this gig, and some of those *crazy fucking rednecks* might be wanting to come and drop a $100 bill on his lawn next to the Sunday paper. The fact that there was to be no money for the hit was a loss, but not a devastating one. He was the only man on the team whose wife knew about everything that he did. She held the purse strings and did a damn good job of it. All he had to do was make it to her and then sweet Betty would know what to do about the rest.

Their boss's plane had been late, and that was the reason that they were now late. Director of Sales Tom Sloss and Assistant to the Assistant of Promotions Kenneth Hyland weren't pressed for time; they just wanted to have a little of it to play with. *Working on the Fourth of July sucks*. It is hard on the kids, the wife, and the marriage. Sloss checked Hyland's speed, a reasonable sixty-seven miles per hour. Technically two miles per hour over the legal limit, but Sloss wanted to get there too, and as long as they were both sober Sloss figured that they were safe. Home by dawn was the thought that pervaded both their minds.

But the world has its own design, and it had most rudely failed to properly notify the Director of Sales and the Assistant to the Assistant. At their current rate of travel, the imminent future was only five seconds out.

Dave Sacra had drunk only as much as he thought was enough to get a good buzz. But that *goddamn bitch of a girlfriend of his*, Sara, was still harping on him *as if she was his goddamn mother*.

"What the fuck do you want from me?" he asked rhetorically as he pounded his fist down on the center of the steering wheel. The impact of his fist engaged the horn, but did nothing to change the trajectory of the truck. It was only when Dave turned to his passenger and his elbow caught the inner notch of the steering wheel that he began to career recklessly.

Dave gripped the wheel hard and began an attempt to right the vehicle. His efforts initially seemed to be rewarded, but when the right front tire blew, Dave and Sara shared one last glance. The argument was forgotten. It gave way to a moment that conveyed sympathy and ultimately, love.

Speed, weight, and pilotlessness drove the vehicle into one of those white picket Crosses that are supposed to remind people of how dangerous the nation's highways can be. The broken Christian cross-smacked the hood of the truck, shattering the window's glass but leaving it intact within its aperture. The broken crucifix then lay atop the fragmented glass, shielding from Dave's view the next hazard that lay in his path.

The advertisement agency had insisted that the road sign be made of steel, and despite the price, this was done. The First Baptist Church held the current lease of the space and their admonition "PORN DESTROYS FAMILIES" was mounted upon a beam of Bethlehem steel. The tender moment inside the truck was over now; terror gripped the two occupants as their blindness was coupled with all that speed. Sara had not been wearing her seatbelt, and when the signpost sheared off the passenger's side of the truck, her

172

body tried to exit through the doorframe. This did not happen in an attractive manner.

Dave was luckier than Sara, if you can count losing the only thing you love as lucky. It was the pain of his head injury that woke him up, but the sight of Sara's mangled body threw him into shock. Already incapable of making rational choices, Dave's position wasn't improved by the rapid swelling that was occurring within his cranium. The internal bleeding was squeezing off desperately needed oxygenated blood. Dave Sacra was dying rapidly but was incognizant of it.

On a bright and sunny day, his actions might have been a success, but on this dark night, those same actions were irrational. Trying to flag down a car from the side of the road is one thing, but trying the same technique from the middle of the road is quite another. For the rest of his days, Kenneth N. Hyland would hold the image of that nebulous man at the far end of his headlights, his hands held up in a gesture of surrender. Nor would he likely forget the sound of human bones cracking against the grill of his car or the sight of blood splattering across the windshield. But that was not the worst. He had applied his brakes as fast as he could, and when the SUV had come to a halt, Kenneth had exited the vehicle with a senseless desire to help the man that he had hit. The sight beneath the front wheels was far more gruesome than the windshield. The man's body was caught in the wheel well. *Just hamburger.*

Hyland yelled for Sloss to put the truck in neutral, then tried to push it off the body. The realization of where he was and what he was doing hit him. This man had been killed because he was standing in the highway. Hyland looked over his shoulder and understood that the man was dead and *he* was now in danger. He ran in front of the SUV and down the embankment to safety.

Another motorist, too afraid to stop, but not too indifferent to help, called 9-1-1 on his cell phone, thus accomplishing something that Tom Sloss and the Assistant

173

to the Assistant could not. The Bourbon County Sheriff's Department and the Missouri State Highway Patrol were contacted. They dispatched two of their finest patrolmen to the scene of the accident. Sergeant Colt and Corporal Ross hated responding to accidents. It was always gruesome, and took them away from what they deemed to be "real" police work. Tonight was a night that real police work needed to be done. A barnburner of a firefight had been taking place a county or two to the South, and they were stuck *at some damn DWI wreck.*

Regardless of what the two troopers thought of the situation, they had to stay and perform the mundane task of traffic regulation. The County Mounties on the scene had the gruesome task of dealing with the horrifying injuries, and so Colt and Ross dealt with the nuisance facet of the fatality wreck.

Interstate 44 was not heavily populated at four in the morning, but there were motorists, and they needed to be redirected away from the incident. Because it was a multiple fatality accident, the patrolmen had to close the entirety of the road while photos were taken, skid marks measured, and the meat wagon was filled. Once that had taken place, the left-hand lane was opened to allow the considerable amount of backed-up traffic to pass. And therein lies the rub for the Highway Patrol and for the passing motorists alike. Both groups want the vehicles to pass as quickly as possible, but once in the position to view the scene of an accident, the passing motorist is no longer so eager to pass. Instead, they are consumed by a macabre desire to see the result of a steel-on-flesh conflict. The casual passerby is not so much inclined to get out of the car and look, but to glance just long enough to impede the flow of traffic. This very phenomenon would change the course of this newborn day for Patrolmen Ross and Colt.

Sepp's departure from Fort Ozarks was far less dramatic than his entrance. He quickly stole to the water's edge and located his mooring line. That led Sepp to his SCUBA gear, where he submerged beneath the din of gunfire. The .50 cal. had stopped along with all the other supporting fires and he knew that this confluence of non-events meant only one thing. With one last look to the far side of the water and the men busy there, Sepp's world went black and cold. The only sound was his own breath: his only pursuant curious fish. The watertight bag strapped to his chest was more of a bother than the one that he had practiced with, but that was because it was filled with more cash than he had anticipated. *Some problems are good to have.*

Two weeks prior to the Battle of Fort Ozarks, Sepp Lokken had gone through all the steps to set up a kayak trip from the headwaters of the Mississippi River to the Keys of Florida. Lake Winnibigoshish, Minnesota is where he had decided to start from, and that had been where had gone that last week before the Hit. He had to be there and get his papers signed and his picture taken with the Park Rangers. The paperwork and photos were sealed in watertight storage bags and sunk along the lower Current River along with the rest of the necessary accouterments.

It was to the submerged kayak that Sepp now found himself navigating. It would take the rest of the night and a good chunk of the morning to get there. The lazy current would make it an easy dive. But between Fort Ozarks and the kayak there were many chances for a slip. His Dräger bubble-less regulator would allow him to complete the trip without leaving a trail of air bubbles in his wake, but fresh tanks had to be procured along the way. Sepp had strategically placed said tanks in the weeks prior to the hit. Still, his nerves were taut.

Sepp had not known for sure that the hit would degenerate into a goat-fuck, but he had planned for it. Standard Operating Procedure for the State and local police would ensure that all the roads would be blocked, and the river would be patrolled for surface craft, but there would be no searching for a scuba diver. Helicopters and boat propellers were the threat to Sepp on this leg of his journey. The water was generally deep and the air cover would come too late to spot him. He knew that the mentality of the southern Ozarks would never be looking for a scuba diver. There might be a skilled diver or two, but there would never be any concentrated effort beneath the water. Unlike the coastal regions, there was not a sub-marine mentality in the Ozarks. In this, Sepp's planning was brilliant. No one alive knew of his exit strategy. He had practiced his underwater navigational techniques on his last vacation. Valuable lessons had been learned in Belize, and Sepp always learned from his mistakes. As with any complicated task, the most important aspect is mental. If you know the task at hand and have prepared yourself for it, all things come easier.

During his "fam" training, Sepp had achieved a great deal of skill at underwater navigation. Practice makes perfect. Sepp knew all too well that there were still many dangers to this type of exit. His depth would never be greater than twenty feet, but that was not the factor that posed the most danger for Sepp. The duration that he would be under the water was. Sepp figured it would take him at least six hours to provide the kind of miles between Fort Ozarks and himself. Six hours beneath the water at an average of ten feet was his expectation. At that depth and that duration, another case of subcutaneous emphysema would cripple him if he had to ascend too quickly.

The maps he had made on his last dry run proved adequate for the task. It took Sepp a little longer than the anticipated six hours to reach the kayak, but he did it without missing a single air tank. The re-fittings went poorly at first; Sepp had not considered the growth of moss and algae on the tank's screw threads. Regardless, he accomplished the task belatedly, but without detection. That was the only aspect that concerned him at this juncture of his mission.

The ever-cautious Joe had been the last man on the team to leave the objective. Of this, he was sure. He was there when Killer and Matt had made their heroic, yet ill-fated stand. When the fifty-caliber sniper fire went still, Joe was still there. He provided covering fire for Sal and Dognut as they made a commendable push through the perimeter and to safety. They had not noticed, but Joe had done much to provide for their security. It was after that when Joe first noted the absence of Sepp, but there had been no time to wonder what had become of the team leader. A Fort Ozarks guard had yelled something to the effect that there are cops in the AO. It was then that Joe knew that he had to execute his own Plan B.

Joe, like Sepp, always had a secondary way out of every objective. Secondary only in the sense that it was a plan of escape that only he knew of. And this one was the offspring of a little snooping into the team leader's comings and goings. Joe had followed Sepp on his last foray downstream and noted that while the Boss was keen on the route to Fort Ozarks, he was far more interested in the waters to the south of the OBJ. It was then that Joe was sure that he had found Sepp's secondary, or perhaps his primary avenue of egress. And so, Joseph decided to model his late-blooming plan after that of his leader. Time and energy would be saved by the emulation.

Like fresh wood thrown on the embers of a dying fire, a reborn firefight arose out of a waning one. The majority of shots originated from the police, but there were elements within the Fort that had fight left in them. Joe saw his opportunity and took it. He dashed from his hide just within the breached wall and made for a large tree near the river. It was a maneuver that effectively flanked the police. From his position he could have killed them *in mass*, but that was not his intent. One of the greatest advantages in ground combat had presently knocked on Joe's door. Enfilading fire is achieved when the enemy's line is in perpendicular convergence with one's own gun line. The benefit is that if you miss the first man, your missed shot will probably strike another further down the line. As Joe moved into the advancing line, to his left and to his right lay a line of potential targets. Had he desired to shoot in either direction, Joe could have collapsed the entire police line. None of their positions afforded any protection from *within* their own perimeter. They might have been good cops, but these were not soldiers. As it was, Joe had zero interest in stopping the assault of this cop party. He instead had an idea about how to make their formation useful to his own cause. Joe carefully unhooked his M4 from his Ranger Body Armor, set it against the tree and then in an act of true fearlessness, took off the armor.

Joe Shifflett was a man who thought tactically. He never wore urban or woodland camouflage, only black. He never wore face paint, only a Nomex balaclava facemask. Even in the humid heat, Joe adhered to his doctrine, and here, along the river, it paid for itself in full. Affixed to the back of his body armor, Joe pulled out the reflective tab that read US MARSHAL, pulled off the balaclava, and donned a black ball cap that he kept folded in the small of his back. He then heaved the armor back on and rejoined the fight. Waiting for the police to continue past his position, Joe let loose an entire magazine at the only belligerent guard tower left. He made sure that his rounds were all low and that his fire was obvious to the police. Joe noted that a slim blonde woman was leading the police toward the Fort. She paused, let loose a controlled burst of fire, and then moved her element toward the fight. *Sexy, that.*

178

Predictably, his fire drew fire, but by that time Joe was safely behind the tree, and out of the view of both combating elements. It was time for him to act and act he did. Simultaneously retreating toward the river and firing wildly at the Fort, Joe started yelling out. "I'm hit. I'm hit!" he said as he slid with a sheet of loose rock down the embankment into the cool air just above the river.

There, crouched behind the heavy rocks of the lower shoreline was an injured officer. Agent Brown said, "I'm hit, too. What the fuck." Brown had a compression bandage on his face, blood dripping from its swelled bulk, making it look like an overwhelmed Maxi-Pad affixed to his chin.

"I'm getting the fuck out of here, man. Good luck." Earplugs were still muffling the sound of Joe's own voice.

"You too," was the only audible response as Agent Brown popped off a 40mm smoke round from a M-79 grenade launcher that he had taken from a subordinate. Joe caught a last glimpse of the lawman in the light of his 40mm discharge and allowed himself to be dragged downstream into the darkness, and away from the reborn fight. And so, it was there, with Joe pulling off his boots with the help and hindrance of the river's current, that the last remnant of the team finally withdrew from the Battle of Fort Ozarks.

Jenna eventually wrested control over the situation. She was lucky in that the mercenaries had severely weakened the manpower of its defenses. Her twelve-man element faced a bleeding and bruised contingent that was now leaderless. Dan Brewer had abandoned his men as soon as it had become the practical thing to do. She did not know this, but its effects were obvious to her. After the rest had conceded defeat, a lone man was still vigorously defending the battered structure from a tower. Her team had no explosive weaponry, so Jenna found herself in a pickle. She was faced with the decision to storm the tower or to attempt to negotiate with the man. The first option was a classically stupid move. To assault a position that was on the high ground was akin to suicide. The man had nowhere to go. He was a trapped animal and would probably fight as such. The second option, to try and talk the man down was about all that she figured she could do. Agent Britton was still in transit, and with him laid the real authority over the operation, but the Task Force was answering to her now regardless. Detective Penning was the only one who had displayed any real tactical acumen thus far.

Seeing that the situation was untenable, Jenna surveyed the area for a solution. Amidst the random gunfire, she saw the carnage that had been wrought. The old-time fortress was a shambles. Several walls were breached. Dead and dying men lay about haphazardly. *There*, affixed to a man long dead of a gunshot to the head, Jenna saw the solution to the last tower's resistance. She reached into the muck of seeping brain matter and unhooked a Flash Bang from the man's tactical harness. She had never used one, but thanks to her investigations, she knew what they were capable of. As her arm went back, Agent Mabe grabbed her wrist.

"The safety, Ma'am," he said, pointing to the small paperclip-like safety that keeps the spoon affixed even when the pin is pulled. It was the second time the man had come to her aid. After popping the thin wire off the device, Jenna gave it a hook shot up and into the tower. A flash and a bang later and the Battle of Fort Ozarks was finally over.

Floating in the near weightlessness of the river, Joe slowly yet smoothly discarded much of his battlefield accouterments into the gentle water that pushed him downstream. Eventually, he was left with only his weapon, two extra magazines and his NVGs. He held the latter to his face as he treaded water upstream from a blazing riverside campfire. All the elements were in place. Drunken men, oblivious to the happenings upstream, no weapons in view, and a truck with in-state plates.

Joe adjusted the focus on the Night Vision goggles as he kicked toward the shore. But no. A killing here would do more harm than good. Joe let the water's force usher him further downstream until a good inlet presented itself. Sharp stones hurt his feet as the weight of his body was transferred from buoyancy to ball of the foot. Joe made his way to the trees as noiselessly as possible. Moving parallel to the swampy water of the inlet, Joe knew that he only had one or two real options. Option one was to make his way back to the campers, kill them and flee in their vehicle. There were some really good reasons to want to leave, but Joe knew that he could not possibly navigate his way along the dirt roads of the Ozarks. He could as easily drive right on up to a checkpoint before he made it to the Interstate. The second option was one that Joe knew to be possible. It would be tough as hell to pull off, to be sure, but it was still possible. And with that flicker of certainty, Joe low crawled back to the ooze from which he had sprung forth. Along his way, Joe tried to recall the last time he ate, drank, pissed, and shat. All of this would be very important in the days to come.

Joe found a plastic soda bottle, cut the wide end off, unscrewed the lid, and then placed it in his mouth. Then with a deliberate slowness he began to ease himself into the slime beneath a low hanging tree. It would be days before he could emerge. He would have to drink the fetid, brackish water of the inlet, and his bodily functions would be held close by his clothing. Few men have the patience to undertake such an endeavor; still fewer have the discipline to accomplish such a feat. Joe was not completely sure that he would remain undetected, but he was sure that for the next few days, he was not going to voluntarily give his position away. Pulling some moss around the jagged opening of the bottle, Joe adjusted his body and began a very long period of inaction.

Just before the light of day, Sergeant Colt and Corporal Ross helped to spur the rubberneckers on their way. There was not a great deal of traffic, but it was steadily growing in volume. In the distance, toward the end of lined-up headlights, Corporal Ross saw a van pull off to the side. *Odd.* He was about to point it out to Colt. Vehicles that stop and turn around at any choke point are suspect, but these people only seemed to walk around the van as if to change drivers and then proceeded to get back into traffic. It was probably just a tired driver taking advantage of the situation to take a break, but one never knows. Ross decided to check the van as it passed.

Sal and Dognut had indeed switched out drivers, but they did something else as well. They had been checking out the van for anything out of the ordinary. Sal had stayed inside to activate the turn signals and then depress the brake. It would not do to be pulled over for a broken light at this point. All the lights had checked out, so the two men had decided to change drivers and wait out the traffic. St. Louis was only an hour away. It pleased them to snort a line of meth off a CD case while watching the flashing lights of the police.

As the flow of traffic brought the van closer to the scene of the wreck, Corporal Ross knew that he had seen the van before. *Somewhere. Oh, yeah, those hippies. Probably stoned again.* Ross mentioned it to Colt and then returned to waving a hay-laden eighteen-wheeler beyond the scene. The van edged forward, consuming the gap.

"Fucking Cops, man," Sal declared as he eased the slide back on his Ballester-Molina .45. Sure enough there was a round in the chamber. Sal was not looking to start anything with the police, but he wasn't a man who liked surprises either.

Corporal Ross paid attention as they passed by. Sal in the passenger seat was closest. Whoever it was in that van, they weren't the hippies, and they definitely weren't interested in looking at the wreckage. Two well-built, serious looking men occupied the van. The men did not fit memory, and further, the men did not fit the van. The driver had a tattoo on his left forearm. The ink was dark green and formed a familiar Arabic script. Ross's curious face watched in silence as the van passed. On the back of the vehicle, within the red cross of the Deadhead "Steal Your Face" Corporal Ross noted a crease in the metal and flecked paint that a grazing bullet had made.

"We got trouble," Ross called out.

That was all that he had to say. Colt noticed the change in his partner's posture and demeanor. "Let's go get 'em," he said, and they headed to their patrol car.

After a hindrance, like an accident, traffic tends to speed up and then taper back on the gas. Traffic is not unlike an accordion in that regard. It was just as the flow of traffic was beginning to level back out that Corporal Ross visually reacquired the hippy van. Their cruiser was held way back. He wanted to get as close as he could before turning on the lights.

"Cop car, 700 meters, closing," Sal spoke as he turned in his seat, staring out the back of the van's rear window. There was no reason for a direction to be given, and so it had been omitted from the situation report.

Sal climbed into the back of the van and began to set up a hasty fighting position by piling up the duffle bags of dope in the rear of the van. He used them as sandbags, resting the barrel of his weapon on them for support. Dognut looked back again as Sal was hoisting their body armor over the duffle bags to reinforce his defensive position. Sal then trained his weapon toward the threat. Dognut couldn't see the cop car, but knew it was only a matter of time.

183

"Pull out into the fast lane, will ya, Dognut?" there was a thought brewing in Sal's mind.

Neither Ross nor Colt knew what to make of it when they witnessed the van apply its brakes and begin to slow toward them, right next to the hay truck. Ross popped the siren and rollers. The van pulled tight against the eighteen-wheeler, and its side door slid back. Corporal Ross recognized the machete-wielding man in the doorway as the passenger. *What the fuck is he doing?* The man sliced at the heavy nylon strap that held fast the last row of hay bales. The arm was strong and the machete was sharp, and so the task was easily accomplished. The strap was immediately pulled into the truck's slipstream, but the hay remained in place. That is until Sal put down the combat machete and picked up the shotgun. The buckshot tore into the rear tires. As they began to shred the momentum change rippled up to the stack of hay bales. They toppled rapidly.

Dognut cocked his arm outside the driver's window; his gun hand was backward and the firearm upside down. It was a haphazard shot meant only to scare, but what it did was open a legal doorway for the police. They promptly returned fire.

Swerving in between the hay bales Colt did a magnificent job of negotiating the hazards. The cop car's customized suspension aided immeasurably in the task. The eighteen-wheeler had lost half its load before coming to a stop on the side of the road. The driver thought the pops were fireworks. He was startled to see a cop fly by, guns a-blazing.

Sal had not bothered to close the side door. The turbulence forced the two into yelling back and forth.

"Why aren't you shooting?" Dognut screamed. He could see that the cops had overcome their obstacles and were still in pursuit. The van was faster than he had expected, but still pegged out at 95 mph. Tink, tink, tink, tink. They were taking rounds and still Sal had yet to fire.

"What the fuck?" Dognut was about to chastise his friend when he turned and saw the reason for the delay. Sal

184

had formed a fighting position in the rear of the van and was slapping the belt into the feed tray of his Squad Automatic Weapon. *It wouldn't be long now,* Dognut thought.

The implication of what he had just witnessed took hold of his consciousness; he frantically looked about the van for anything to plug his ears. He pulled a cigarette butt out of the ashtray and began to shove its moist bulk into his left ear. It was too late for that, though. Every window in the van, save the hardened windshield, was shattered by the violent over pressure exuded by the SAW.

A hail of bullets peppered the patrol car. It was a hellish few moments that ended only when Sal could no longer control the recoil. Neither officer was hit, but the patrol car would need some serious bodywork. Ross had stayed on target, returning fire the whole time. Colt had to roll the window down and stick his head out to see, but he, too, was still on mission.

Ross came back in the car to change mags, and upon reloading, said in a calm out-of-body manner, "Fuck this shit."

He knew what needed to be done. Ross cleared out some glass from the shattered windshield and carefully took aim. The right rear tire of the VW decompressed rapidly. Dognut wrestled with the steering wheel in a fight for control that he could never have possibly won. The van swerved, tried to right itself, and then became top heavy. Dognut felt all of it in real time, but for Sal, who was unbuckled, the sensation crept through time.

Colt hit the brakes and watched the hippie van as it somersaulted through the barbed wire fence that ran parallel to the road. The Volkswagen van held up well throughout, but Colt and Ross had to wince as they saw a human shaped ragdoll eject from the swirling white powder that consumed the van's wild rotation.

Sal's body was broken in many places, and when the van came to rest atop his mortal coil, the two officers knew that there could be only one remaining threat.

Dognut was disoriented by his upside down-ness. His eyes stung from the white dust that seemed to be everywhere. Breathing deeply, the pain and shock gave way to a sense of absolute invulnerability. His knife sliced through the seatbelt and his fall was arrested by the strength of a single arm. *Superman!*

On the ground beyond the shattered windshield lay a pistol and a rifle. They were both lying in smashed corncobs, speckled with blood. Lowering himself to both, Dognut quickly ascertained their combat readiness. *Ready to roll.*

He crouched into the cover of cornrows surrounding his side of the wreck. Panting in the humidity, Dognut was thrilled to see his shoulder covered in crystal meth. He buried his nose into the fabric and inhaled deeply. Dognut did not notice that a thick layer of blood had oozed out of his ear and covered his arm with its doom.

"Damn," Sargeant Colt spoke as he halted the patrol car behind the decimated row of fence posts pointing the way toward the now immobile van. Beyond it lay a large red barn. A faded white paint advertisement for Meramec Caverns was still visible on its weathered panels.

The two cops used an abbreviated bounding over-watch technique to approach the vehicle. The patrolmen were as quiet as possible while moving to the van. At the rear of the V-Dub they saw one of the men's bodies. It was torn and tattered; half pinned by the van and covered in a white powder they both knew too well.

"Meth, if you wanna get high, do it tonight," Colt let some gallows humor whisper out as he inspected the interior of the hippie van.

"Driver gone, blood trail...front right." Ross was in no mood for jokes. He checked the deceased for vitals. He shook his head, indicating to Colt what was already evident. He was stepping over the broken remnants of a SAW and its belt of ammo when the van was peppered with a series of controlled bursts of pistol fire.

186

A verbal assault followed. "Fuck you, cops!" The troopers instinctively used the sound to triangulate its source. They then shot wide to the left and right in an attempt to channel their prey into the tight sector that lay between their fires.

Cha-chink, Boom! Colt's 12 gauge reloaded and then exploded with violence as he eyed movement in the tall corn. The double-ought buckshot scattered through the heavy blades of thick vegetation, but at least one of the pellets had found its mark. There was a wail of discomfort from within the corn and a return of fire that ended with five tracers. Ross knew what that meant. He charged headlong into the chin-high field, M4 ablaze.

Dognut reloaded as he closed the gap to the old barn. The thick green stalks of corn ended about fifteen feet from its open doors. The last leg of his journey was without cover. He dove through the doorway with shots whizzing past his body. Even in the early morning hours there was a latent heat within the barn. Surveying its interior, Dognut noticed a wooden set of rungs that led to the second floor of the massive structure. He felt the pain of his newest injury as he hoisted himself up the worn timbers. Once on the elevated platform, he moved two hay bales into a fighting position just as he saw a shadow move across the dirt floor of the barn.

Colt was trying to draw fire; he knew that the suspect had taken the high ground, and that Ross was the better shot with the rifle. It was not a pleasant task, but one that he was familiar with.

Outside the barn, Ross had dispensed with his drill sergeant hat, thrown the rifle over his shoulder and was pulling himself up a rope that someone had strung up the barn to hoist a weathervane to its roof. His boots were unexpectedly loud against the wooden slats of the barn. A fierce exchange of gunfire came from inside the barn. Ross used the deafening clamor to hurry up the rope to the single open window above.

187

Inside the barn the air was still. Smoke from Colt's shotgun blast hung heavily around him, mixing with the dry, dusty air. Colt had heard Ross along the wall and exposed himself to draw the perp's attention. The guy was up on the second tier, behind the hay bales. Colt knew that his shotgun had no chance of hitting him, but that did not matter. He was simply providing covering fire. Colt reloaded the shotgun while he still had one round in the chamber, then let loose another barrage at the bales of hay.

Using a trick he had learned in the Service, Ross twisted the running end of the rope beneath his foot, freeing up his arms to use the rifle. Adjusting his face behind the scope, Corporal Ross centered on his partner and followed the line of Colt's shotgun back to the shooter. *There, covered in blood, was the man with his back to the window.*

All it took to end things was a single shot to the head and the chaos ebbed toward order.

Inside the barn, Ross found Colt inspecting the various weapons strewn about the crime scene.

Colt picked up a .45 caliber pistol. It was a 1911 chassis. "Hey, look here, a Ballester-Molina, excellent condition, too." He had the calm of a man adjusted to gunplay. "You know they made this out of the Graf Spee, a Nazi boat they sank off of South America," he stated as he dropped the mag, cleared the chamber and safe'd the weapon.

"You would know something like that, ya freakin' history nerd." Despite the jab, and perhaps because of it, a pleasant silence began anew between the two patrolmen as they each assessed their readiness before calling higher command.

Dan Brewer knew that with the introduction of the police into the fray, the Fort was lost. This enabled him to focus all his energies and intellect on his real concern: the physical security of his boss. Leaving the men to fend for themselves in a situation that was rapidly deteriorating. Dan headed to Douglas' living quarters. As soon as he saw the dead bodies of Doug's security element, he feared the worst. Only the frantic wailing of Doug's mistress led him to his master.

Brewer appraised the situation. The boss was dead, and so now he was the Boss. *The King is dead, long live the King!* The ample bosomed woman now clung to the bloated corpse. Dan never had liked that gold-digging bitch, and he was in a position to do her the way he had always wanted to. He wrenched her from Douglas and then pulled out his sidearm, a Beretta 9mm. She was left in his wake with two hollow points in her chest. It had been an easy thing to do.

Dan looked around the closet and knew for sure it was a robbery. The Bancroft tape was missing from the safe. It was an insurance policy, and one of those was desperately needed. *Especially now.* He had a new fear. Had Bancroft arranged this raid?

The muffled exhaust of the two-seated Sea-Doo poured a soft smoke onto the water within the Boathouse. Beneath the din of gunfire, it was relatively inaudible. Dan decided that *speed was security* and so he throttled it back. He had Jon-boated this section of the river for years. Navigating the route upstream was easy. The cover of darkness became comfortable. Dan took one last look at the life he was leaving and was pleased to see only a white rooster tail. He turned back to navigate when a huge fireball consumed a cabin in front of him. Sepp had reset the team's cabin to blow long before the standard time had elapsed. Dan figured that the explosion had something to do with the attack on the Fort. He made a mental note to begin his hunt at the burned-out cabin by the river.

Twenty minutes later he scuttled the small craft and headed to an old barn that sat aside Acker's Ferry. The red doors of the barn opened slowly with the nudging of the fender and seconds later, his blue pickup truck was shuttling him to safety. As he drove through the night, Dan truly began to appreciate his newfound position. He knew the contacts. He knew the bank codes. He was now the drug lord. There was trouble to be sure, but nothing that he could not surmount. He smiled a sly grin as he made his way south. He would head to the villa outside of Cancun and then send some men to investigate that cabin. *The old man would have approved.*

The first town of any real size that Chicken recognized was Memphis. Chicken took comfort in the sign, but he dared not slack off in his quest to get home. His whole body was tired; the vibrations of the road numbing him like a massage chair. Reluctantly, Chicken popped the only two pieces of Ranger Candy that he had ever been foolish enough to possess. The prescription methamphetamine worked just as Sal had told him it would. The east-west expanse of Tennessee went by in a blur. It was only about fifty miles north of Birmingham, Alabama when Chicken first noted that a gargantuan high chair was steadily keeping pace with him. He took comfort from that chair for a few leagues until his senses told him that chairs normally do not follow cars. Chicken had been awake for more than thirty hours and was in the midst of a wild hallucination. He took the next dirt road that presented itself and decided to get some rack.

Four hours later, in the relative cool of the southern evening, Chicken changed out his stolen Missouri license plates and screwed on his own Alabama tags. *It always pays to have local plates.* Tossing the stolen ones into a drainage ditch, Chicken took up the road again. Soon, he was within miles of his house. Chicken placed a call on one of his prepaid, disposable phones. After three rings his woman answered it. The voice asked, "Is this the Blackthorne house?" Betty politely replied that he had the wrong number.

Betty shook so violently that she had trouble placing the receiver onto its hook.

She had known that this day would come, but its sudden presence was a bit of a shock nonetheless. Betty took a drink of cool water straight out of the faucet with a dirty glass that she had just begun to wash. She never even noticed. A quick prayer calmed her nerves before she gathered up the few things that time allowed. She drove her little ole red Honda Civic up to the filling station. Forty minutes later, at the quarry, she drove up the steep inclines that led to the clay pit's deepest pools.

Chicken finished removing all his electronics from the van and was in the process of tossing the devices into the abyss of water seventy feet below. The radar scrambler made a comforting splash as the Civic crested the hill. Betty didn't wait for the dust to settle. She was coughing as she hugged her man.

"Is it really over?" she asked.

"Yeah, Babe, it's over," he told her as he stroked her hair, holding her face close to his. "And we didn't get no more money neither."

"What?" she pulled herself away from him and gave him one of her cold stares. Chicken knew this was going to be hard for her to hear, but there simply was no cash from this one.

"But Baby, it is over. Most of them mother-fuckers is dead, and I ain't never doing that shit again." Chicken was relieved to say it. The finality of his words hit home with her. She began to smile and move toward him again.

"Where we headed?" she asked softly, the tears in her eyes beginning to well up.

"Did you bring the money?"

"In the trunk," she said, gesturing to their car.

"We're headed north, Baby." Chicken wanted to get as far away from Sepp as possible, but not out of fear.

"Is somebody looking for us?" Betty was not talking about the cops. What worried her were the white devils he associated with.

"I think Sepp made it out. Maybe Joe, too. And it's possible Chuck did too, but don't you worry 'bout Sepp or Chuck. They ain't crazy," he left a lot unsaid.

"Oh, I ain't worried 'bout those two." Betty had met each of them and had rightly placed her fears in Joe.

"Let's get ghost, Baby." Chicken pulled her tight and pressed his lips to hers. After the kiss, Betty climbed into the Civic's passenger seat. Chicken always drove. There was never any question there.

Chicken watched her ass as she went. He then turned to the van, reached in through the window and started it up. The engine roared to life and then settled into a quiet purr. He shook his head in regret as he maneuvered the automatic gear stick into the D position. He could not bear to watch his beauty slowly drive itself off the cliff. The disruption of the placid waters below made Chicken cringe. He hopped in his shitty car and drove on in his personal mission of evasion.

Joe awoke encased in muck. He instantly recognized the danger of being awake. It meant that he had been sleeping, and in sleep, there was no security. The pile of leaves still concealed his head, though he had rustled them enough to let in the light. *Have I snored?* Joe felt it difficult not to move his body as the adrenaline was released within. It was time for fight or flight, and he willed himself to do neither. Such was Joe's dedication, his training, and his strength of mind. Joe told himself that he had not been caught. He then began to concentrate on slowing his breathing. It was Daylight, the sun was at about a 45-degree angle to the east, which meant 8 or 9 in the AM. *Day three in this freaking mud hole.*

The real danger had passed though, and Joe was acute enough to know it. There had been a foot patrol near enough to hear on the second morning, but nothing since. Joe knew that he could only last so long, and so began fashioning his escape. He decided to wait till nightfall or during a rain shower if one presented itself. Flexing his muscles to prepare them for activity, Joe fixed on an overland movement. Following the river was a no-go; if they caught Sepp then the authorities would most likely be more vigilant there. Joe was sure that Sepp planned to ditch the team by heading downstream. *Sitting in an estuary, immobile for three days, it gives a man time to think.* Joe went over scenario after scenario.

Sepp was almost sure to have made it out. The Hit had been orchestrated around something that Sepp failed to share. The team had been set up for failure, and Joe chastised himself for missing the obvious. He should have been more attentive to Sepp's disdain for street drugs. Then there was the pressure put on Sepp to start looking at the dope as a financial asset. In retrospect, Sepp had gone along too easily with that alteration of what he saw as *his* team's purpose.

Sepp would have had more than a month to prepare his betrayal. Yes, Joe was sure that Sepp would have made it out. *As for the rest?* Chicken had the best odds of all of them to survive the evening. But Chicken was no threat to Joe, and he knew it. Other than that, Joe knew that he could have no idea of whom if anyone made it out. Chuck was dead or had been wounded. The fifty cal. had become poignant in its silence. Matt and Killer were dead; Joe had seen that with his own eyes. Something within his warrior sense told him that Sal and Dognut had made it out. He had no basis for this assumption, but he believed it nonetheless.

Sepp had tried to kill him. Just as surely as all those Hajis. This made Joe an angry man. That anger, that growing hatred, gave a vile birth in the mind of Joe. He had his White Whale to hunt now. More than the service or the hits on dopers had given Joe this monomaniacal sense of purpose,

193

to escape the area and then begin the hunt for Sepp was the clearest idea that Joe had ever experienced. It was the right thing to do. Put a $100 bill in his windshield wipers and then pop him as he recognizes its venomous bite.

A rain cloud began to pepper the leaves around Joe's head. The sound of the droplets slowly increased to become a noise resembling a steak sizzling on the grill. It made Joe hungry. He worked his torso slowly back and forth to make room for his body to slide out of the morass. A gently sucking sound was replaced by a much louder farting noise. Joe froze momentarily and then began again to wiggle out of the mud and into the rain darkened Ozark evening.

Leaving the AO was surprisingly easy for Joe. Everyone seemed to be going about their business. He was sure there were still checkpoints to be negotiated. Joe made it to his stash spot where a gym bag of fresh civilian clothes and a pistol waited. He had one for every mission.

Joe cleaned up and hitched a ride with an elderly man to Rolla, Missouri and from there a quick bus ride took him to Biggart's Army Surplus Store. After buying a few essentials, Joe took a taxi to the gates of Fort Leonard Wood, or as it is more commonly known to those who serve there, "Fort Lost in the Woods." Unlike most military bases, there is no town of any real size for more than a hundred miles from its main gate. It was at that main gate Joe flashed a DoD ID card that an active-duty friend had made for him and was quickly shuttled to the Bachelor Officers Quarters. It was a bold move, but one that he was sure would work. A wartime military has a heightened security, but they also have a lot of officers going to and fro. Joe was white, he knew the lingo, and this *was* southern Missouri. He fit the type, a cursory check he could pass without a problem. To augment his passing through the MPs, before each mission, Joe generated military orders on his home computer. For this particular mission, he would be on orders to Fort Sill, Oklahoma. This would allow him to stay at a variety of Army posts throughout the region. His ID card would not stand a

194

washing through the real Army database, but Joe knew that it should not have to. He was betting on the fact that he would only have to flash it once at the gate and then again to get a room. It was a bold move, just like the decision to stay in the area after the firefight. *Fortune favors the bold.*

The BOQ was a safe place to rest for a few days while he gathered intelligence on the fight at Fort Ozarks. Brevet Captain Joe Shifflett then caught a taxi ride to Union Station and then took another to Lambert International Airport just outside downtown St. Louis. From there he used his real ID and flew to his personal safe house in Oregon. It was in the pristine woods of the Siskiyou Mountains that Joe began to plot his next move.

Patty and Linda Lu were waiting for Sal and Dognut at the Travelodge when a procession of cop cars began to converge on the outskirts of town. From what the receptionist said, a couple of the guys involved in that gunfight on the river had been killed just down I-44. The girls walked out of the office on their way to the car. They were stunned by the reality of it as they watched the cops and news vans stream by the hotel. By the time they got to the rag-top Mustang, a simultaneous moment of clarity hit them. The drugs and the cash they were holding was now theirs. It was crystal clear to the two young women. They were rich, had lots of coke, and they needed to get the fuck out of Dodge. Linda Lu fished out the keys to a '67 Mustang and they tore off in the opposite direction of the crash.

WRITTEN ON WATER

"Well. that sucked!"

An soldier's first words upon returning from Iraq.

The sea kayak still lay anchored at the bottom of the brown water river, secluded beneath a lightning-shorn willow tree. Twenty feet down, concealed by the depth and further shrouded within a camouflage net, Sepp had trouble locating it a scant three weeks later. This was encouraging. Sepp had a ten-digit grid to the watercraft and a state-of-the-art GPS. If he had trouble finding it, then it was a safe bet that others had too.

The establishment of a bivouac was hard work. Good planning and execution, not the vagaries of fortune, were what Sepp counted on. He had, of course, ensured that hydration was waiting. He left a water filter within the river bag attached to the kayak, as well as a full bottle of fresh H_20.

Sepp found himself gently singing as he worked the filter's hand pump. He had to sing, for whistling had never come easy to him. The lyrics were from an old Kingston Trio song that his mother had played for him when he was a child. The lyrics moved him to a safe place, even if that safety was a mirage.

Contrary to the tune in his mind, Sepp drained the water bottle within seconds of opening it. After manually working a few pints through the filter, he attached his empty bottle to it. The clean water began to rise, making Sepp all the thirstier still. When the filling was completed, Sepp drank the entirety of its contents down. It was the first treated water consumed since the Battle of Fort Ozarks. He downed the H2O like he had in the 125-degree Iraqi heat. *Swimming is thirsty work.*

The infrared blocking camo net that he had reallocated from the government while on active duty was still in good condition. There would be protection from the probable arrival of the Helos. He had not rushed in setting up his camp. Method was the watchword for this phase of operations. The watertight bag and the netting were raised from the depths, but he left the kayak for the last minute.

Sal had not felt the oppression of *the Fear* since his days in the war. Every creak of a tree, each splash of feeding fish. Each noise gave him the sensation of *imminent Doom.* Those were the words that he and his brothers in arms had given it then, *the fear, doom. The Fear is a big dark purple monster behind you, lurking like a stalking butler. It waits on its own time. To strike without warning. And that goddamn beast will not sleep either.* Sepp had been under fire numerous times in his mercenary career, but for some reason, this time was more like "over there" than he cared to think about. The only solace came from within his watertight bag. In there was more money than he had time to count. It felt like there were forty-plus pounds of hundreds. And then there were the tapes. He was sure something good was on those tapes, if only by the way Douglas had acted indifferently about them.

Every time Sepp thought that he heard an engine's rumble, a retreat was made to the safety of the camo netting. Several times he thought that the black helicopters were about to pounce. But they did not come on the first day or the second, and so Sepp judged it appropriate to leave on the third day. He swam down to the submerged kayak and released the compressed air canisters that were attached by an algae-draped cord. The submersible overcoming the mooring lines on its way to the surface. But the vessel was detained in its accent. Straining against the cords, the kayak's futile struggle slowly became visible as the bubbles faded. After the river cleansed the area of muck, Sepp swam beneath his ride and inspected her for flaws. All was in order, so Sepp cut the five-fifty thick cord and she breached like a whale. Pulling her ashore, Sepp began to prepare for the voyage.

Three and a half hours later the newly named vessel, *the Chub,* nosed to a halt within the loose gravel and broken concrete that lay just below the Missouri HWY 19 bridge embankment. The water was deep and the current devious, but this was a stop that Sepp felt that he had to make. He tied off, popped open one of the two cans of beer that he had stashed in the kayak and started up the hill. Of course he was armed, but to the untrained eye Sepp was just one of many river rats having a beer on his way to buy supplies. The beers were kept in a mesh bag towed behind the kayak to cool in the river water, but the Current River does not run that cold in mid-July. As a consequence, the beer was none to pleasing to the taste, but *beer is beer.*

With postage paid, a package was slipped into the drop slot of the co-located US Post office. Sepp then collected the necessary food and obligatory beer. Buying spartan amounts of the former and ample bottles of the latter, Sepp also retrieved a newspaper and began walking to the store exit that faced the river, not the road.

"Hey Sir, can I speak with you?" an unfamiliar voice called out.

It was the "sir" that alarmed him. *Cops, it has to be the cops.* Standing next to him *was* a National Park Ranger. They are still cops, and Federal cops at that. Sepp had learned that lesson as an underage drinker, an experience that he had no desire to repeat. He turned slowly, ready to drop the grocery bag and pull out the pistol concealed within his fanny pouch. Cop or no, Sepp was leaving this place. He had never killed a cop himself, but that was only because he had never really felt that he had to.

"Sir, you can't transport bottled beer on the river no more. Gotta be cans. I strongly suggest that you follow the new state law here. Bet'cha Marlene will let you exchange 'em if you ask real nice." The young Ranger looked barely out of high school and very conscious of his own sidearm. Since the gunfight up the river, the rules had changed. Ranger Nantz took all men under the age of forty, physically fit, and especially the ones alone, quite seriously these days.

"Yes, sir officer... 'er Ranger," Sepp played it cool. The Ranger stood near the refrigerator reserved for bait. *How did I miss him?* Sepp asked himself, not wasting the effort to answer.

"Sir, were you on the river six days ago, around Fort Ozark, by chance?" the Ranger was young but not stupid. Sepp had the look of a man that hadn't had a shave or a washing in about that length of time.

"No, sir, been on the Black 'bout a week. The Current's too damn ugly for my taste," he said as he lay the bottles on the counter and motioned to Marlene if it was OK to get cans. *It was.* She hadn't told him about the law because she had not liked the look of him, but now she saw how polite he was and felt a bit sheepish for not telling him about the cans.

The Ranger stayed at the counter as Sepp made the exchange. He was looking over Sepp's purchase with an inquisitive eye. "This got something to do with the papers?" Sepp motioned to the headlines that were reflecting on the "Gunfight at Fort Ozark."

"I am sure it doesn't, Sir," Nantz replied. "Sorry for takin' your time."

His knowledge of the river confirmed the plausibility of the haggard river rat's story, and so the rookie made an error that he never would have with a few more years on the job. Many a mistake is made in just that manner, and it is altogether fitting and proper that things are so.

Later that same day another agent of the federal government came to *Marlene's Grocery and Bait Store* and took the contents of the mailbox to the town's distribution center. From there, Sepp's package made its way toward its final destination. The CD had the name Bancroft written on it, and Sepp was sure that his Dad's wife would know what to do with it. She worked for the big newspaper in St. Louis and had a reputation as a bulldog when she was on a story. He had put the 8mm film and the VHS along with it.

Later, the postmark and the Park Ranger's incident with the river rat would be examined at length, but only after it was far too late to make any difference to Sepp.

The Clark County Elementary School's gymnasium had its air conditioning unit cranked on MAX for six hours straight, and still it was not enough to stem the tide of the summer's slow attack on the bodies. Even the locals were asked to bring in block ice so that it could be placed up in front of the large school fans. Jenna had the County Coroner line the bodies on the children's lunch tables that now served as makeshift mortuary slabs. The Sheriff's Department was busy identifying their own dead, as well as the local. The known deceased were placed on the western side of the gymnasium. There were twenty-three bodies, so many that each seat's backrest had to suffice as gurneys for the inanimate. The police dead were all taken to the proper morgue, and the rest stayed at the gym.

Those who could not be readily identified by familiarity, and those so grievously wounded as to be unrecognizable were placed on the east side. At present count, there were seven of them, and two more were on the way. The Highway Patrol was sending them along with their State Forensics Team. They had been gunned down by a pair of Troopers along I-44. Walking up and down the eastern row, Jenna was still piecing together what had happened. The corpses were helping to fill in the blanks.

The two bodies being ferried down by the State Police were the ones that got away, but were there more?

Jenna was sure there were. The locals had insisted that they had them all, but when she suggested that the far bluff be checked, they had returned with yet another body. There would be more, of this she was quite certain. Once on site, Agent Britton saw the look in her eyes and asked, "Is it over?"

"For them," she let her eyes fall on the bullet-ridden man sprawled out on the table. Death had not been kind to Chuck, his limbs and face were distorted by the reaper's blade, "It is." This crew has seen its last fight. But we know that at least one of them made it out."

"Agent Brown's statement," Britton was referring to the wounded man that Agent Brown had seen, well, he had seen no wound, but it was clear that someone escaped *into* police lines. And if that could happen, *then anything was possible*, he guessed quite correctly.

"I suppose that it is your call now, Agent Britton," she said turning to him, but he was not paying any attention to her now. Britton was listening intently to the earpiece attached to his cell phone. Jenna was abashed at catching herself talking to no one, but then Agent Britton's eyes lit up and his face became crimson with embarrassment.

"It's for you," he proffered the detached phone to her and smiled.

The lower reaches of the Mighty Mississippi were even fouler smelling than Sepp had imagined. By the time the Ohio and Missouri reach it, the wastewater of the Great Plains and the Rust Belt are combined. For Sepp the stench would prove to be the most grueling part of the travel. The rest was simple navigation and tedium. His small boat was caught in the inevitable eddies and swirled around more than a few times, but never was there any real danger. The great boats of the river paid Sepp no heed, and it wasn't until he reached Baton Rouge that he was even hailed.

Louisiana's Governor Huey P. Long halts all ships coming up and down the river and thereby lines the pockets of his state with tax money. The U.S. Coast Guard hailed Sepp. This was another expected stop for Sepp, the last on his itinerary.

The rendezvous with the USCG was a planned and coordinated event. They would provide the necessary documentation for Sepp's departure from the United States. After he was hailed, by both sight and sound, Sepp and his kayak were hauled aboard for a safety inspection. Sepp was treated to a well-prepared meal rather than intense scrutiny. The crew seemed more interested in the psyche of a man who planned to make it all the way to Marathon, Florida on a kayak, than with said person's recent history. The paperwork all checked out and Robert L. Smyth was allowed to proceed. He even had his photo taken with the crew, although he was careful to leave the beard and long hair in their rough-hewn state.

Most men would have taken the Mississippi all the way down, but at a road-crowned levee in Louisiana, Sepp decided to portage his gear over to the waters that lay to the west. It would not save any time, but it was more solitary. Atop the mound, Sepp watched as a car approached. It was old, obviously not a cop, and so Sepp decided to wait for it to pass before dragging his boat across the road. The black car began to slow as it approached. Its rooster tail of dust shrank into a wisp as the vehicle came to a smooth halt.

The driver of the antique Cadillac, a hollow-eyed man with pale skin and a timeless yet weary look to him, asked Sepp if he'd like a ride. Maybe it was the fact that the old guy was drinking and no threat, or because he needed a change of scenery, regardless, Sepp took the man up on his offer. He agreed to a lift but protested that his boat would also need to come along. The man took a pull from his flask and gestured to the trunk. It took some doing, but Sepp fit

203

the majority of the kayak into the trunk. He sank in the leather of the passenger's seat slowly closing the door as he did.

If it was company he sought, Sepp would have been disappointed. The old guy only spoke when he asked for a light for his cigarette. Ten minutes passed blissfully as the best country music that Sepp had ever heard played softly on the radio. The man took a deep pull from his flask, not offering his passenger any.

During a pause in the music, the pale man spoke. "Drifter, you need to get right, right by yer self." And that was that, and nothing more.

An intersection lay ahead with five different roads to be chosen from, six if one counted going backwards. The driver turned the car around and came to a halt mid road.

"This is where you get off, boy, 'cause I'm going back to..." but Sepp could not make out the last of the sentence as the door squeaked too loudly upon its opening.

As Sepp alighted from the man's ride, he stopped to say, "Mister, many thanks."

His hollow eyes glared at Sepp as he said, "You don't have to call me Mister, Mister."

Sepp pulled his kayak from the trunk and started down a road marked with a pictogram of a boat landing.

The second leg of his trek was the Gulf Intracoastal Waterway. Spanning the distance between Carrabelle, Florida and South Padre Island, Texas, it was specifically built to allow for a consistent width and depth for inter-state marine transport. The waterway was now being used to transport a notorious killer to an island safe haven. He tossed the travel documents and almost did the same to the pistol but thought better of it. That would have been too much, so Sepp took the semiautomatic pistol apart.

It was the seventh night on the coastal water when Sepp was paid a visit by the local law, Texas style.

"Where you headed, son?" It was both a question and a statement. Sheriff Porter wanted to know where the raggedy man was heading, and let him know that he *was* indeed headed. *You don't have to go home, but you sure as hell can't stay here.* Porter was a physically imposing man. In his late fifties, there was a hard strength to him. He had a presence about him that only a life spent enforcing the law can give.

"Vera Cruz, sir, I am heading toward Vera Cruz, Mexico," Sepp looked pained as he said it, rubbing the scruff that had formed on his chin and neck. The Sheriff eyed him knowingly before asking.

"You got some sort of ID?"

Sepp pulled out an old desert camo-colored neck carrier from beneath his well-worn T-shirt. The tan and black holder had OIF stitched on it, the Sheriff noted. *Operation Iraqi Freedom, huh?* Sepp then produced three pieces of ID, which he conveyed in this order. First was his incredibly expensive and incredibly fake "Retired-Medical" US Military identification card. The second was his Veterans of Foreign Wars membership card, and the third was a damn good fake passport. Sepp had done this once with his genuine credentials, and it had worked. He had the sneaking suspicion that it would again work today.

"You had a tough time over there did you, son?" the lawman had a real look of concern on him.

"I did," Sepp said as truthfully as he had ever said anything.

"What outfit was you in?" there was still the business of the bona fides. Lots of men say that they served, few actually do.

"One-Six-Two Infantry, Oregon Army National Guard, had a hell of a hard time in..."

"Fallujah," Sheriff Porter kept up with the war. He felt he owed it to those boys.

"Yes, Sir." *You have to add the sir, real servile the "sir" is.* It was working, Sepp could tell. He hated using a Unit he had not served in, but he had seen the 2/162 after their action and had been impressed by how they held themselves. Fallujah is a name that can safely be dropped, and once you throw the National Guard into the mix, even the savviest of men can get confused. What the Sheriff saw was real, a genuinely disturbed combat vet. Sepp was saying some things and omitting others.

"Where's yer gun?" the Sheriff asked. It was not accusatory; it was asked out of concern and Sepp knew then that he was safe.

"I ain't got no gun sir," he was lying and it was obvious.

"Son, I know that you have a gun, or that you are needing some help." Again, it was fatherly, not prosecutorial. "Just tell me what you got so that me and the Missus don't have to worry about you out here, see?" the lawman soft-balled him.

"I got a Glock, a forty-five. It's over there," Sepp pointed toward the kayak on the water's edge, well out of reach. "It's disassembled," he added lamely, but truthfully again. The calm of the ocean had made him forget a lot about his past over the preceding week. The officer knew that he was in no immediate danger to himself or others. He had felt the same way when he came home from Vietnam; sometimes a man just needs to get away.

Sheriff Porter knew that he had a disturbed man on his hands, but this fellow was trying to simply leave, and that was exactly what Porter was going to let him do. Still, there was something decidedly not right about the *boy*. It was like he was playing it up for a VA paycheck, although he was fully capable of pretending that everything was all right. Well, Sheriff Porter thought, he had done almost the same damn thing, hadn't he? *Don't all combat vets play it or hide it as the situation dictates?*

On the ride home, Sheriff Porter was forced to relive the first few months of his life when he had just got back home. It was not the most pleasant of memories for him.

"Hey baby, how's it going?" Chicken asked as he entered their new apartment's small kitchen. A disproportionately large picture window above the sink let streetlight bleed through the thin curtains, softly illuminating her face.

"Good, Clarence," Betty never called her man by his nickname "Chicken." Especially not now with their new life and all. Betty was all smiles as she turned to the trashcan on the other end of the slender kitchen.

"Did you leave some money above the sink this morning?" she asked. The wall that she was now facing distorted her voice. Chicken's chest took on the weight of lead, but he might have just heard her wrong. She turned to him, pulling a neatly folded $100 bill out of the chest pocket of her apron. The sight of it froze him with *the doom*.

A small white clump, about the size of a wad of bubblegum, exploded in the center of the widow. The blast did not kick much glass into the residence; it was only supposed to eliminate the distortion of depth caused by the window. It was an old trick employed by snipers. This Chicken knew all too well. The blast merely cleared the way for the bullet that was already in flight.

His darling Betty was struck in the side of the head by a high velocity round. It took the top off of her cranial mass. As her body fell, Chicken just stood there. His love, his world was gone. He did not rage against the inevitable.

Joe was checked in at Mexico City's Commodore Hotel. He, like his prey, had stashed his wealth away. Joe had fluid assets, easily exchanged for hard currency. Diamonds were his thing. Small, easily transported and concealed. The small translucent rocks were funding his quest, and could continue to do so for years, if that is what it took. Joe had nothing better to do, and a lot of advantages over his quarry. He was traveling incognito, bypassing a great deal of the territory. He knew that Sepp would not move to Alaska, or to some uninhabited place. Sepp had bragged about his worldliness. Sepp had never gone home on military leave. He always took a transport bird to someplace exotic. Joe believed most of the stories, but still didn't think that Sepp would go that far. You gotta start somewhere, and Central America is as good a place as any. He waited out the necessary arrangements, and then booked a flight to Tegucigalpa, Honduras.

Joe figured Sepp to be in the company of Europeans rather than Americans. They would definitely be Caucasian. As magnanimous as he was, Joe always smelled a hint of racist bastard in Sepp. Plus, a guy has to fit in with the background. The community would be neither too large nor too small. *A place to start would be one where people of wealth are welcome, not suspect.* The way Joe figured it was that if Sepp was in the Caribbean, then he would be in a small tourist town, living on a boat, or near one. Sepp would have altered his appearance and could be living quite well considering the money that he had heisted. He certainly would not be poor, for Sepp had shown the world that if he could not earn it, he would simply take it. There were many ways to slowly section off places that Sepp would and would not be.

Joe smiled as he surveyed the view from his hilltop apartment. Sepp was out there. He checked to make sure that his sidearm was loaded, tucked it into the small of his back and then took the stairs to the hotel lobby. Joe did not partake in the generally mellow mood of the city as he started to amble down toward the commercial pier. He had booked passage on a day-tripper to the islands the day before. At the fisherman's cantina, Joe pulled out a pack of French Royale menthol cigarettes, placed one between his teeth and tried to extract his Zippo, the one with the Moby Dick scrimshawed on the front. But his ham-fisted approach forced him to fumble the now flaming lighter. It skidded off his boot and

208

then twisted on the ground. The chewed-up leg of a barstool ultimately halted its movement. A barstool occupied by an ardent and established imbiber of hardened spirits. The barfly picked up the still flaming lighter, turned it around and noted the engraving on the opposite side of the white whale. It read, "You can't kill a man who was born to hang." A drunken smile.

"Stupid," was the single utterance given by the drunk as he extinguished it with a closing and handed it back. Joe cared little for the statement, but he was pleased to have his Zippo back. He gave the old coot a cross glance and continued his walk to the marina. He had chartered a boat to the Islas de la Bahai, and then the isle of Roatan.

The task was not so great. Sepp could be tracked. It was a complicated matter to be sure, but not an impossible one. As with any task, if you break it down piece by piece, and devote enough time to it, then the odds of success greatly increase. It really is as easy as pie, cutting one that is.

The approach to Belize was uneventful, and that in and of itself was a surprise to Sepp. He leaned back to relax, taking in the view. The now all too familiar bow of the kayak *Chub* was surrounded by a vision of paradise. Small structures on the Island's shore were masked by palm trees. Sepp fired up his GPS and waited for the palm-sized apparatus to acquire enough satellites to pinpoint his location. The map screen went from a question mark to an aerial image of Caye Caulker within a minute. Sepp dug the paddle blade into the emerald sea and began the end of his trek with an emboldened spirit.

Even as he neared the shore, Sepp elicited nothing more than a few smiles from people eyeing his approach to *Patty's* dock. Sepp smiled back and then proceeded to steer his kayak around a swimmer. He maneuvered his vessel smoothly up to the diminutive jetty. Not minding to tie up or anything, Sepp stretched briefly before approaching his favorite bar in the world. He ordered an Ice Pick from Patty. His appearance was haggard, but he had cash and seemed vaguely familiar. Patty mixed up one of her concoctions and placed it in front of him. Sepp drank it down in three gulps. There was already another on its way. *Patty was on it.*

Sepp semi-drunkenly looked around for Elke, but had she been a dream in his periphery? He did realize however, that there were a great many other women at the bar. Sepp allowed his mood to be altered by their simple presence. But first things are always near the beginning, so Sepp tipped Patty's bar-back twenty dollars to watch the kayak for a few hours. He then navigated his way toward a different hotel than before. Sepp procured himself a room for the night, a breakfast of coffee and toast included, and then began the process of surviving in a new life.

Within three months Sepp had effectively consolidated his wealth around his new existence. In Central America cash is king, and Sepp needed to grease a lot of palms in order to rise up from the ashes. There was never any connection made between his arrival and yet another incident of violence up North. Even to the islanders that took note of that one specific detail within the vast array of crime reports from the States, the shootout in the Ozarks was soon forgotten. Sepp became something of an investor on that tiny island. His speculation earned him a small parcel of prime real estate. On it he began to build his dream bar.

The driftwood carved sign read, *Virgin Bob's Ski Lodge.* It was an odd dream that Sepp was trying to bring to life. Antique snow skis and climbing axes hung along the few interior walls. The bar's mirror was frosted, and the drink list was organized by alcoholic content and assigned diamond rankings just like ski slopes are for their danger. The many ceiling fans cost a lot to run, but they keep the place real comfortable. It had only been a few months and the bar was becoming all that Sepp hoped it could be, and more. Patty was none too happy about it, but her husband did not really seem to mind, and that was the critical factor.

Sepp was sitting on the customer side of his bar, watching the pretty ladies lounging in the faint rays of a dying sun. His attention was diverted to the TV mounted behind the bar. There was a story breaking about the Attorney General of Missouri. A scandal was brewing concerning the deceased drug lord Douglas Nelson. The same man killed eight months ago in a desperate firefight in the Ozark Mountains. A devil's grin crossed over Sepp's face, a smile like a cat who had just eaten a canary.

Sepp tipped his head back in pride and then looked back to the bikini-clad girls. They were laughing and having a good time from what he could tell. After a few rum punches were delivered to their table, the two American beauties were approached by two men. It was not a hostile confrontation, but rather a business proposition. One of the dreadlocked Rasta men deftly proffered a cellophane baggie filled with what appeared to be marijuana. The girls smoothly passed money.

Sepp felt that there was something fundamentally wrong about open dealing. It needed ending. He instinctively checked for his knife, and found that he was already in the process of both unsheathing and concealing it.

The Rasta men looked over at Sepp, dismissive of the man they saw. Like all great predators, Sepp was not fully appreciated until he decided to strike. As they exited the soft light of the bar's Tiki torches, Sepp stood and finished his drink. He then slipped into the darkness of the Caribbean night, methodically stalking his prey. *A dog will hunt.*

RALLY POINT

De inimico non loquaris sed cogites

Do not wish ill for your enemy... plan it.

While in the service, Sepp always called a fellow soldier by their last name. That name was the one on the uniform and its use was seen as more professional to the chain of command. There was no Joe or Sepp until after they got out of the Army, and even then, it took a while.

It had started with the intent of a strong drink. Joe Shifflett and Sepp Lokken had wanted to score some hooch for the Christmas party, but their translator had been unwilling to fill the request. Nothing personal, it happened to be a Friday, the Muslim holy day, and Amar had said no to the touching or transporting of alcohol. That was that. But Shifflett had it in his head to jump the fence and walk the four blocks to a haji liquor store, get the damn booze and then re-enter the Forward Operating Base (FOB) via the same small gate to the west. The FOB lay just outside the Green Zone, the living heart of the American occupation of Iraq. Alcohol consumption was prohibited in the entirety of the theater of operations and so only the American captains, sergeants, and privates knew where to score it. The majors, first lieutenants and general officers all feigned ignorance of the liquor store's accessibility. Lokken was no man's fool; he had the store's coordinates plugged into his GPS.

They knew the tower guards, hell, those guys wanted some of the booze too, and so the biggest issue was resolved. Lokken just hoped that the FOB was not renamed in his brief absence. His FOB was currently on its fifth name in eleven months. The *Stars and Stripes* had even run an article on how

213

confusing it was for the helicopter pilots. One day the name was in English and the next in Arabic, and added to that the old timers were always referring to a FOB name that had not been used for perhaps a year.

Lokken had warmed to the liquor run when Shifflett constructed a genuine five point contingency plan. He had even written it up in on a sheet of butcher-block paper that they reallocated from the Company Command Post. It was nailed to a wall of the cramped space that the two lived in.

Operation Iraqi Booze Freedom:
FIVE-POINT CONTINGENCY PLAN

G - Going? Where to? Haji Booze store.

O - Others going, who is? Lokken and Shifflett.

T - Time planned to be? Approx. One (1) Hour from SP to return.

W - What to do if they do not return? Actions to be taken if they do not make it back? - Rogue element is fucked. No outside assistance would be given or expected.

A - Units Actions if contact is made in their absence? - Fight the good fight. Drive on with the mission.

When satisfied that all five of the main issues had been covered, a few other points had to be addressed. Communications were an absolute necessity and would be conducted via Motorola handhelds. Secondary commo consisted of two personally owed contraband Iraqna brand cell phones. These phones were technically illegal to have, but in Baghdad there was no stopping a soldier from getting them. Shifflett and Lokken had purchased theirs in the Mansour District for fifty bucks, even the Fobbits could score one in the Green Zone.

Peter Jackson's *The Lord of the Rings* movies had just come out and 'Fobbit and Hobbit' was just too rich for the American soldier not to adopt. Just as hobbits lived in the Shire with no desire to leave, most soldiers were relegated to spending their tours on the FOB and were spoken of derisively by soldiers that went on combat patrols. Just as *Rear Echelon Mother Fucker* was used in Vietnam, *Fobbit* was used in Iraq and Afghanistan.

The "no-coms," or non-radio communications, contingency would be an IR strobe. The tower element had night vision capability. A cost/benefit analysis was made. Getting some booze was worth risking their lives. It *really* was.

At the gate, the two men donned their Iraqi man-jammies, the loose fitting pull over robe preferred by the old-school men of the Middle East. They made their way out of the sally port and thus embarked on a mission that would interlock their destinies. They had walked the streets of Baghdad many times, but never as alone as they were that night. Every part of the experience was heightened. The few streetlights that worked seemed brighter than ever before. They made their way as calmly as possible, but every car that passed forced them to rethink the wisdom of their current predicament. They could have walked down to the *Pizza Time* store within the Green Zone, but they only sold booze to the Brits. Any American officer there would surely bust them. Shifflett had to tell himself that this was actually safer, operationally speaking.

Behind the concealment provided by a cluster of sun hardened prickly bushes, the two soldiers took off their man-jammies and donned their Kevlar helmets. Now, looking every bit the American occupiers that they were, the two walked right into the haji store. The lone man behind the counter was not especially surprised to see the two Americans, but he was surprised to see they appeared to be alone on foot and, therefore, unsupported. Lokken had two twenty-dollar bills in his left hand. He set the notes on the

215

counter next to the register and pointed up to the row of Absolut Vodka and then over to the row with a selection of whiskey.

The Iraqi national quickly understood that they were here for booze and that they were quite alone. He pulled down a bottle of Swedish vodka and then grabbed the Grand Whisky. Lokken had sipped that stuff before. The label proudly reads "The Finest Industrial Whisky of Lebanon." The Lebanese know little about quality whisky production. *This is a damn fact.* The first and only time the team ever drank "Industrial Whiskey" Lokken was forced to pull rank and have a private drink it first. Lokken thought that Haji was trying to poison him. When the private didn't go blind the rest of the team drank the foul liquor anyway. *Booze is booze.*

"La," Lokken loudly uttered the Arabic word meaning *no*. He met the Haji's eyes and said, "Jim Beam!" in a loud, slow voice. This mixture of languages was not lost on the night clerk. The other soldier, the one who had his weapon pointed to the door, was now turned to him. He looked frightened and dangerous. Abdul rightly sold the infidels their desired booze.

"Let's roll," Lokken said after loading the bottles into his assault pack. And just as quickly as the two Americans had appeared, they were gone.

Abdul rushed to the rear of the store. There, beyond the beaded curtain that led to the family's living space was his nickel-plated AK-47 and his sleeping brother.

"Wake up!" he yelled at Muhammad. It was the mechanical noise of a chambering of a round that got his slumbering sibling to wake up.

"What is it?" Muhammad asked as he instinctively began to reach for his own automatic rifle.

"White infidels, brother, buying liquor and alone in doing so," Abdul responded with eyes of steel. He was not the sort to partake in the insurgency, but he was too proud to

216

see this weakness in his country's occupiers without responding.

"Be silent and wait for me to start the shooting," he commanded his little brother as they walked out of the family store and into the street.

The soldiers were gone. The street was in fact empty of pedestrians. A single pre-invasion taxicab was making its way up the road coming from the direction of the American compound that lay just out of eyeshot. Abdul scanned the street again, knowing that they were out there somewhere.

There! Two figures moved from the cluster of date palms. They were dressed differently now, but walked the same, moving like American soldiers despite the garb, bulky and encumbered with the weight of their armor. One man was walking face front, the other moving slowly behind, his ill-concealed weapon pointing to the rear. Abdul lifted the rifle up to his face and pulled the trigger. The absence of a buttstock on the rifle caused the weapon to jump in his hands as the trigger was depressed. His grip was loosened and his shots scattered, but he trusted Allah to make his aim true.

Shifflett and Lokken needed no verbal communication for this incident. Shifflett had rear security so he immediately returned fire. The man firing at him was at least one hundred fifty meters away, but that was child's play for Shifflett and his M4. The reticle pattern in his ACOG optic was quickly centered on the presented silhouette. His collapsible buttstock was firm against his shoulder, giving him a stable weapons platform. Two of the three bullets that he fired found their mark. Those first two shots had a tight grouping. Abdul had his life snatched from him. The resulting meat succumbed to the simple force of gravity. His little brother was right behind him. Muhammad dropped to the ground taking both cover and concealment behind the oozing corpse of his older brother.

"Got him," Shifflett said as a form of quiet returned to the neighborhood. Gunfire was no stranger to these parts and so everyone concerned knew not to expect any form of law enforcement to respond to the incident.

"Let's get the fuck out of here, Shifflett," Lokken said.

The two infidels got up from the crouched stance and began to run. Muhammad's weapon did not have a buttstock, but it did enjoy the support of Abdul's dead body. When he squeezed the trigger, the shots were far more accurate than that of his brother. *Insha Allah.*

Shifflett took two 7.62mm rounds into the back plate of his body armor. The force of the rounds pushed him flat on his face and into a pool of urine, feces, oil, and engine coolant that is perpetually gathered in Arab streets. Lokken looked back at his companion and saw him face down in the muck, not moving. The taxicab that he had seen earlier was still coming toward the exchange of fire and so Lokken made a quick decision. He fired a single round at the white car with orange quarter panels as it approached his position. Lokken quickly took cover behind the taxi, thus depriving Muhammad of a clean shot. The driver quickly summed up the situation as the whiteness of the man's skin betrayed his clothing. The man pressed his bare hands against the windshield, as experience had taught him. He went in and out of the Green Zone with regularity and knew better.

The barrel of a weapon has a language of its own and the angry gibberish of Lokken only reinforced it. Stupidly the man refused to exit the car; instead, he clung hopelessly to his sole possession of any real value. The taxi driver had briefly forgotten that personal life has a certain value of its own. Just as he reconsidered and was about to surrender his taxi, Lokken let fly a 5.56mm problem solver of his own.

Pulling Shifflett out of the shit-pool by the fabric handle affixed to the rear of his body armor, Lokken had the strength of five and a half men. He moved Shifflett to the ass end of the taxi and then set about to extinguish the threat that was currently peppering him with a controlled burst of small arms fire. Lying on his belly, Lokken inched over to the rear

218

passenger's side wheel and began to scan his sector through the light gathering scope attached to a very familiar rifle. A small, shadowy hump seemed to be hovering over the sprawled-out body in the street. Lokken took his time, remembering his training, his own experience. One shot rang out; it surprised Lokken, just as it was supposed to. He fired three more just to be sure. The last round was a tracer, its arc of red light streaming to the target. *No movement.* Lokken disengaged and moved hurriedly to the rear door of the taxi. Using the provided security of concealment, Lokken assessed Shifflett's physical state. Beyond smelling like shit and being knocked out cold, Lokken found there to be nothing urgently wrong with his compatriot. *That damn armor had just saved another American life.*

After slamming the rear door of the taxi, Lokken tried to get into the driver's seat but was impeded by the bulk of his backpack. He had to push his arms back and jump up and down to get the straps off his armor, but finally it came free. Settling himself into the foul-smelling car, he squinted to see the dashboard. All the lettering on the various gages and dials might as well have been Greek to Lokken but a car is a car. Within seconds he had the vehicle moving in what felt like second gear. Immediately he pulled a U-turn and headed back to the FOB. In all the excitement, Lokken was not sure of the current name, but he called it home.

A passing convoy of US military gun-trucks or 11-14's, had seen the visual effects of the small gun battle and had decided to get in on it. A burst of 7.62mm rounds thundered over the roof of the taxi. Lokken was scared shitless; he prayed to Crom that his IR beacon had not been inadvertently turned on. That flashing light could be seen as a militant act. The gun truck could light him up. Never had he truly appreciated the fearsome nature of those vehicles. Lokken sank low into the seat as the armored convoy passed him by. Battle pleased Crom on that day; Lokken averted a cruel fate.

In the back seat, Shifflett was tossed and turned by Lokken's evasive maneuvers. The crushing pain that he felt awoke him. "Aww shit, man, what the fuck," he moaned as consciousness swept through him.

"Chill the fuck out man, you're OK," Lokken was having enough of a time trying to negotiate his way to the FOB without having to deal with anything more. The immediate threats were in the rearview mirror, but the future held many an obstacle. If he got too close to the FOB while still in the taxi, he could be perceived as a car bomber and thus be killed by his own brothers. *Fratricide is such a horrible euphemism.* He also knew that if he did not get close enough then he hazarded being attacked by still more Iraqis.

Eyeing a busted streetlight approximately 100 meters from the walls of FOB *Gunner/Izdahar/Highlander/Prosperity*, Lokken pulled the taxi to a stuttered halt beneath its umbrella of darkness. He had discarded his man jammies and turned his attention to Shifflett who was struggling to free himself from the tattered mess of his twisted gear and broken armor plate. Using his fix blade Buckmaster to accomplish the task, Lokken made short work of the damaged gear.

"OK, Schiff, we gots to move. You OK to go?" he inquired with all seriousness.

"I can make it," Shifflett responded under labored breath. "I need a dip," he added. Lokken looked down at his friend, took his finger out of the trigger guard and scooped out his dip of Copenhagen snuff. Lokken placed the re-chew into his buddy's mouth. *Man hath no greater love.*

Shifflett smiled up at him and grunted in an attempt to move. Lokken exited the taxi and wrenched open the rear door of the dilapidated car. Helping Shifflett to extricate himself Lokken was doubly burdened by both a physical weight and the gravitas of the situation.

"Is the IR on?" Shifflett asked. *Shit, it wasn't.*

"Good thinking bro!" Lokken had forgotten to turn on the infrared blinker, without which the tower guards

220

would not recognize them. It would have been a deadly mistake to have made. After stopping to turn on the beacon, Lokken hoisted Shifflett up to his feet. Shifflett was in excruciating pain, but there was no way to do it without hurting him.

They began running to the sally port, "Two men coming in!" Lokken communicated as quietly as possible to his booze thirsty compatriots at the gate. They helped him in and gave a discreet call for an off-duty medic who would be friendly to the situation. It was plain to see that Shifflett was injured, but Lokken had indicated that there was no emergent medical situation. As their medic buddy took hold of the situation, the Doc explained again how indispensable the armor is. During the lecture, Shifflett grabbed Lokken by the hand. "I owe you my life, bro. I won't forget it."

The two soldiers then realized that they had become murderers. They both had killed men in the Middle East but that had been done in the line of duty, so technically was not murder. But what they had done that night was indeed murder, and they had no illusions about it. The bond that they had forged out there in the Haji Street was even stronger than that of brothers in arms. Lokken and Shifflett had just become as thick as thieves.

Sepp was still too excited by the killing of the Rasta-men for sleep. He was in a world of awareness. The euphoric high which he had for nine months denied himself had returned, and with a vengeance. The long swim back was cool and soothing. The water felt like nothing else that he had ever experienced. He was swimming in quicksilver. He felt pushed by the exercise, not struggling against any tide. It was also washing off the copious amounts of blood that had spattered about whilst he hacked up the bodies. The messy boat had been easy to scuttle. There was a deep pool a few

221

hundred meters offshore known to the locals as a haven for moray eels. *No one would go near it for days.* He was in no real hurry, for Sepp knew that he had plenty of time to cover his tracks.

Once back ashore, Sepp used a stiff white towel from a nearby hotel's guest hamper to dry himself as he made his way back toward his own bar. There, the usual drunks were mixing it up with a few hard-core tourists. He was gone for nearly an hour, but it had been a crucial time. In the tropics, after the sun sets, there are a few social hours before bed is calling. The mornings are too hot to sleep through and no one wants to miss another beautiful day. Only the newbie tourist stays up late in Belize.

Sepp had Adriana fetch him a pilsner beer and a Bushmills neat. She brought them, and in doing so tried to strike up a conversation with her sometimes lover. It was immediately clear to her that he wanted to be alone and so she left him to his thoughts. Sepp's eyes were distant. She thought he was thinking of the war, but Sepp's mind was really in Atlanta.

It was not their first firefight, but it was their first without the shield of legitimacy provided by the Army. The rigid structure of the military was lacking that night in Atlanta. That lack, Sepp knew, had been the real reason that Nick had lost his leg. He had known also that there was going to be trouble. It was inevitable. Without the clear legal authority of the Uniform Code of Military Justice and the innate sense of duty that the Flag of one's own nation instills; his team was bound to have trouble. In firefights a clearly delineated command structure is necessary, and although Sepp had styled himself as some sort of lieutenant, there was no sense of a chain of command. And that was at the heart of the matter, as Sepp saw it.

They were just outside of Atlanta. Well, close enough that they called it Atlanta anyway. They were to the south of Hartsfield International Airport. The endless drone of commercial flights was supposed to drown out the

222

gunplay. That was a selling point, anyway. Sepp had been real proud of that small advantage. Nick was also one of Sepp's selling points. An ex-Ranger who had gone to and passed the Special Force Qualification Course, Nick was a true Green Beret. Sepp laughed at the thought of a floppy green hat once impressing him. But it had, and that was just the straight hard truth of the matter. There was also something else going on that night. It was a devious construct of Sepp and of Joe. Sometimes people need to fail in order to learn, and Atlanta had been designed to do just that.

Way back in the beginning during the Atlanta Operation, the team was working by committee. They were all tired of being told what to do and how to do it by some goddamn officer. Few men like being ordered around. It had been decided on the outset that they would work as a true team. Sepp said harsh structure was unnecessary because they were all equals in this mercenary life. Sepp knew of course that he never could have sold them on the idea of his being in charge. Sure it was his idea, but these boys hated that side of the military. No, Sepp had to demonstrate that they needed a leader. And who best to fill that slot? Well Sepp, of course. After their failure in Atlanta, Joe had even been the one to "think of the idea." *Thanks Joe.*

Sepp paused to admire his bar. The thick Dutch thatch work that canopied the outdoor seating added to the beach bar theme. The barstools were intricately carved by the native peoples of the mainland, and they looked it. It was no longer a ramshackle beach bar. Virgin Bob's Ski Lodge was the most profitable concern on the island. Comprised quite cleverly of five huge steel shipping containers, the conex box became a staple of the US military. Initially used as storage

223

facilities, they evolved into arms rooms and sleeping quarters.

Sepp had three 40-footers making up the first floor and two more crossed like Lincoln logs perpendicular above them. The first floor was dedicated to the bar, and the second floor was a VIP balcony, a shipping container for the office, and the other for Sepp's residence. Sepp had lived in many converted shipping containers before, but never with such amenities.

He was more than satisfied with his new life. It had taken nine months so far, but things were really coming together. The bamboo framing added a tropical touch to it, but Sepp looked beyond that, to the internal steel latticework of the skeletal remains of craftily chopped containers. The bar area had little framework. The inner walls added an industrial touch. Sepp could shutter the bar safely in the event of a storm. Not even a hurricane would get in. Sepp had stolen the idea from a carnie in the mobile amusement industry. The reallocation had worked out well.

The entire structure was prefabricated in Panama, and barged to the islands, saving money. Sepp did not think of himself as a war profiteer. Offloaded and stacked offset with a nautical crane, the steel boxes took on their present form. A blowtorch here and there later, and the bar and adjoining apartment were ready for a paint job. The electrical wiring and a few plumbing challenges later and the new and improved *Virgin Bob's Ski Lodge* was ready for business.

Without removing his sandals, Sepp cooled his feet in the running water spittoon that ran by the feet of patrons at the main sit-down bar. The Australian waitress used a small bridge to move from the serving area to behind the bar. Sepp remembered that the piping for this little river extravagance had been a bitch to plumb. But soaking his feet, he was reminded that it both cooled the customer and kept the level of sand and small rocks down to a minimum in the bar itself. The only real troubles with it lay in cleaning the filter and keeping the really drunk ones from peeing into it.

Sepp particularly liked to relieve himself into it, and so he was especially hard on the ones he caught in the act. *Ah, the joys of hypocrisy.*

"What can I get you, Love?" Adriana asked the chubby American man two seats from Sepp. Her accent was exotic, sexy as hell. It had invited no small number of marriage proposals. Sepp figured that some of them thought that they might have a shot with Adriana, but he knew that he was gonna be the one to tag that Aussie tonight. The Japanese tourists clustered at the far side of the bar were obviously taken with the statuesque blonde as well. Sepp could not hear them well, and his Nipponese was rusty, but they were clearly impressed with her elegant shape. Everyone was.

"Beer." It was all that the man could muster. He was unprepared for her, taken aback by her beauty. Although he did not normally consider himself the timid type, this Australian goddess was a force of nature. *Yet another move I played well*, Sepp noted as he watched the man's stuttered response.

"Your name isn't Chuck is it, Love?" Adriana asked coyly.

"No," he said. "Why?"

"Because if your name is Chuck, and if you are sitting in that chair there, then this beer would be on the house." She scooped up his US dollars while pointing to the brass tag on the chair to the side of him. All the barstools had name tags on them. The tourist took a good look at the name next to his and laughed.

"DOGNUT, What kind of name is that?" the customer inquired.

Sepp laughed, for Dognut was an odd name. Looking across the way, the man saw that a small brass plaque was affixed on each chair. He asked Sepp who they were for. Sepp explained that they were the names of twenty fallen Rangers, their dates of life and death, and their ranks were all displayed. They had not all been friends, but they were

225

brothers. The man was an American and although he had never served, he raised his glass to Sepp and toasted him for his service. It made Sepp feel a bit ashamed, but he never let on.

"And those?" The man pointed to the six stools on the short side of the bar, to the ones with only nicknames. Sepp told him that they were all members of his squad. They were all men that he had been close to.

"That's the difference you see," Sepp commented. "If your name is one of 'em you get a free beer, friend. But to date, no one has owned up to the name Dognut. There are lots of 'sure I'm Chuck' admissions, but not a single 'call me Dognut', not even for a free beer." Sepp smiled at that. He was the kind of guy with a friend named Dognut, not this pencil-pusher from the States. Out of contempt, Sepp bought the man's drink for him and then told him to have a nice stay in Belize. He also plugged his bar's lobster breakfast deal before excusing himself to the main side of the bar.

Making his way up to the long bar, he ordered another tall pilsner and in doing so shot Adriana a look that said *I need you*. She smiled at him with her soulful eyes. Serving him a tall draft of his favorite beer, she politely but firmly began to usher the midnight revelers off. A few of them seemed to get the picture and Sepp enjoyed the disgruntled looks that were passed his way.

They went back to her place, they always did. Adriana had been to his apartment but did not like the AC on so high. Sepp always swore that when he got back from Haji-Land that he would never be without air conditioning, and he had been true to his word on that score. Knowing that Sepp would satisfy her and then do her the small courtesy of leaving, Adriana could convince herself that not everyone on the island knew. It was fiction, of course, but we all live by the lies we tell ourselves.

They were on each other before her door was closed. He kissed her passionately as they fought to remove each other's clothes. The sex was incredible. Sepp had been rough

226

with her before, but rarely like this. *Manly, take charge aggressive*. Adriana heartily approved. PTSD-Sex she called it after reading up on his condition. This was no time for foreplay. Sepp had her up against the wall with her back to him. He kicked her legs out wider and held her hands firmly in place. The pounding he gave her was relentless. He rubbed her clit to the rhythm of his thrusts.

Sepp knew she was getting close when she aggressively bit at his neck. He concentrated on coming and timed it nearly perfectly. She joined in as he was finishing.

They collapsed on the floor, their breathing syncing as one.

She did not want him to leave. Adriana asked him, for the first time, if he would rather stay the night. Sepp was pleased, flattered even, but he had other things to do. A new life had just been joined by the old. It was odd for him, but in an exhilarating way. Sepp needed a strong drink and solitude.

He tucked her into her bed, kissed her forehead and let himself out.

The streets were deserted. There was a waning crescent moon rising in the star filled sky. He walked slowly down the sandy street, but bounded up his own stairs with a youthful exuberance he had not felt in months. After slipping his key in the door, he felt something was not right. The tiny hairs in his ears stood straight up, stretching to raise auditory acuity. *Nothing.* The knife was instantly in his hands. Cold air swept over his hand as he opened the door to his residence. *Still nothing.*

Inside was cold. The air conditioning had been on full blast. His movement across the floor made no sound. Thick Persian rugs covered his tracks. They looked clean, it was hard to keep them that way, but he could tell if someone had been there because of it. *No one had*, but it was cold comfort. There were ancient artifacts placed around the apartment. Nothing was out of order. Sepp took the Arabic scimitar off his wall. It was a fully serviceable weapon and would serve him better than the knife. His pistol was in the desk, twenty feet further. Security is nothing more than a constant process of upgrading technological advantages.

Sepp hit the main switch, lighting up the mahogany-paneled room. *More nothing.* He lay the sword on the desk and fished for the gun in the main drawer. Without having to look, he inserted a magazine and chambered a round. Sepp patrolled his home, cutting angles just as with any room clearing. There were no signs of a disturbance, not even an errant smell.

His adrenaline receded as he headed for the liquor cabinet. A fifth of Johnnie Walker Gold was calling him over. He grabbed the bottle and poured himself a shot to calm his nerves. The sweet, honeyed whisky did just that. Back at the desk, he tucked the pistol into his shorts and went to grab the sword. It was expensive and needed to be on its wall mount. Reaching over the desk, he noticed it. Right in the middle of his day planner, between Monday's note telling him the bar's electricity bill was due and the weekend entry marked "fishing trip," it lay. A single, well-worn, federally minted portrait of Ben Franklin. *Aww shit.*

ACKNOWLEDGEMENTS

My late mother, Molly, was a lover of Letters. She was also a strict enforcer of many esoteric regulations imposed on our language by men famous for authoring rule books, and all the entertainment found in such. She always supported my efforts, fighting or writing.

Professional acknowledgment for this tale goes to those with whom I served with. From B Co. 3/75th John Rafferty, Zuber, Cash, Pickering and Martindale. From D Co. 3/187 IN Eric Duncan, Karl, Lima and Rocco. And from C Co. 1-161 Infantry O'Boyle, Fred, Hyland and Bley.

As for Sal, Dognut, Matt, Doc, Killer, Chicken, Joe and Chuck.... Well, it is enough that we know who we are, isn't it?

This page intentionally left blank

This page intentionally left blank

Twice dismissed from Westminster College in his hometown of Fulton, Missouri, Phillip Holt enlisted in the U.S. Army in 1995. He served as a Forward Observer in Bravo Company, 3/75th Ranger Regiment.

From 2004-05 he served in Baghdad as a M249 gunner during OIF II. After completing his bachelor's degree and Officer Candidate School, he volunteered to serve in RC East as a Rifle Company's Fire Support Officer. His first command was in the Shah-i-Kot Valley.

Phillip has a Bachelor of Arts from The Evergreen State College. He allegedly wrote *The Irony Chancellor: Bismarckian Socialism explored via Interpretive Dance.* Having no grades at Evergreen, his transcript reads "He explored the space."

He earned his Master's Degree in Military Affairs from Hawaii Pacific University. His thesis became a refutation of his original thesis statement.

Phillip's hobbies include guns, travel, and Persian rugs.